There Can Never Be Enough

More Fiction by David Arnason

Baldur's Song

If Pigs Can Fly

King Jerry

The Demon Lover

The Dragon and the Dry Goods Princess

There Can Never Be Enough

New and Selected Stories
by David Arnason

TURNSTONE PRESS

There Can Never Be Enough
copyright © David Arnason 2014
(© 1982, 1984, 1989, 1994, 1995, 2002, 2014)

Turnstone Press
Artspace Building
206-100 Arthur Street
Winnipeg, MB
R3B 1H3 Canada
www.TurnstonePress.com

MIX
Paper from
responsible sources
FSC   FSC® C016245
www.fsc.org

"The Raffle," "The Unmarried Sister," "The Drunk Woman Is Singing in my Office," "Square Dancers," "The Circus Performer's Bar," "Do Astronauts Have Sex Fantasies?," "Girl and Wolf," "The Figure Skater," "Sons and Fathers, Fathers and Sons," and "A Girl's Story" are from the collection *The Circus Performer's Bar*, Talon Books, 1984. "Driving Through Montana," "The Happiest Man in the World," and "The Naiads" are from the collection *The Happiest Man in the World*, Talon Books, 1989. The stories from *The Happiest Man in the World* and *The Circus Performers' Bar* by David Arnason, published by Talon Books. Used by permission of the publisher. "The Sunfish," "Fifty Stories and a Piece of Advice," "Owl on Cairn," "Over and Over," are from the collection *Fifty Stories and a Piece of Advice*, Turnstone Press, 1982. "The Dragon and the Dry Goods Princess," "The Cowboy: A Tale of the Old West," "The Waitress," "The Girl of Milk and Blood," are from the collection *The Dragon and the Dry Goods Princess*, Turnstone Press, 1994. "Once in a Small Bar in Odessa," "At the Grave of Taras Shevchenko," "Tansy from My Garden," "Bad Girl," "Fifth Gait," "Southern Cross," and " In the Garden of the Medicis" are from the collection *If Pigs Could Fly*, Turnstone Press, 1995. "In Paraguay" and "Prelude to America" are from the collection *The Demon Lover*, Turnstone Press, 2002.

Turnstone Press gratefully acknowledges the assistance of the Canada Council for the Arts, the Manitoba Arts Council, the Government of Canada through the Canada Book Fund, and the Province of Manitoba through the Book Publishing Tax Credit and the Book Publisher Marketing Assistance Program.

Printed and bound in Canada by Friesens for Turnstone Press.

Library and Archives Canada Cataloguing in Publication

Arnason, David, 1940-
[Short stories. Selections]
    There can never be enough : new and selected stories / David Arnason.

Includes previously published short stories.
ISBN 978-0-88801-450-4 (pbk.)

    I. Title.

PS8551.R765T54 2014   C813'.54   C2014-903006-1

In Memory of Judith Rempel Curto and Mark Curto

Contents

There Can Never Be Enough

Getting It Right

I t's a bright March day, colder than it should be but still not
very cold. The sun is bright on the snow that fell all day yesterday and then through the night. My grandmother was born
here a hundred and twenty-six years ago, but I have no idea
what the weather was like. Probably something like today.

Everybody had come down with smallpox. Well, not everyone but pretty close. Her two older sisters had it and came out
marked, but my grandmother was somehow immune through
all that tragic winter. It was mostly infants and old people
who actually died, and because the ground was frozen and
there was no way of burying them, their bodies were piled on
the roofs of the makeshift huts they lived in. That was so the
wolves wouldn't eat them before spring came and they could
be planted in the earth.

That's the story my mother told me, and I believe it. Looking out over the lake from where I sit it is easy to believe that
you are at the North Pole and nobody else exists in the whole
world. My mother knew a verse in Cree that one of the children from the reserve near where she lived had taught her on

the way to school. She said she thought it was a dirty verse, because he laughed when she recited it aloud. She never forgot it and after she taught it to me, I never forgot it either. I know some Cree speakers but I don't dare recite the verse for them, because it might just be nonsense, or so corrupted by my mother's memory and then my own that it might make no sense.

My grandmother died in 1964. She was eighty-eight years old. The night she died I went to the beer parlour in Libau with many of the mourners, including my uncle who lived with her and took care of her. Everybody left, and then there were only the two of us. He didn't want to go back to the house where his mother had died, so I took him home with me to Transcona, where I lived at the time. The next day we went to the zoo, and the following day to the planetarium. When I finally took him home to Libau, everybody was upset because no one knew what had happened to him. Now he's dead too.

Last year I lived for several months in Kiel, Germany. The weather wasn't much better than it is here in Gimli. But I was happy because nothing in Kiel triggered memories. Everything was brand new and none of it tied to a past that meant anything to me. We travelled all around Europe in the wonderful trains, and we visited cathedrals laden with history, but it was somebody else's history and so it did not weigh on me.

My grandmother's house had a parlour, a room reserved for special visitors, and it had an old piano that was hopelessly out of tune, one of those strange desks with hundreds of tiny drawers and a curved slatted front cover that went up and down. There was a small chesterfield with an antimacassar and my grandfather's books, untouched since the day he put a shotgun in his mouth and pulled the trigger some fathomless time ago. I used to go to his grave on a summer's day and marvel at the granite slab that marked it. It was only years later that I learned that the granite slab marked his father, and my grandfather was in a grave nearby marked only by a row of white stones.

My mother grew sweet peas in her garden. My father planted wooden stakes, then weaved a web of string for the sweet peas to climb. On the south side of the house she grew hollyhocks, red and yellow and white. There was a plum tree in the bush near the house, and my mother picked it to make jam every September. She planted two small spruce trees that she found in the ditch in the curved flower garden near the road, one for me and one for my brother. They are still there, though many other families have grown up in that same place.

We had a ghost. Her name was Ricka, and she had come from Iceland around the turn of the century. My mother had nursed her in the nursing home, and she came to live with us when I was only about three. I remember her sitting in a rocking chair with her long grey hair braided and singing to herself. She had a picture of the baby she had in Iceland and who had died before he was a year old. I didn't know at that time that death came to children, and it was a frightening revelation. She ate oatmeal porridge and she broke up pieces of toast into her cereal. Then one day she was simply gone. No one explained to us what had happened, and we didn't ask in case she had died. I still don't know.

We used to shop at the Lakeside Trading Company on the corner of Centre and Main in Gimli. You could buy anything there from food to hardware, and the building smelled strongly of leather from the horse harnesses that hung from the walls. I remember barrels of flour and of raisins and of oatmeal. You made a note and gave it to the clerk, Then he walked around the store gathering up your merchandise, and he wrote down the numbers in a book. I never saw any money change hands, though it was wartime and my mother tore out pages from my ration book to give to the clerk. I loved my ration coupons, those brightly coloured scraps of paper, and I hated to watch them disappear.

I fell hopelessly in love in the first grade with a bossy little girl named Irene. She always made me carry her books home, though she lived only a couple of blocks north of the school and I lived a mile and a half away in the country south of town. I was always thrice-a-dreams those days, and though my parents knew my penchant for getting lost in daydreams they became worried when I didn't get home till well after dark. Then one day, I was told that I could go home with Irene and play with her until nine o'clock when my parents would pick me up. We played all sorts of games, all of them of her invention and all of which involved her dominating me in subtle ways. The next day at school she did not appear. She was missing for a whole week. Finally I asked a classmate about her, and he told me that she had moved away to Winnipegosis. I still fall in love with bossy girls.

And I suppose that is why I am telling you all this. The amplitude of these anecdotes is proportional to their distance from me in time. I think I am growing old, and I don't want to. I have been blindsided by life. Just moments ago everything was expectation. I had plans. I lived in many different futures in my imagination, and I slept well at night and dreamed dreams of power and success. Now, I want to live in the past. I would be willing to live my life over exactly as it happened, taking the good with the bad, as if it were a favourite movie that I could replay whenever I wanted.

But of course life doesn't do you that sort of favour. I remember riding an Icelandic pony high in the mountains of Iceland. The trip was seventeen kilometres, and the highest eight were in deep snow. We followed an ancient trail marked by cairns, and the horses took us through a landscape so rough and jagged I would never have set out on it if I had known in advance what to expect. Still, every moment of that ride is as fresh in mind as if it had just happened.

I look forward to spring, though it will take me to my birthday and to the knowledge that I cannot recover all those things I have lost. My unplanned future is hurtling towards me and I am helpless to resist it. Lately I have begun to dream of houses with secret rooms that contain artifacts from the nineteenth century, gas lamps and old irons and lockets with pictures of beautiful women carved in ivory. I am unreasonably happy in these dreams, and when I waken from one of them I am desperate to recover it.

Sometimes my children arrive in my dreams in the guises of their former selves, but never as they are now that they have moved on and made their own lives. Sometimes I am a child myself, and those are the most troubling dreams. Once, my brother and I found eight puppies in a brush pile in the spruce bush across the road from where we lived. The mother was a yellow dog of indeterminate breed and she let us approach and pet the puppies. In memory, this is one of the happiest moments of my life, but in dreams I am full of trepidation. I sense how powerless I am to save those pups, though in real life we did save them, bringing them home to mother and finding new homes for them all.

Rabbits. I remember rabbits in the bush near home. I set snares for them and skinned them for their fur, and Mother cooked them and we ate rabbit stew. They seemed distant and other then, deserving of their fates, but now I have rabbits living in the back yard of my house in Winnipeg, and I am concerned about them, fearful of dogs on the loose and feral cats. I have given them names and learned to identify one from the other. I bring them food, sunflower seeds and rye bread. They have become so tame that I can walk close to them and they will not move. It bothers me that they are so trusting.

Since I was young, I have wanted to buy a convertible and drive through our too short summers with the top down. I always thought that I would get one, some time in the near future. I rented one in California and drove through the starry desert night in February and I was happy. But I have not yet bought one, and it looks as if I probably never will. It was a small dream and easily realizable and yet it failed and continues to fail me.

I should make lists, try to figure out what I want and what I need and put my life in order. But I know that I would lose the lists, that the priorities I set would never arrive in the correct order. I know because I have tried. I have bought electronic organizers and failed even to learn how to use them. I miss important meetings and forget about important dates. Yet if I do remember, I am always punctually on time.

And meanwhile important events occur. Countries go to war, and thousands are slaughtered in the most inhumane ways. Innocent people are tortured together with the guilty without anyone much noticing the difference. Whole galaxies are spinning out of control. Black holes in space are swallowing stars and spinning them into some unimaginable other place. And I am living in the past, living in memories that need careful examination and I don't have much time to get it right. So, a beginning.

The Bad Samaritan

It was still snowing as they moved past the car dealerships and doughnut shops at the edge of the city, but the wind had dropped and there was less snow here than back at the cottage. They passed the new hospital and Sam remembered the phone call he had got from there one night a few years ago. The girl's name was Pamela, and she was high on some drug they had given her, for her cancer. She wanted to talk about the class she had taken with him a few years ago, a first year class in English. She was very excited, and Sam was not sure whether the last thing she had said was that she loved him. It sounded like that, but he had been too embarrassed to go and see her, and about a month later he read that she had died. Now every time he passed the hospital he remembered that phone call and wondered why he hadn't gone to see her. She had asked him to come, but he was afraid to see her dying.

The road widened to three lanes, and Sam turned the Jeep into the lane by the median. There were two lanes of traffic between him and the sidewalk, and the traffic was heavy, though just then they were stopped at a red light. A man on the sidewalk lurched in a crazy sort of dance and fell full length in the snow. He got up and fell again. Then he was out into the street, lurching through traffic, falling and rising as if he were some sort of wounded animal.

"We've got to help him," Amanda said. "He's going to get himself killed." She was leaning forward in her seat as if she could get closer to the man that way.

"Do you think he's drunk?" Sam asked.

"No. I think he's having some sort of fit. He looks sick, not drunk."

The man had made his way back out of traffic and was churning his way up past a set of gas pumps towards a little variety store. He moved amazingly fast, considering how often he fell. The light had changed, and the traffic began to move. Sam signalled his intent to change into the middle lane, but none of the other drivers seemed eager to let him do that.

"Look," Amanda said. "A woman has come out of the store and she's helping him up."

"I can't change lanes," Sam said. "Nobody will give way, and it's too slippery."

"He'll be fine. He's got help."

Sam thought he should turn around and go back, but the traffic kept moving, and soon it was too late. They had come to Notre Dame Avenue, and turned left towards the city centre.

It was nearly Christmas, and Sam had not yet begun his Christmas shopping. He had promised Amanda that he would pay for a trip to Paris that she wanted to take with her sister. But that was a couple of months later, and he supposed that he should buy something to put under the tree, only they had decided that this year, they would not have a tree. All the children had asked for money rather than presents. They were grown up now, starting their own families, and all three had moved to distant cities. It made sense to send money, particularly since Sam seemed unable to package anything so that it arrived intact at its destination.

Amanda had bought a vase for her son, who was not Sam's son but the remnant of an earlier relationship that Sam had not asked Amanda about, and now, after fifteen years, it was too late to discuss. She had packed it in a box with a lot of kidney-shaped pieces of Styrofoam and sent it off in the mail. Sam had no doubt that it would arrive intact, but he knew that if he had packed it, however carefully, it would have shattered in some distant postal delivery truck.

Neither spoke the rest of the way home. It had become the way they travelled, in silence, unless Sam put on the radio, and he didn't do that very often, because the music didn't seem to have anything to do with him. The love songs, whether country and western or operatic, seemed addressed to someone he might once have been but was no longer.

Christmas passed, and the new year opened without any sense of occasion. They visited friends. They went out for dinner to restaurants they had not visited before. Sam even got drunk on New Year's Eve, and floundered around in the Harpers' hot tub, singing the dirty versions of folk songs he had learned thirty years before when he had worked on the survey gang up north. For a short while he was happy, but the next day he had a hangover that lasted until late in the day, and he vowed he would not do it again.

Amanda went up to the lake by herself for a few days. She said she needed to recharge her batteries, and she needed some solitude. She increasingly went places by herself, and sometimes Sam wondered whether she was meeting someone else, but it seemed unlikely. She had settled so comfortably into her life since she had given up working that Sam couldn't imagine her living any other life. He wondered whether he was even capable of being jealous any more.

Amanda took the dog with her. It was the one point of contention in their relationship. Jake was an old dog, but he had to be walked every day, and he was growing increasingly incontinent. Amanda thought they should put him down, but Sam was unwilling. And yet it was Amanda who cleaned up after the dog, and who stuffed pills down his throat and saw that he had food and water. The dog was Amanda's dog, had come with her as a puppy, and was now preparing to die painfully because Sam couldn't stand the thought of killing him.

Sam had no classes on Wednesday, and so when Amanda asked him to drive out to the lake for lunch and bring her computer with him, he agreed. He had a meeting, but nobody actually cared whether he came or not. It was the library committee, and he had been on it as long as he could remember.

He realized that he had no money with him. When he bought his sandwich yesterday, he had searched all his pockets to come up with enough to pay for it. The bank just down the street from where they lived had an instant teller, and so he stopped there. It was early, only seven-thirty, and it was still not bright. When he stuck his card in the door and opened it, he saw a woman sleeping on the floor. She was wearing a blue twill suit and a white blouse and her head was resting on her white purse. She had on a pair of pumps, but no coat and, she was not prepared to walk out in the cold winter weather.

Sam tried to see if she was breathing, but her chest did not seem to move. She was off to the side, not directly between him and the machine, and so he put in his card and punched in two hundred dollars withdrawal while he tried to figure out what he should do. The woman did not move. Sam knew he could not just walk out of there. He would have to do something.

"Are you all right?" he asked. There was no response.

"Are you all right?" he asked again, this time louder. The

woman stirred and groaned. She said something incoherent in a deep, male voice, and settled back into sleep. Suddenly, Sam noticed that her hair was coarse and strange, and he suddenly thought that she must be a man. He backed out of the bank and walked quickly to his car. He thought that he should call the police or an ambulance or something, but he didn't. He got into his car and he drove all the way out to the lake without stopping.

On Silver Pond

A mile south of Gimli on the west coast of Lake Winnipeg, there's a small marsh. I grew up on the edge of that marsh in a white house on Highway 9, just where the road curves. If you've been that way, you've probably seen it. I remember the red-winged blackbirds and the yellowheads in spring, the soggy greenness of it in summer and the will-o'-the-wisps in fall. But I remember it best one cold November day when I was twelve. The lake was high that year, and we'd had a three-day blow from the northwest. The lagoon, normally a half-mile away, had flooded, and the water lapped over Mother's garden all the way into our back yard. A small flock of fall ducks landed right in the corner where the rhubarb grew.

We went to bed that night to the unaccustomed sound of waves breaking on the lawn. Overnight the temperature plummeted and we awoke to a dazzling sheet of ice that stretched to infinity. The air was so clean and clear that impossible details were visible: a muskrat sitting on his reed house a quarter-mile away, clusters of cattails and reeds at the far edge of the lagoon. The sunrise was red, the sky a colouring-book blue.

Every so often the world delivers a moment of grace, and that was mine. It could have been any day of the week, but it was Saturday. I ate my Sunny Boy Cereal with my skates already on. I wore my Montreal Canadiens sweater and a new blue toque, and when I took my first strides on the fragile new ice, I knew what freedom meant. My rink had the same boundaries as the world.

I wasn't alone. Skating alone has its own special attraction, and I guess there's a way in which you always skate alone however many people are around, but that day in 1952 my brother Gerry skated with me. The wind from the northwest was still strong. We skated at a speed I don't dare estimate. After the ice had formed, the water must have receded to the banks of the lake, and our ice hung suspended by the marsh grass over which it had frozen. As we skated, the ice collapsed in sheets behind us. It growled and moaned and made rifle shots, and we shouted at each other, laughing as we fell when our skates touched reeds that poked through the ice. We were out of control, creatures of the wind and the ice, and I'd like, just once, to be that much out of control again.

I played hockey that year, and we were good enough to make it to the provincial Bantam B finals. We lost, though we might have won if I'd been a slightly better skater. I jumped onto the ice for my shift and the puck landed on my stick with nobody within yards of me. I headed for the opposition goal, an interminably long distance away it seemed, just glancing over my shoulder to see the entire enemy team closing in. The goalie in front had turned around to talk to the goal judge behind him, leaving me the open net. I could hear the breathing of the enemy behind me, so I fired a quick wrist shot and raised the puck over the goal into the third balcony of the Roland arena.

Growing up in the country with a set of chores to do each day, I didn't get the same chance to practise that the town kids got, and so the tightly disciplined series of sudden bursts and stops that characterize hockey seemed to me oppressive and claustrophobic. They wouldn't let you practise stops and starts during open skating, but that was fine with me. I preferred the slow, rhythmic grace of skating to music. Besides, I was always in love, and sometimes I'd get a chance to skate hand in hand with the girl I dreamed about. Or some other girl might be bold enough to ask me to skate with her, and whirling around the rink to the music of "Rosemarie," I'd fall in love again. Few things can equal the excitement of taking a warm hand, removed from a pink mitten for the occasion, and holding it while you skate to a scratchy recording. It was certainly better than keeping out a wary eye for body checks.

The result, of course, is that I am still most comfortable skating counter-clockwise, as we were then required to do, and certain songs, like "Mockingbird Hill" and "How Much Is That Doggie in the Window?" can make me nearly swoon with remembrance. The smells of powder and perfume are clearer in cold air. They were then and they still are.

For some reason, I used to think of skating as something especially western Canadian. Pictures of people skating on the Rideau Canal in Ottawa or in front of Toronto City Hall seemed to me inauthentic versions of the real thing, which could only be done on the Prairies. But I spent a couple of years in Fredericton, where I lived next door to an old fellow who had only one eye and a colostomy and a three-legged cane. One day he invited me over, passed me a warm beer that he took out from its hiding place in the wall behind a flap of wallpaper, and told me the story of his courtship.

In 1906, just before Christmas, the whole town of Fredericton turned out as it always did to clean the snow from the St. John River and make a skating rink that stretched for miles. They lit a gigantic bonfire in the middle of the river, and everyone brought picnic lunches.

My neighbour, who had just turned twenty then, had never been out on a date before, but he saw the prettiest girl he had ever seen, dressed in a snow-white cloak with a fox-skin hood, and he asked her to skate with him. They skated out to the end of the darkness, where she kissed him, then back to the warm glow of the fire. They'd been together sixty years since then, and he loved her still. His wife, hefty and bad-tempered now, showed no sign of being the skater of his heart's desire, but I knew what he meant.

We're a northern people, and skating is at the heart of our notions of our own innocence. My grandparents, when they want to conjure up an image that will show once and for all how far the present age has fallen into decay, will tell stories of skating in their youth. Their stories will be like my Fredericton neighbour's story, a tale of community and shared joy. They'll evoke hoarfrost and icicles, fur collars and laughter. And of course they'll forget the problems of the present in their rich remembrance of the past.

A couple of years ago, I lived in France for a while. My wife and I rented a little studio in Strasbourg, and we lived there happily enough, though a little homesick. It was early March, and though it was one of the coldest winters in European history, there was no snow.

We decided to treat ourselves to a weekend in Paris, and we arrived on a cold, clear day to the bustle and excitement of the Left Bank. The bus dropped us off right at the marketplace, at the corner of Boulevard Saint-Germain and Rue Monge. We made our way through stalls loaded with vegetables, mounds of shrimps, oysters and fish, and mountains of wine. We decided to dump our bags in a little hotel and make our way back to the centre of international life.

We found a two-star hotel which, surprisingly, had a television set. I turned it on to see if it worked, and suddenly there were skaters. I was watching the World Championships, and it had come down to a choice between Brian Boitano of the United States and Brian Orser of Canada. Boitano was just finishing his performance, and I saw only the last few figures, a controlled and elegant series of spins and jumps that brought him to a confident bow before the judges. The French announcer seemed to feel it was over, that Orser would provide a fitting denouement to Boitano's victory.

But Orser skated like a man possessed. It was his greatest moment as a skater. He whirled around the ice, dancing, sailing through the air as if he'd made some private agreement with gravity to release him from its laws for this performance. I've watched figure skaters all my life, and loved them all, from the tiniest winter carnival angel to the great goddesses of the sport, but I've never seen a more moving program. It was all freedom, it was all control, it was all that skating can be.

When it was over the crowd cheered wildly, and even the flinty hearts of the judges were melted and Brian Orser was the champion of the world. Then we went out into the streets of Paris, past the lovers along the banks of the Seine and the hushed candlelight of Notre Dame cathedral into all that history.

But we went out confidently now, because we knew just a little better who we were, and we knew it had something to do with skating.

Fifty Stories and a Piece of Advice

I t didn't happen right away. First he was sick like with a flu, and of course he wouldn't go to the doctor. Then he could hardly walk, and he was spitting blood. Finally, when all the brothers got together to make him go to the hospital, he said "just a minute," and went into the next room and put a shotgun in his mouth and pulled the trigger. The doctor checked him out later and said it wasn't cancer or anything, just a bad ulcer, so he didn't have to do it after all. He used to give me a ride home sometimes. He always whistled "The Isle of Capri," sort of through his teeth, and when I said thanks for the ride, he said yessirree. I never heard anybody else say yessirree.

*

Once when Jerry and me were lifting our snares in the spruce bush, we met Harry carrying his twenty-two. He shot into the tree just over our heads and really scared us. He used to shoot rabbits in the snares and say they were his because whoever killed them owned them. He said he could shoot the eye right out of a squirrel, and he could too. I saw him do it. He's in jail right now because one night he shot just about every dog in town.

*

One time in August, Jean and Sharon phoned up and said I should come over and take them for a ride. They were two grades ahead of me, and I hardly knew them, though I think Jean was some kind of third cousin. They weren't drunk or anything, just sort of really crazy. We drove down to the beach at Camp Morton in Frank's Pontiac, which I shouldn't have been driving, since it was only parked in our yard. We turned the radio up high and opened all the doors and I danced with first one and then the other on the sand. Then they took off all their clothes and went swimming, and I just sat there on the beach, not really watching. Afterward I took them home, still giggling, and they both kissed me goodnight. If there'd only been one it would have been all right, but I didn't know what to do with two of them.

*

You probably don't remember Donna, the fat girl in grade five who moved away to Winnipegosis. She was in love with you. She always walked home with me because she lived in the same direction. She kept telling me about you and made me promise not to tell you. I didn't either, because I used to keep secrets until I figured out that nobody told you secrets unless they wanted other people to know.

*

I used to have this crazy habit of trying to keep my direction clear. I'd figure out how many times I'd turned left, and then I'd turn right enough times to make it even. I'd wait till all the other kids had gone into school after recess, then just stand there and spin until it was right. One day the teacher caught me and asked me what I was doing. I didn't tell her, but I never did it again.

*

One day I picked up this hitchhiker. He told me he was going to visit his aunt on Matheson Island, but he wasn't Indian, or I don't think so. He had a switch knife, and he kept flicking the blade in and out. I loaned him two dollars and dropped him off by the bridge just outside Riverton. A couple of months later they found a body in the river about half a mile away of a guy about the same age with a switch knife in his pocket, but nothing else. They couldn't figure out who he was. I guess I should have told the police about it, but the police were always trying to catch us with liquor in the car, and I didn't like to talk to them.

*

They say a dog won't bite you unless he thinks you're scared of him. I got bit three times one week by dogs that I didn't even see until after they bit me. How did they know I'd be scared of them?

*

I always got picked first, but somehow I never got to do the picking.

*

When we were about sixteen, Harve went out the whole summer with a girl from Calgary who was staying with her aunt because her parents were getting a divorce. They used to pick me up and we'd all go to the beach and drink a bottle of red wine, then they'd wander off into trees and make love and we'd all go to the Chinaman's for coffee. I don't know why they always came to get me, but there wasn't much else to do that summer and it was better than staying home with a houseful of kids. I met a cousin of hers a couple of weeks ago who said that Sheila had told her that I used to be her boyfriend, but I wasn't. It was Harve.

*

Once we were putting up a TV antenna at a farm out in the country about five miles from Rembrandt. There was a girl there, about thirteen years old, dressed in a frilly white dress. She asked us all sorts of questions and I was teasing her, just like I always teased my sisters. All of a sudden, her mum came running out of the house and threw a panful of dishwater over her. It was all dirty and full of potato peelings. The girl started to cry and ran into the house. She never came out again. She was about the prettiest girl I've ever seen.

*

My grandfather had a dog named Sport. He was a mongrel, but Grandpa used to claim he was a rat terrier because he was so good at catching rats. Once when Grandpa went over to visit Elli Johanson, Sport killed old Elli's dog. It was a tiny thing, about four inches high and nothing but hair. Sport thought it was a rat and bit its head off. Elli was really mad and insisted that Grandpa should kill Sport because he was a menace. Grandpa wouldn't, but it didn't matter because Sport was run over by a car a week later anyway.

*

There were two sisters who lived just down the road from us, Irene and Eileen Johnson, who were both albinos. They had white hair and pink eyes and thick glasses that made their eyes look huge. Irene had lots of boyfriends and finally ran away with an airman. Eileen never went anywhere except to school and ended up with a nervous breakdown. I could never tell the difference between them.

*

Old Gus, I forget what his last name was, but he lived a mile west down the Davidson line, was a cowboy out in Alberta before he came back to take over the farm when his brother died. He had a six-gun with four notches in it for guys he had killed. I never believed that, but that's what they said. Anyway, he went out to Krezanski's farm to buy a calf. He offered ten dollars, but old man Krezanski wanted fifteen, so Gus took out his gun and shot the calf and offered ten dollars again. This time old man Krezanski took his offer. At least that's what they say.

*

Bill Gretchen won a TV set on a raffle a week before he died of leukemia.

*

I was hunting out by the Bachelor's once and shot a bird like I've never seen before. It had a funny great big beak and was all different colours, red and blue and green. Nobody else knew what it was either. I even got a book and couldn't figure it out. I gave it to Sammy and he stuffed it. He's still got it in his living room, sitting on an end table, and nobody ever figured out what it was.

*

Sometimes I can't believe how dumb I used to be. I was in love with Myrna Gislason and she was a really good-looking girl. One day when I was washing the floor in the furniture store, she came over and sat there all day talking about her graduation which was on Friday. I didn't figure out for a week that I was supposed to ask if I could take her. She went with Tom Schwartz instead, who I never could stand and still can't. I don't even like to think about it.

*

Jerry and me were throwing stones at a Helldiver in the ditch, but it was too fast for us. It would stick its head up for a minute, and then it would be gone for half minute. Finally, we just waded into the ditch with sticks and tried to hit it on the head when it popped up. It was great fun, and we were laughing and shouting. Finally we got it, and then all of a sudden it was horrible. We had this tiny little bird, and it was all soggy and dead, and I got terribly scared because I knew that that was going to happen to me and to everybody. All of a sudden we were going to be dead. That Helldiver was the deadest thing I ever saw.

*

When they took little Siggi to the hospital because of a pain in his stomach, the doctor took out his appendix, but he died because it wasn't his appendix at all. He was having a heart attack.

*

Uncle Joe got stuck out on some tiny island with a bunch of Indians when the ice started to break up early. They were there for ten days and had nothing to eat but muskrats and willow tea. He says the muskrats were delicious, but I don't know. He hasn't eaten any muskrats since.

*

I was staying alone in the cottage after we had the trouble. J.J. was fishing off the point, and one day he dropped in on his way home and we drank a few beers. He told me hundreds of lies about what a good hunter he was. He said he shot fourteen teals with one shot from a sixteen gauge. Nobody likes him very much because of all the lies, but really, he's not a bad guy. He even includes you in his lies. He told Len that he'd seen me kill a wolf with a twenty-two at four hundred yards, and I've never even shot at a wolf.

*

Women are crazy. I never met one that, if you got to know her, didn't want to squeeze your pimples. I think that's disgusting, squeezing somebody else's pimples.

*

Dad always said you could tell when a woman was pregnant from the look in her eye. He used to tell women they were pregnant before they even knew it themselves. I asked him how he did it and he said it was just a joke, but he was almost always right.

*

When I worked in the garage, old Jon Grim used to come in drunk and watch me change tires. He was a funny old guy and I used to tease him. One day I said that he was so old that he was probably as bald down below as he was on top. He stuck his hand down his pants and pulled out a bunch of hair and said what do you think that is, badger fur?

*

Tom had the craziest thing going with Jamie Kopchuk's wife. They had a tent out at Crow Island and they'd meet at the bridge over Willow Creek and paddle out in a canoe. Tom would park his Coke truck just off the highway and she'd park Jamie's old pink Buick beside it. They only did it on Mondays when the store was closed and Jamie went to Winnipeg for supplies. The only person in town who didn't know about it was Jamie. Some days there'd be ten people with binoculars at the landing, watching them chase each other around the tent.

*

The first goose I ever shot, I was fourteen years old and I was hunting with one of my uncles and his friend from the city. This flock came over low from the south over a little bush. I picked one that was off to the side, and when I pulled the trigger, it dropped like a stone. I was just starting to run for it when my uncle's friend shouted I got it and ran out and picked it up. Everybody knew I shot it including him, but nobody said anything, except my uncle gave me a big drink of rye from his mickey. Why do people do things like that?

*

Once on Sadie Hawkins, Wanda phoned me up and asked if she could take me to the dance. She wasn't really ugly, just strange, and everybody made fun of her. I pretended that I didn't believe it was her, and that it was somebody else playing a joke on me. A few minutes later she phoned back and said had somebody phoned pretending to be her. I said yes and she said it was her crazy cousin playing jokes. I felt kind of mean about that at the time, but what if it really had been a joke? I got enough things I don't want to remember without that.

*

Grandma was always strange about animals. One time a heifer that was just about to have its first calf knocked her down and tried to gore her with its horns. She was hurt pretty badly and could hardly walk. Grandpa wanted to ship it to the stockyard right away, but Grandma wouldn't let him. Instead she went out to the barn the same day and talked to it and petted it. When it had its calf she wouldn't let anyone else milk it. She wouldn't even let Grandpa cut off its horns.

*

You can kill a gopher by holding its head in one hand and its body in the other and giving a little pull. It breaks their necks.

*

When the cows got into wet alfalfa they'd get so full of gas they blew up like balloons. There'd be eight or ten of them lying on their backs with huge fat bellies and their legs sticking out like on kids' toys. Then you'd have to go out and stab them in the stomach with a butcher knife. The air would all come out with a whoosh, and it really stunk. Sometimes they lived, and sometimes they didn't.

*

You'd think your hands would get cold, dipping them into freezing water under the ice. The trick was to have a pailful of water boiling on the stove in the caboose. You'd put on a pair of hot, wet mitts, then when you'd finished lifting the net, the mitts would be all frozen and you'd throw them in the pail and pick out another pair. It was warm as toast.

*

Jerry got into a fight one time with a guy from the city. They both wanted the same parking space, and Jerry got it. The city guy was little, but he ran up to the car and grabbed Jerry and swung at his head. Jerry stepped out of the car and hit him a couple of times and he fell down and didn't move. Jerry helped him back to his car and his friends drove him away. Somehow, he managed to tear a little rip in Jerry's shirt. Mum fixed the tear, but from then on she called it Jerry's fighting shirt.

*

It's easy to lose a duck if you've only wounded it. It will dive under and grab onto a reed with its beak. It will hold onto the reed until it dies, and even after it is dead, it will still hold onto the reed and won't come to the surface.

*

One time this crazy lady fell in love with me. She used to follow me around and telephone me every day and give me little gifts, cactuses and little china dolls and tablecloths, things like that. She'd be waiting outside the door when I got off work, even if it was the middle of winter. She was about forty years old with a big nose and buck teeth and she was always dressed as if she were on her way to a party. She was actually pretty scary, and for a whole year I had to hide and sneak around like a criminal. Now, she just seems sort of pitiful, but the really scary thing is, what if she'd been pretty? She'd have been just as crazy, but she'd probably have got me.

*

The cops are another thing altogether. I got stopped by this great big cop one time, for going through a stop sign. He was so mad when he came over to my car that I thought I was in real trouble. I didn't realize until he was halfway through that he was drunk as a fart. Then suddenly he gave me a warning and ran back to the cruiser and vomited behind it. He didn't think I saw him, but I did.

*

The Leduc boys were the funniest guys I ever saw. They were always drunk, but still always neat and clean with their hair slicked down with Brylcream, so it didn't even look like hair. Whenever they borrowed money off you for beer, they would arrange the exact day that they were going to pay you back, only they never did. They were very serious and never laughed or talked even to each other. Still, I kind of liked them. Then one day the police came and took all four of them away for raping their little sister.

*

No-account Swenson had six daughters when his wife ran away with the foreman of the gang who were putting in the waterworks. One day at a bingo he met a woman from Riverton who also had six daughters, but whose husband was

32

dead. He was a bush pilot, I think. They got married and had another six daughters. Eighteen girls altogether, all of them beautiful and all of them horny. No-account had to quit his job and stay home on welfare just to protect them. Every night there were so many cars parked around his house, it looked like a picnic. It worked out all right though. They all got married and moved away. Now there's only No-account and his wife, but he's still on welfare.

*

One time Mum gave me hell for going out with Helgi Thorson's daughter. Mum said she was nothing but a cheap tramp, and I should keep away from her. She said Lena Gibson had seen me and her driving out to Devil's Curve. The thing is, I didn't even know that Helgi Thorson had a daughter. It turned out that Helgi was divorced and his daughter had been living on the coast with her mother. Her name was Joanie, and she was a really nice girl. I suppose I should thank Mum for that.

*

At Lenny's wedding, there was a church right next door, not the one he got married in but a Catholic one. We were all pretty drunk and during the intermission we sneaked into the church through a side door which was open. Johnny and Dolores said they wanted to get married, so I took a Bible and stood up there like a preacher and repeated the service as well as I could remember it. They both said "I do," and I declared them man and wife. We went back into the hall, but Johnny and Dolores never showed up again. A couple of years later they did get married, but Johnny still says he considers that marriage at Lenny's reception the real one, and he calls me preacher. Dolores insists that it never happened and that Johnny and me just made it up.

*

In about the middle of July, the fishing boats would come in from up north, and then the pub would be full of drunk fishermen for two weeks and the taxis would be full of drunk Indians, just cruising around because they couldn't go into the beer parlour. One year there was this beautiful Indian girl. She was about sixteen, with long black hair and a beautiful face. She was about nine months pregnant, and she used to walk up and down in front of the beer parlour, waiting for this fifty-year-old white guy who'd stagger out drunk, and she'd carry him back to the boat. She walked with her back straight and her chin up and when the guys would drive by and shout at her she wouldn't even glance at them. She was real proud. That's what she was, proud.

*

When Cam and Bruce were little, they used to sneak out my twenty-two and shoot birds in the spruce bush. Then they'd hide the twenty-two in a hollow tree and forget where they'd put it. I lost about six twenty-twos that way, and I could never figure out what happened to them. I was having a beer with Bruce the other day and he told me about it. We both thought it was funny and laughed about it, but I'm going out to that bush as soon as I get the time. It's full of hollow trees with twenty-twos in them.

*

When we lived out by the marshes, the animals used to keep getting caught in muskrat traps. Once we had two three-legged cats and a three-legged dog. We also had a cat with only one eye, but that wasn't from the traps. People used to ask if we were running a home for crippled animals. I liked those animals, though. They all came home with broken legs and chewed off the leg, then licked the stump till it was better. They had a lot of spunk, and it didn't bother them, having only three legs.

*

I'm not going to any more funerals with open coffins. Every one I've been to, I can only remember what the person looks like dead. That's a hell of a way to remember someone.

*

I met Laura Ryzik at the Teulon fair this summer. She was in the same grade with me the whole time and I don't think I ever spoke two words to her. She was terribly shy, her family being so religious, and she wasn't allowed to go out after six o'clock. She's married now and got two kids. She came right up to me and started to talk about how much fun we used to have in school and wanted to find out how you and everybody else was doing. I remember a lot of things, but I don't remember Laura ever doing anything but sitting in her desk or walking back and forth in the hallway, running her hand along the railing.

*

After that bad accident at the plant when those two German guys got killed, a man from the newspaper came out and talked to everybody. I was right there and saw it all, and I told him exactly what happened. Then when the story came in the paper it was all wrong. If you didn't know, you couldn't even tell it was the same accident. You can't believe nothing you read in the newspaper.

*

It's hard to figure out. Mostly women just pretend to be mad because they think they're supposed to, but sometimes they get a hard lump of anger in them and nothing you can do will make it go away. Then you're in real trouble.

*

Sometimes I think I'm always the last person to find out anything.

*

I went out with Sheila for about a year. For the first six months it was really casual, like just good friends, and we had a lot of fun together. Then we started making love, and all she wanted to do was make love every minute, no matter where we were. We never went anywhere or did anything. It got so that everything, even food, smelled like her. Finally, I told her it was all over and went up to Thompson to work for three months. I had to. I couldn't breathe. When I got back, she was married to somebody else and gone to live in Winnipeg. I haven't seen her since.

*

When I used to work in the garage selling gas, it would get so boring that I'd pretend I was a super gas attendant. I'd fill up a car, check all the tires, check the battery and the radiator and the oil, wash the windows, check the fan belt, I'd do everything but polish the guy's shoes. People were really impressed and some of them even wrote notes to the manager telling him what a good employee I was. Those were mostly Americans. But only one guy ever gave me a tip and that was a quarter. I only did it because I was bored anyway.

*

I should never have got married. I was always falling in love with somebody, and I should have known that wouldn't change, even if I was married. We're still friends though. Sometimes I meet Liz in a store or at a wedding and even though she's married again and got a kid, it's still embarrassing. She always straightens my clothes and picks little pieces of lint off me.

*

The Solmundson boys had a talking crow. They'd split its tongue and taught it to talk. I went over to see it, but it was a terrible disappointment. All it would say was what they'd taught it to say, and all they'd taught it to do was to ask for food.

*

I'll tell you a secret. If you look in a mirror, you don't really see yourself, because everything's backward. I know a guy who wanted to learn to sneer like Elvis Presley, so he practised in a mirror. What happened was, he got the sneer on the wrong side of his face, but he'd practised so hard he could never get rid of it.

Owl on Cairn

From where you turned, looking over your shoulder, it is only a stone's throw to the white rock. Green billows on the lake, terns falling in impossible dives. Somewhere, it is impossible to say where now, is the cairn we built that summer, four flat white rocks piled one on the other, an impossible monument that anything might destroy. And it was gone. Only a month later I was back, and it was near enough to the time to remember. Something had been by, a badger, a man's careless feet, or only the wind, though I think the rocks were too large for the wind to take.

That's how memory is. You walked right by the spot where we built the cairn, and you didn't look for it, or if you did, I missed your looking. But you turned, looking over your shoulder to where I stood on the shore, calculating how close I might stand to the waves and still be safe.

You were wearing your red jacket, the one you wear when it might rain, though it wasn't raining. Billows of cumulus in a low sky.

But it's the cairn I want to talk about. Your standing there, looking over your shoulder, is only an excuse, and no one else will know whether it happened or not. I'm sure it did, it must have, the gesture is yours. And the cairn is there in memory, as surely as if we'd built it out of rocks somewhere in the Arctic, say, where nobody ever goes except for the odd Eskimo, and they care too much about cairns ever to destroy one.

Let's say the cairn really was in the frozen north, and an Eskimo saw it with an owl sitting on it, and he painted a picture of it. Then, years before I ever met you, you bought it as a hedge against the future. That would be right. Later, we might sit in a classroom and listen to an expert explain that the cairn was made in memory of a departed spirit, and the owl was the soul of the dead person returning to the place it was most comfortable. He might, in order to make his point, draw it on the blackboard, owl on cairn.

And I think now, it was probably an owl that took our stones, a spirit conjured into being by our declaration, because a cairn is always a message, a declaration, a contract with time and whatever other worlds there may be. We walked to the beacon the other day, and we saw an owl being harassed by crows. There's a message there for sure, but it's too easy, the white owl, the black crows, good and evil. That's not what it's about.

Though it's not so easy to say exactly what I mean. Let me go back to the gesture. Looking over your shoulder. I'd just come back from Germany, I remember, though there's more in the idea of coming back from Germany than I intend to mean. It's only a fact. And what I remember now is unimportant. Handles on the doors instead of doorknobs. Ruined castles, which must have been as hard to take apart in the thirteenth century as they were to assemble. Young green wine and beer that tasted like honey.

There was more love to be made that day than human

bodies could handle, and so we made our love with stones, piling them into a cairn under the eye of the imaginary owl. And there was a litany of birds: white pelicans, terns, gulls, sandpipers and wrens. Blackbirds flashing red or yellow or purple. Waxwings and warblers, wrens and vireos and teal. It was that day I learned you knew the names of birds, could tell them by their calls. It was worth knowing.

Virtue is not that easy, and I know it better now than I did then. The simplest thing is naming. I'd like to make a list of things we saw that day we made the cairn, and say, "Look, these are the things that were there. Stone, rock, gull and cairn. All the crawling and the flying things that leave their signatures in the sand."

But naming is never enough. The owls nest in the clump of trees at the edge of the swamp in the hay meadow. Beneath the trees, you can find hairballs, small treasure troves of fur and feathers and tiny perfect bones, the remnants of mice and gophers, warblers and wrens. These too are messages.

That day, I skipped flat white stones across the mirror-flat water. You find them high on the beach where the waves throw them, a limestone alphabet waiting to be shaped into cairns, waiting for the inevitable owl to consecrate them.

Looking over your shoulder. In Germany, I climbed to the top of a ruined castle. The walls were eleven feet thick, those walls that remained. The castle was on the top of a hill, surrounded by a moat. In the thirteenth century it must have seemed impregnable, but it was ruined for all that. Now only a few tourists will climb to the top of the highest wall, or perhaps, when there are no tourists, an owl will sit there, looking for mice or simply watching the flat stones splayed down the hillside.

This is simply to remind you of the cairn you failed to see, there by the white rock. Or perhaps you did see it, but thought it not worth mentioning. In Germany, I dreamed of you, in your red jacket, looking over your shoulder. I was standing by the shore, skipping flat white stones over the water. There was more to the dream, but that's all I remember.

And now you are here, on a rainy night, sitting by the fire. I built that fireplace myself, collecting the flat white stones and arranging them just so. I mixed the mortar by hand, built the foundation and piled up the bricks. When we came, an hour ago, there was a nearly-dead owl in the fireplace. It must have got in through the chimney, but it couldn't have been there for long. It didn't resist when I took it in my hands and carried it outside. I put it on the lowest branch of the ash tree just outside the window, and now it is gone. It sat there, without expression, facing the lake, but looking over its shoulder.

The Unmarried Sister

The Unmarried Sister is outrageous. She gets too drunk at parties and tells stories that make the men blush. She's some girl, the husbands say. The wives say it's no wonder.

The Unmarried Sister buys a red sports car. Nobody knows how she can afford it. She drives too fast and gets two tickets the first week.

The Unmarried Sister goes to Hong Kong. She has an affair with the Chinese tour guide and nearly gets stabbed in a back alley. The wives don't believe her. The husbands say she can do better.

There is a party. Somebody brings an Unmarried Brother, tall and shy with big hands. The Unmarried Sister says, "I've got enough troubles without taking on a cripple."

The Unmarried Sister is weeping. The Brothers want to know what to do They want to beat somebody up, but the Unmarried Sister says, "No, it isn't anything like that."

The Unmarried Sister goes to showers for younger women who are getting married. She comes with whiskey on her breath and leaves early. She brings the most expensive present and everyone is angry.

The Unmarried Sister decides to go to medical school. The Father fixes up a room for her in the basement with a separate entrance and a kitchenette, but the Unmarried Sister goes to Finland instead.

Finally, there is a man. Nobody sees him, but there are rumours he is in the white slave trade. Suddenly, the Unmarried Sister has visitors. Questions are asked. She tells them, "It's my life. I'll lead it the way I want."

The Unmarried Sister tells a joke. It is a very funny joke, but when everyone talks about it later, it seems to be a gay joke. Is the Unmarried Sister a lesbian?

The Unmarried Sister will not come for Christmas. She says she can't afford to buy presents. Everybody agrees that she shouldn't have to buy so many presents. She does come, and her presents are better than anyone else's. She doesn't know what to do with her money.

The Unmarried Sister is beautiful. Well, not beautiful, but very pretty if she'd just lose five pounds. Why will nobody marry her?

The Unmarried Sister is pissed off. Not angry or depressed, just pissed off. Why? She says it is her mother's fault. The Mother always liked the Younger Sister who is married. Why does the Mother not love the Unmarried Sister?

The Unmarried Sister

The Unmarried Sister makes friends with the Ex-Wives. Is this treachery?

The Unmarried Sister is hurt in a car accident. The accident is her own fault. Everybody visits her in the hospital. The nurses say she is the funniest patient they have ever had. The whole hospital loves her. After that, she doesn't get very many visitors.

The Unmarried Sister refuses to eat white bread or red meat. She disapproves of sugar. What can the Family do about this?

The Unmarried Sister dyes her hair black. This makes her look tough. Nobody knows how to tell her.

The Unmarried Sister disappears. The police are brought in. A week later, she is found in Grand Forks, North Dakota, with a married Real Estate Agent. The Unmarried Sister is furious. Is this fair to the Family who worried so much about her?

The Unmarried Sister has allergies. She cannot enter a house where there's a cat or a dog. She cannot sleep on feather pillows. She cannot eat strawberries or anything with coconut in it. She sneezes in clothing stores. When she goes to Australia, her allergies disappear. She says she might go to live in Australia, but everyone agrees this would be a mistake.

The Unmarried Sister has a dream in which all her hair falls out. She moves to another apartment.

Rapists and murderers stalk the Unmarried Sister. They hide in parking lots and peer through her windows at night. She doesn't seem to notice, but everyone agrees it would be better if she would move home and take care of the Failing Mother.

The Unmarried Sister dances. She dances the rhumba, the samba and the tango. She does foxtrots and old-time waltzes and heel-toe polkas. She can do the twist, the bunny hop, the schottische, the Charleston, the quadrille, the square dance, the cotillion, the gavotte, the minuet, the jig, the galliard, the mazurka, the butterfly, the stomp, the cakewalk, the stroll, the jive and the Highland fling. Sometimes, late at night, alone in her room, she dances, but this dance has no name.

Girl and Wolf

I t is morning. The possibilities for the wolf are open and endless. The paths through the forest run in every direction.
The pale green new leaves on the trees are welcome after a
hard winter. The breeze is gentle and ruffles his fur. The wolf
is hungry, he is always hungry. That is what it is to be a wolf.
The wolf is sleek and limber. As he runs, he admires his own
grace.

The red-haired girl is going to see her grandmother. The
weather is the same for her, same morning, same breeze, same
new green leaves. The girl is tall and well made. She has
already forgotten all her mother's cautions. She is ready to
talk to strangers, she is eager for strangers and adventures. A
girl's life is surrounded by cautions, she is circumscribed by
rules. Only a forest offers freedom.

The paths through the forest run in all directions. They
meet and intersect. They double back on themselves, inter-
twine. There are a thousand nodes, a thousand crossings. At
any one of these crossings the girl might encounter the wolf.

There are so many crossings that it is inevitable that at one of them the wolf and girl will meet.

When they meet, the wolf must ask the question, the girl must answer. Where are you going? To visit my grandmother. It is the question all wolves ask, the answer all girls give. The girl's path is the path of needles, the wolf will follow the path of pins. Needles and pins, the path leads to the grandmother's house, all paths lead to the grandmother's house.

The wolf is there first. He is always first. He runs with his easy gait down the winding path. The girl is distracted. She strays from the path, she picks flowers, she stops to drink at a stream. The wolf is early. He must wait for the girl. It is only the start of his waiting. The wolf eats the grandmother. He must pass the time somehow, and he is hungry. Even then, and that takes some time, the grandmother is old and stringy, he must wait. He lies in the bed.

The girl knocks at the door. The wolf, in the bed, is nearly mad with impatience. He is sick with desire. "Come in," he shouts. The girl enters. The girl likes entrances. She is fresh and perfumed from the flowers she has picked. She dances in the door, her dress swirls, her red hair swirls. "Grandmother," she says, "see, I have picked you some flowers."

"Bring them here," the wolf answers. She gets a glass of water from the kitchen. She puts the flowers in the water and brings them to the bed. She knows that the wolf is not her grandmother. She recognizes him as the stranger she met in the forest. Still, she is calm. She seems to know what she is doing, or else she is caught by some force that makes her operate against her will.

"Come, get into the bed with me," the wolf tells the girl. It is a desperate ruse. If she recognizes him all will be lost. And how can she fail to recognize him? He is not even masked. All his life it has been like this. He is never properly prepared. He never has the disguise he needs, the mask he should wear.

"What shall I do with my coat?" she asks.

"Throw it in the fire," the wolf tells her. "You won't need it anymore."

The girl takes off her coat and throws it into the fire. "And what shall I do with my dress?" she asks.

"Take it off and throw it into the fire. You won't need it anymore."

She slips the dress over her head and throws it into the fire. She is wearing a white slip and red shoes. "What shall I do with my shoes?"

"Take them off and throw them into the fire. You won't be needing them anymore."

The girl sits on the edge of the bed to take off her shoes. She bends with an awkwardness the wolf finds touching. She slips off one shoe at a time and throws them into the fire. "What shall I do with my slip?" she asks the wolf.

"Take it off and throw it into the fire. You won't be needing it any more." The girl pulls the slip over her head and throws it into the fire. She has on black panties and a black brassiere. Panties and brassiere are edged with lace. They look expensive.

"What shall I do with my brassiere?" the girl asks the wolf. Her red hair spills over the whiteness of her shoulders.

"Take it off and throw it into the fire. You won't be needing it any more." The wolf is tense. Is he perhaps too eager? He is trying to make his answers part of a ritual that will complete itself out of its inner necessity. One false step now and the charm might be broken.

The girl takes off her brassiere and throws it into the fire.

Her breasts spill out, or at least the only words that come to the wolf's mind are "spill out." The girl's breasts are high and firm and very large. They accentuate the slimness of her waist. In the cool air of the room her nipples grow firm.

"And what shall I do with my panties?"

"Take them off and throw them into the fire. You won't need them anymore."

The girl slips down her panties and flips them into the fire with her toe. She stands there, entirely naked. The little triangle is a paler red than her hair. The girl gets into the bed and snuggles up against the wolf. Her hair seems even redder against the white of the sheets.

"Why do you have so much hair on your body, Grandmother?" she asks. She rubs her hands along the wolf's body, and he feels rising in himself something that might have been hunger if he hadn't just eaten.

"It keeps me warm," the wolf replies.

"And why do you have such large eyes?" she asks, and as she asks, she looks at him with her own wide green eyes.

"The better to see you with," the wolf says, though he knows the inadequacy of that answer. He can feel her firm breasts pressed against his body.

"And why do you have such large teeth?" she asks. It is his moment. The wolf knows there will be no more questions.

Everything depends on his answer now. He hesitates a moment, but there is really no option. There is only one answer, and there has never really been a choice. He says it reluctantly: "The better to eat you with."

"Nonsense," the girl replies, sliding under the wolf and pulling him on top of her. Her hands slip down to his hindquarters, easing his entry. The girl likes entrances. The wolf moans in his delight, a moan that blends with the ecstatic moans of all his ancestors. The girl is inexperienced but active, and when it is over, the wolf doesn't know whether what he feels is joy or pain.

Girl and Wolf

The girl lights a cigarette from a package on her grand-mother's table. She sits cross-legged on the bed, looking at the wolf. "That was nice," she says. "We're going to get along fine."

She blows the smoke out her nostrils and flicks some ashes onto the floor. "It's a pity about my clothes, though. I'm going to have to get an entire new wardrobe. You don't have a job, I know that, but it will all work out. You can work at my dad's service station until something better comes along."

Just then there is a knock at the door. The girl finds a robe in her grandmother's closet. She slips it over her nakedness and goes to the door. A woodcutter stands there, his axe gleaming in his hand.

"Is everything all right?" he asks.

"Just fine," the girl says.

"I was wondering about your grandmother."

"Grandma's gone to Tucson, Arizona, to live with my aunt," the girl tells him. She's given the house to me and my fiancé. We're going to be doing some renovating, so if you're looking for work, why don't you drop around in a couple of weeks."

The wolf already knows the ending. It is the last of his wolfhood. His morning runs down the winding and criss-crossing trails of the forest are over. Already, his legs ache from the concrete on which he will stand. His fur is begin-ning to smell of oil. And so it has always been. What is the good of cautioning young girls? Grandmothers cannot be trusted. They are always somewhere else. The woodcutter is always too late. Whatever is lost is lost forever, and the for-est trails, though they wind and cross, are searching for some-body else's meetings.

The Figure Skater

What magic there is left in the world is wholly in the possession of figure skaters. You remember the scene in *Carnal Knowledge* where Jack Nicholson is talking to Art Garfunkel and they are overlooking a skating rink where a figure skater swirls in delicate arabesques. Nicholson and Garfunkel are both playing seedy characters. It is difficult for us to forgive Nicholson for having seduced Candice Bergen when they were in college, and just as difficult for us to forgive Garfunkel for allowing himself to be cuckolded before he has even got married. We are presented with friends, but we know that a betrayal is at the core of their relationship, making it unstable. The figure skater swirls.

The figure skater, of course, is in all respects in opposition to the carnal knowledge of the title. She is engaged in her art. She whirls and pirouettes, and is quite as free from sexual attractiveness as an angel. There is no doubt that she is a pretty girl and that her body is graceful and attractive. Nicholson and Garfunkel look down on her from above. Ann-Margret is at home. She has become fat and bad-tempered, and just now either Garfunkel or Nicholson is explaining how unsatisfying his marriage really is.

The ice, of course, has a lot to do with it. The background against which we see the figure skater is cool and smooth. Her movements are clearly made without effort. There is no question of her perspiring. She herself is neither warm nor cold. These distinctions have nothing to do with figure skaters. There are both male and female figure skaters, but when we use the term we are always speaking of women. A male figure skater, however good, can never be more than a parody. The director knew that, and there is no male figure skater in the film.

In our part of the country, winters are bitterly cold. There is no shortage of ice, but it is impossible to figure skate outdoors because the freezing arctic winds sweep down from the north, chilling the bones and piling the snow in drifts. The ice heaves and cracks. Inside, in covered skating rinks, the figure skaters change, and lace on their white boots in dressing rooms still sour with the smell of the sweat and beer of last night's hockey players. The room is rank with the smell of maleness, and the warm air blowing from the grate in the floor provides no solace.

The skaters are preparing for the town's winter carnival. Every morning at six o'clock the three senior skaters practise for two hours before they go to the high school. The younger girls will meet with their parade-marshal instructress at three in the afternoon. The school allows these girls to leave early. At four, the younger boys will practise hockey. Outside, other preparations are underway. The Kinsmen met last night to put the final touches on the pancake breakfast. They have ordered the bacon, the flour and the milk. They have chosen their shifts.

Ticket sales are going well. We have three candidates. The

blonde girl is supported by the high school, the dark girl is supported by the Chamber of Commerce, and the redhead is, of course, supported by the volunteer firefighters. Whoever sells the most tickets will have their candidate become queen. The dark girl is the doctor's daughter. There is a rumour that the doctor will buy however many tickets are required to guarantee her victory. Right now, the drawings of thermometers, gauged in dollars, indicate that she is running third. We all agree that this is the best way of choosing our queen.

The money will go to enlarging the dressing rooms. Only the bitter tears of the two losers will deny us, and those will disappear when the pillowcases are washed.

The figure skaters have no fear of loss. They know their moment will come. The lights will darken in the arena and the spotlight will pick them out at the door of the penalty box. There will be one second of hesitation before they push away from the wooden boards, and then they will be released into the freedom of their dance. Already they have begun to change in preparation for this metamorphosis. They are silent in the hallways of the school. They clutch their books in front of their breasts with both arms. They do not speak to their friends, scarcely recognize them on the street. At home, it is no use to talk to them. They have entered the dream. Already, they are starting to glow, like sacrificial victims before some great event, and we treat them delicately, like something fragile that might break.

Art Garfunkel and Jack Nicholson, trapped in their betrayals, their disappointments and their lust, do not even see the figure skaters. At home, Ann-Margret weeps and fights with the flesh that threatens to overwhelm her. I hurry past the snow sculptures: dinosaurs and seals balancing snow balls, snow horses pulling snow sleighs, a castle made from ice with coloured lights inside. My skates are wound around my hockey stick, the stick rests on my shoulder. I drag my canvas equipment bag over the snow. I know I am not late, but I hurry as if I were.

Most of the other players are already in the dressing room when I get there. I find an open spot on the bench and start to unpack. We make the usual lewd jokes, we elbow and jostle each other, but there is a tension that makes our uproar seem subdued. The animal of a crowd out there sobers us. We are accustomed to playing before a couple of hundred people. Tonight there will be nearly three thousand. They will be jammed so tight they cannot move, and when they shout we will feel their breath on our necks.

We are, of course, playing the ancient enemy, the Other Town. They were our fathers' rivals decades ago, and they are ours now. We will win; we always win at our carnival. They win at theirs, when we are the enemy. We are inhabited by the will of that fearsome crowd. When our energy flags, the inarticulate language of its cry will enter us and give us power. We know it in our flesh.

And we do win. I am aware of the brightness of the ice, the whirl of the bodies that surround me, the jolt and crunch of the collisions. I see the black crowd that surrounds us, three thousand bodies melted into one flesh, speaking with one voice. The score is close. With moments left to play, I am afraid the coach will not put me back on the ice. We are short of defencemen, and I have already played to exhaustion. Then I am slapped on the shoulder, I tumble over the boards onto the ice, out of position. By some miracle, the puck is on my stick. I lunge toward the enemy's goal, fed by the roar of the crowd. I cannot make the decision to shoot, but will alone puts the puck into the net as I fall. Then my friends fall on top of me. They grasp me in their love. Their hands, their bodies, press against me.

The Figure Skater

In the first silence after the game, I vomit alone in the washroom, unsure whether my body is reacting to my effort or to my newfound heroism. For there is no doubt, I am now a hero. But I am the wrong hero, I was not destined for this. I should have been the silent helper, and I know that others have done more heroic things during the game. But my act came at the moment of the crowd's greatest desire, and there is room for only one hero. Later in the dressing room I am showered with sacramental beer. I dress slowly, not wanting to relinquish the moment. I have seen other heroes and I know what to do. To all congratulations and insults, I respond with quiet modesty. When I leave the rink, the crowd has gone and workmen are already installing the throne for the queen and flooding the ice for tomorrow's figure skaters.

The next day, I am up early. Heroes don't last long around here, but I am safe for the time of the carnival. Everybody knows me now. People I have only seen from a distance are my friends. They shout, "Great game," and, "Way to score." I eat the Kinsmen's pancakes, I go over to the curling rink and sample the preserves on display, talk to the farm wives selling cakes and cookies and pies. I go over to the park to watch the races. The skiers have already left, winding down the river to the lake. A half dozen dog teams yelp and fight as their owners get them ready for the dog sled race. The snowshoers walk around stamping their feet, anxious to begin. They are haloed by their breath and ice has formed on the fur of their parkas. Ordinary girls are made beautiful by the circle of white fur that surrounds their faces. I am invited to join, if not to race, at least to take part in the tug of war. I refuse. I cannot take the chance that some small loss might diminish my glory.

I wander the day in a dream. Like royalty, I grace every building I enter. The slackness of the day tightens as evening approaches. The crowning of the queen, the figure skating and the ice dance all await. Then, there is the stomping line-up at the door to the rink, the excitement and the bustle, the smell of hot dogs and hamburgers. Before we are even into the bleachers, we are in a tight crush. I can smell the alcohol on the breaths of the older men, the perfume from the women. I find a place on a bench, the third row, and squeeze in beside my friends. I am still treated with courtesy and awe, but I can feel that I am already losing myself and becoming part of the crowd.

The program begins with a comic broomball game between the volunteer firefighters and the Chamber of Commerce. The firefighters wear their fire hats and long red underwear. The Chamber of Commerce is dressed as a brigade of bartenders with vests and bowler hats. A clown on skates drops the ball, and the game begins. Men, out of shape and out of breath, run in a pantomime of play. We shout out their names and professions. We insult them out of our love for their goodness, their generosity, their willingness to be there on the ice for our entertainment.

Then the game is over. A tie. It is always a tie, the scorekeeper flashing numbers on the scoreboard at his own whim, without any concern for the goals scored. After that, a master of ceremonies in top hat and tails skates out to the centre of the ice. He announces the crowning of the queen. The loudspeaker plays triumphant music. The blonde girl from the high school comes from around a cardboard screen at the end of the rink. She is beautiful in a long blue dress, and she walks on the arm of the high school principal, who is still wearing his brown suit. Then, as the trumpets blare once more, the dark-haired beauty from the Chamber of Commerce comes on the arm of the manager of the Bank of Nova Scotia. Her dress is long and white. Finally, the red-headed hairdresser who is the hope of the volunteer firefighters arrives on the arm of the postmaster, who is also a firefighter.

The Figure Skater

A little figure skater in a ballet costume skates out to the master of ceremonies and hands him an envelope. The whole building is hushed, and he would not need his microphone. Still, his voice rattles through the rafters as he announces the name. It is the dark-haired girl from the Chamber of Commerce. The other two, reduced now to princesses, embrace her. They too know the models of behaviour. They ascend the throne, queen in the middle, princesses a little lower and to the side. It is clear now that if the dark-haired girl was not prettier before, she is more beautiful now. Her crowning has given her beauty, and her father's contribution has nothing to do with it.

After the fundraising amounts have been announced, the volunteers thanked and the merchants singled out for their generosity, the figure skaters begin. First, under the full glare of the lights, a dozen tiny dancers in pink hop and skip around the ice. No one falls. It is carnival, and no one falls at carnival. Then the middle group arrives. They do more difficult tricks, they form phalanxes and arrays, they swoop and dip in imitation of their older sisters. Finally, and we have all been waiting for this, the lights go down and the solos begin. The girls are of no age, their age is unimportant, they are only beautiful and pure. They are ice made flesh and allowed to dance. We who live most of our lives on ice recognize them immediately. For Nicholson and Garfunkel, the skater is mere background. They do not see her. For us, the figure skaters are the point of focus. They hold the six thousand eyes of the crowd, and it is a wonder that the focus of so many eyes does not set them aflame.

The first dancer is dressed in red. She is birdlike, swooping, hopping, spinning off in surprising ways, seeming never to come to rest. The second dancer is in blue. She moves with a slow deliberate grace, long strides, jumps that we think must bring her to disaster until her landing transforms her into a gently spinning flower. And the white dancer. There is no hesitation. We have not even seen her begin. Suddenly, she is there, skimming the ice so that she hardly seems to touch it. She leaps high in the air, weightless, and lands skating backwards, as if direction had no meaning for her. She pirouettes, she whirls, she draws our cries of delight out of our throats. Time stops completely during her performance. Then she is low on the ice, her hand holding her skate, her leg extended. She spins slowly as she rises, speeding up faster and faster until she is a blur of white, what you see when you stare at a distant star. At last, she unfolds her spiral into a sweeping bow and is gone. We roar for more, and she is back. Whenever she tries to leave, our yearning voices draw her out of the darkness into the circle of spotlight in which she dances. Finally, the master of ceremonies in his top hat and tails braves our disappointment to announce that the party will begin as soon as the orchestra can set up on the stage at the end of the rink.

For just a moment the crowd holds, but then individuals separate out onto the ice, a river of movement carries people into the waiting room and cafeteria, conversations begin, the focus is lost. All the lights come on, and, suddenly isolated, we reach out to the people closest to us, asking them if they are staying for the dance, conjuring up the day's activities. Did you take part in the snowshoe race? Did you enter the snowmobile derby? Yes, yes.

Already the band is tuning up its instruments. Mack Harvey and the Deep River Boys break into "In the Mood." My heroism permits me to claim the queen after she has danced with the mayor and the members of the Town Council. She has put on a Hudson's Bay parka over her white gown. Her black hair curls over her shoulder. I have known her for years, since we were children. Her father delivered me, sat up all night with me when I had diphtheria, the last diphtheria case in town, my main source of fame until this carnival. We dance a polka, then join the line for the bunny hop, slipping and falling on the ice. When I hold her tight in my arms for the "Tennessee Waltz," I can see tiny beads of sweat on her upper lip.

I have a mickey of rye whiskey in my father's half-ton truck. At intermission we sneak out the side door for a drink. It is freezing cold in the truck, but the whiskey warms us, and in a few minutes the heater begins to warm up the cab. I kiss her, and she moves tighter, pressing her body against mine. We should go back to the dance, but we know we will not. Instead, fumbling somehow through our heavy clothes, we make love. We know each other. It is a rapid coupling, and if there was any joy, I can't remember it now. After it is over, we drink some more whiskey and hold each other, shivering, but not from the cold. It is her first time, and it is also mine.

The dance is over. People pour out of the skating rink into their cars and trucks, shouting good-byes. The exhaust from their motors hangs in the air, a thick blue fog. Through it, headlights look like moons on a cloudy night. We wait until most of the cars have gone. Then I slip the half-ton into gear and begin to move slowly down the street. I flick on my headlights, and they pick out a thin wisp of a girl hurrying across the road, carrying her white costume on a coat hanger. It is the figure skater, going home.

The Sunfish

Dawn was just spreading its red glow across Lake Winnipeg when Gusti Oddson reached for the buoy to pull in the first of his seven nets. And what was he thinking, that second cousin once removed of my great-grandmother, on a June morning in 1878? Perhaps he was thinking of the smallpox epidemic that had recently taken his wife and three children, or perhaps he was thinking about nets and why they sometimes caught fish and sometimes didn't. He wasn't thinking about talking fish, or at least the scattered diaries he left behind give no indication that he was thinking about talking fish, and why, after all, should he have been? That's why he was startled when the sunfish he had just pulled into his boat, the first sunfish of the day, spoke to him.

"Gusti," the sunfish said, its silver scales bright in the first rays of the rising sun, "listen to me. I have much to tell you."

Gusti did not answer right away. He was a man of common sense, and he knew that fish do not speak. Still, in the past three years, his faith in common sense had been somewhat shaken. Common sense worked perfectly well in Iceland, but it seemed to be of less value in this new country. Common sense had told him that when water is covered with ice, you do not bother to fish. Here though, you fished underneath the ice, and when you pulled fish up through the ice, they gasped and froze solid in the winter air. Common sense told you that land which could grow trees fifty feet high could also grow potatoes, but that was apparently not necessarily so.

He had come to the Republic of New Iceland three years ago. The first year, he had nearly starved. The second year, his family had died in the smallpox epidemic. The third year, religious argument had split New Iceland into two warring camps. Seri Bjarni argued that the struggle between God and the devil was being fought out for the final time on the shores of Lake Winnipeg. Seri Jon argued that there was no devil, that Jesus was not the Son of God, but only a religious leader, and that God was a spirit that was in everything in the world, but was not a person.

So, when the sunfish spoke to him, Gusti asked it, "Are you of the devil's party?"

"Don't talk nonsense," replied the sunfish. "There is no devil, or God either, for that matter."

Gusti pondered for a moment, then asked, "Are you then a Unitarian?"

"I am a sunfish," said the sunfish, "and I'm not here to give you any selfish wishes. Greed and lust," he went on sadly, "that's all you find nowadays."

"Then you are one of the Huldafolk," Gusti said, "or maybe a Mori raised by enemies to bring me bad luck."

"More nonsense," the fish replied. "Ignorant superstition. How could your luck be any worse than it is? Everybody you love is dead. You haven't got a penny to your name. You hardly catch enough fish to eat, much less to sell. Everybody

in New Iceland calls you Gusti Foulfart because you live on
dried beans and never wash your clothes. No woman will
look at you."

"There is no need," Gusti told the fish, "to be rude. Things
have not gone well for me in the last while, it is true, but that
is not to say that they will not soon improve."

"Progress," sneered the fish, if indeed his opening and closing his mouth could be counted a sneer, "delusion, a snare
and a trap, the vast enslaving device of the Western world.
Only peasants and fishermen and fools believe in progress.
Things never get better, they only get different."

"How is it that you speak Icelandic?" Gusti asked the fish,
who seemed to be having some trouble with his breathing.

"A better question might be, 'How is it that you come to
speak Sunfish?'" the fish replied, flopping around on the bottom of the skiff, as if to get a better view of Gusti. "Or indeed,
it might be more to the point to ask, 'What is the nature of
language?'"

"There are plenty of preachers on land," Gusti told the
fish. "Already the sun is well above the horizon, and I have
seven nets to lift. In New Iceland they have taken to calling
me Gusti Madman because my wife sometimes comes to me
in dreams and I cry out for her. I have no time to argue reli-
gion with a fish."

"Wait," cried the fish, with what might have been real fear,
"I am speaking to you. Is this not remarkable? Do you not
want to know what I have come to tell you?"

"I believe the evidence of my senses," Gusti replied, "when
my senses give me evidence I can trust. I know that fish do
not speak. Perhaps there is a voice-thrower on the shore, or
perhaps I am still in my bed dreaming of fish. The least likely
thing is that I am actually in my skiff talking with a fish. So, I
am going to hit you on the head with my oar, and I will take

you in and boil you and eat you with potatoes and butter. You are not a large fish, but you will do."

"Wait," the fish almost shouted, alarmed that Gusti had picked up an oar and seemed to mean business. Gusti had let go of the line and they were drifting away from the net toward the southeast. "I'll give you a wish. Not three wishes, but just one, and try to be reasonable."

Gusti put the oar down. "I'll have my wife back."

The fish groaned, or made a sound that was close to a groan. "I asked you to be reasonable. Your wife has been dead two years. How could you explain her return? Bringing people back from the dead destroys the natural order of things. Besides, you fought like cats and dogs when she was alive. Let me give you a new boat instead."

Gusti reached for the oar again.

"No, wait," the fish continued. "I can give you Valdi Thorson's wife, Vigdis Thorarinsdottir, instead. She's the most beautiful woman in New Iceland and you know you've lusted for her for years, even when your wife was alive."

Gusti pondered for a moment and then replied, "No. She is a fine woman, but a man shall cleave to his wife. It is either my wife that you give me, or I eat you for supper this very night."

"Okay," the fish grumbled, "but it's not the way you think. She won't be there waiting for you when you get back. She'll arrive in two weeks as a young woman, the cousin of your wife. Her name will be Freya Gudmundsdottir and she'll claim kin and come to live with you. But you'll have to woo her. And you'll have to shape up or else she'll marry Ketil Hallgrimsson, and then you'll have neither wife nor supper."

"Good," said Gusti, "that's fair. Now what have you come to tell me?"

The fish appeared to be sulking. "It's ridiculous," he

complained. "I appear at great personal risk to offer mankind wisdom, and I get petty arguments, greed and lust. It's always the same. And I don't suppose you'll pay any attention to what I tell you anyway. Do you think I like to breathe air? Do you think it's comfortable here on the bottom of this boat? I don't know why I do it."

The sunfish fell silent. Gusti felt a little sorry for it and he asked gently, "What is it I should know? I will listen carefully, and if things work out as you say and my wife returns, I will try to carry out your instructions."

The fish seemed a little mollified at this. "Okay," he said, "listen carefully."

Gusti leaned forward, attentive. "It's over," the fish told him. "Done. Finished. Kaput. They're closing down the whole show. Moving on to bigger and better things. Cutting their losses."

"What do you mean?" Gusti asked the fish, who by now was slowly opening and closing his mouth.

"All of it. Everything. Sun, moon, stars, trees, birds, animals, men, dogs, cats, the whole shooting works."

"You are telling me then," said Gusti, "that the world is going to end."

"You got it," said the fish, "go to the head of the class." He flopped once and continued, "And not a moment too soon. Nothing but greed, lust, dishonesty and pride. And self-righteousness. If it weren't for self-righteousness, they might give it another go. If you knew how often I've flopped around the bottom of boats trying to explain things, talking to selfish louts with no more in their minds than their own little comforts, it'd make you sick."

"And when is this to happen?" Gusti asked.

"I don't know. Maybe tomorrow, maybe a couple of millennia. They're busy, they've got things to do. Anyway, I've done my part. I've delivered the message. Now if you'd must heave me over the side, I'll be on my way."

Gusti ignored the fish. "This," he said, "is no great news. Everyone knows that the world will end some day. What matters is to live a proper life while you are here."

"Makes no difference," said the fish. "Proper or improper. What one man does is of no concern. If the whole world changed then maybe they'd reconsider. But it's far too late now for that. Go ahead, rob, murder, steal, it isn't going to make any difference. And if you don't get me in the water soon, you're going to have my death on your conscience as well."

The fish's eyes had started to cloud over. "Just one last question," Gusti went on. "What day will my wife arrive?"

"You see," said the fish, as if addressing someone not in the boat but in the blue sky overhead, "you see what I have to put up with. I bring the most important message in the history of the universe and I have to answer foolish questions. Friday. Or Wednesday, or maybe Saturday. A week or a month. I've given you your wish. I'm not in charge of travel arrangements."

The fish had ceased to gasp, and lay in the bottom of the boat like a dead fish. Gusti picked it up gently, and slipped it into the water. The fish lay on its side, drifting slowly away from the boat. Gusti watched it for a long time, until finally, with a flick of its tail, it disappeared under the shining surface of the lake.

The next morning Gusti did not go out to his nets. Instead, he hauled water from the lake and heated it over an open fire. He took every article out of his shack and washed it. Then he washed the entire shack, inside and out, including the roof. He rechinked every crack he could find with clay, and then he whitewashed the shack inside and out. The entire community came out to watch him with wonder. The children began by singing the song they always sang when he came near, "Gusti Foulfart, Gusti Foulfart, smells likes rotten meat. Stinky beans and stinky fish is all that he will eat." Their parents hushed them and threatened to send them home unless they stopped.

Vigdis Thorarinsdottir was the only one brave enough to speak to him. She knew she was the most beautiful woman in New Iceland and she had seen Gusti look at her out of the corner of his eye.

"Gusti," she asked, "what happened? Are you expecting someone?"

"There has been a change," he replied. "The world will end soon and so a man cannot mourn forever. I will fish no longer. From now on I will be Gusti Carpenter. If you will make two blankets of the finest wool, I will repair the leaking roof on your shack which your husband will not repair because he prefers to sit on the dock repairing nets and telling stories. And, Alda Baldvinsdottir," he went on, "you have a cow. If you will give me a jug of milk each day for a year, I will put another room on your shack so that the twins will not have to sleep in the same bed with you and your husband, and you will not have to worry that he will roll over and smother them."

In this way, Gusti conducted business with the entire community. Halli Valgardson exchanged a year's supply of firewood for a new boat. Inga Gislasdottir agreed to make him a new suit in exchange for a brick chimney. The fishermen agreed to provide him with all the fish he could eat if he kept the dock in good repair. When the sun went down that day, Gusti was the richest man in New Iceland, and everyone had forgotten to call him Gusti Foulfart or even Gusti Madman.

One month later, twenty new settlers arrived on Hannes

Kristjanson's boat. They told frightening stories of the trip, how their ship had nearly foundered on the rocks on the coast of Scotland, and how a marvellous silver fish had appeared and led the boat to safety; how, coming up the St. Lawrence, they would surely have crashed into another ship had not a marvellous silver fish come to the captain in a dream and warned him in time. Just that morning, coming down the Red River, they had run aground in the delta, but a school of silver fishes had bumped into the boat until it floated free.

Among the passengers was Freya Gudmundsdottir. She was eighteen years old, with blonde hair that hung down to her waist and eyes so blue that from that day on, no one in New Iceland called anything blue without explaining that it was not as blue as Freya's eyes. She looked like Gusti's wife had looked when she was young, but Gusti's wife had only looked pretty, and Freya was beautiful.

Ketil Hallgrimsson was the first to meet her when she got off the boat. He asked her to marry him then and there, and he vowed to devote his life to making her happy. Ketil was a handsome young man, only twenty-three years old, with hair that hung in curls and muscles that rippled when he moved. The smile with which Freya answered him made Gusti's blood freeze. Still, she said she had not come to marry the first man she met, and she asked for Gusti. She told him she was the orphaned cousin of his first wife, and asked if she might live with him until she could support herself. Gusti's tongue was so tied in knots that he could barely stammer yes.

She gave him her trunk to carry and followed him down the street to his newly whitewashed shack. The first thing she said when she got into the shack was, "I can see there hasn't been a woman's hand around here for a while." Then she scrubbd the table that Gusti had scrubbed until the top was thin. She sniffed the blankets that Vigdis Thorarinsdottir had just made and which had never been used. She screwed up her nose and hung them out on a tree to air. Then she swept the cleanest floor in New Iceland, threw out the fish that had been caught that morning, saying they had gone bad, and she started to make bread. Gusti sighed and thought, "Yes, this is my wife all right. The fish has delivered his part of the bargain."

And that was pretty much the way things went until the following spring. Gusti found himself occupying a smaller and smaller part of the house. He left early in the morning to do the jobs he had promised the others, and he came back late at night to find the house getting cleaner and cleaner. Freya made him new clothes. She cut his hair and clipped his fingernails and toenails. He had almost no time to write in his diary, but what he wrote pretty well describes his life. "Thursday, January 11. More snow, the weather very cold. Freya is cleaning again. Worked all day repairing Helgi's roof. I may no more chew tabacco." Any entry reads like any other.

Then that spring, Freya was chosen to be protector of the god in the wagon. Gusti should have expected it. Each year the prettiest young woman in the community was chosen, and Freya was certainly the prettiest of the young women.

Things changed very quickly. One morning Gusti awoke to find that his breakfast had not been made and Freya was not in her bed. He thought, because it was spring, that she might have gone for a walk, but she was not on the beach, nor was she in the garden behind the house. He walked to the dock and asked the fishermen if she had gone by. They laughed and said it would be some time before he saw her. He asked the children on the road, but they only laughed and ran away. Finally, he knocked on the door of Vigdis Thorarinsdottir, and she told him not to be a fool. "When the god in the wagon comes you will see her," Vigdis said. "Now go away and act like a man."

Gusti knew then that he was in trouble. The protector of the god must marry that spring and Gusti had not begun his wooing. Though they had shared the house for eight months, they were no closer than the day she had arrived. Gusti had been silenced by her wonderful beauty and even more silenced by her terrible temper. Still, he had changed for her. He was clean, obedient, sober and hard-working, an ideal husband. Ketil Hallgrimsson, on the other hand, had given up all work, and did nothing but sulk on the dock and wait till Freya came by, when he would leap to his feet and do tricks of strength until she had passed.

It was time, Gusti thought, to consult the fish. He walked all the way out to the south point and around to the channel, where the water was deep and he knew that fish liked to sun themselves. He stopped near a large white rock and shouted to the gentle waves that lapped at the shore. "Sunfish, come out of the water, I have to talk to you." The only reply was the splash of a tern diving for minnows. He shouted again but still there was nothing but the quarrelling of gulls. He was about to leave, when he decided, "No, I have walked all this way, I will try once more. Sunfish," he cried, "come out." With a splash, the sunfish landed at his feet.

"If you would read something besides the newspaper," the sunfish said, "you would know that you have to call three times. Now what's wrong? Is the wife I brought you not good enough?"

"Oh, she's fine," Gusti replied, "even more beautiful than I remembered, though her temper is strong."

"You just forget," the fish said. "She is exactly as she was. You were just younger and didn't pay as much attention to her."

"Well, said Gusti, "she has now been chosen as protector of the god in the wagon, and so must marry this spring. What shall I do?"

"Marry her."

"I am not so sure she will marry me."

"Well, that's your problem, isn't it?" said the sunfish. "I've fulfilled my part of the bargain. Face it, you're getting on, you're not a young man anymore. And besides, you've become incredibly dull. You've given up tobacco, you don't drink, you work hard all the time, you've even shaved off your beard. What woman would give you a second glance?"

"There is no need to be insulting," said Gusti. "I have only asked you politely for advice."

"I'm busy," said the fish. "The world is coming to an end. I've got things to do. I have no time to give advice to the love-lorn." With a flick of his tail, he flipped himself back into the lake. Then his head appeared, silver in the sunlight, and he added, "Give her a philtre," and disappeared.

"What kind of philtre?" Gusti shouted at the waves, but the sunfish was gone and the waves didn't answer.

For the rest of the week, Gusti stayed in his house, watching the dishes go dirty, the dust begin to gather on the table and the floor. He stopped shaving and began to chew tobacco, spitting the juice into a basin on the floor. Freya did not appear. She was gone wherever the women had taken her to prepare, and he knew there was no reason to expect her. Once, Ketil Hallgrimsson came over and they shared a bottle, but neither had anything to say. In the community, women were frantically baking, and the men were decorating the doors with willow boughs. The first green leaves were starting to sprout on the poplars and maples, and already in some yards, the poppies were starting to bloom, white and yellow and red.

On Friday at dawn, she arrived. The whole community, men, women and children, had gathered in the street to await her. She came down the road from the south, dressed in a flowing white robe, her long golden hair ruffling in a slight breeze, her blue eyes flashing. Gusti thought he had never seen anything so beautiful. She was leading Helgi Gudmundson's white ox. The ox had a garland of flowsers around its neck and was pulling the wagon with the god. The god was the largest Gusti had ever seen. He towered above the wagon and swayed with every step of the ox. His heavy hands, pams upturned for rain, rested on the front of the wagon. His shirt was a brilliant patchwork of colour and his great painted face beamed at the whole community. The wagon was filled with flowers, and there were flowers and branches with green leaves sticking out of every crevice in the enormous body. Gusti noticed that one of the legs was draped in the blanket that Vigdis Thorarinsdottir had made for him. "Where," he wondered, "where do the women find so many flowers, so early in the season?"

The ox stopped right at the foot of the dock, and Freya climbed into the wagon and seated herself in the lap of the god. She began the oration, and all the community sat down on the ground to listen. Gusti was so entranced by her beauty and her frailty, there in the lap of the god, that he hardly heard what she said. She spoke of rain. She spoke of sunlight and crops. She spoke of trees bursting out of the earth, of animals in the fields, of nets dripping with fish. She spoke of love and of little children. Her voice mingled with the voices of birds and the lapping of waves. And then she was gone.

Then the women brought out the steaming vats of coffee and plates full of *pönnukökur*. They brought out turkeys glazed with honey and chockecherries, chickens and pigeons and ducks. They brought out roasts of venison and roasts of beef, plates of boiled sunfish and fried pickerel and broiled whitefish. They brought out *hangikjot* and *rullupylsa*, *lifrapylsa* and *slàtur*. They carried out bowls of *skyr* and ram's heads pickled in buttermilk. They brought out *vinarterta* and *kleinur* and *àstarbolur*.

The men pulled corks out of bottles and threw away the corks. They said, "It is never too early for good whiskey," and they aimed the bottoms of the bottles at the sun. The children were into everything, laughing and crying and squealing, but no one paid any attention to them. Husbands and wives who had hardly spoken for months kissed like young lovers, so it is no surprise that no one noticed that Gusti had slipped away and returned to his house.

Freya was there. She had changed from her white robe into an old blue housedress. She was staring out the window and hardly noticed the mess in the house. "You were wonderful," Gusti began. "Never has there been such a beautiful protector nor so clever an oration."

Freya glanced at him, then looked out the window once more. "I shall marry," she said. "In nine days, I shall marry."

"And who shall you marry?" Gusti asked, his heart wrenching inside him.

"There are many I might marry," Freya responded, though without enthusiasm. "In the meanwhile, it is not seemly that I should live longer with you. I will go to stay with Vigdis Thorarinsdottir until my wedding day." Then she packed her trunk, and Gusti carried it down the road to Vigdis's house.

The next day was quiet as the community rested from the celebration, but by Monday the town was buzzing with rumours. Who had Freya chosen? Would it be Ketil Hallgrimsson, or one of the other young men of the community? Or had she perhaps betrothed herself to an outsider who would arrive on the wedding day? There was even a rumour that the priest was angry becaue they had received the god in the wagon, and that he would refuse to perform the wedding ceremony. Ketil Hallgrimsson was dressed in his best clothes, and stood in the road before Vigdis Thorarinsdottir's house, doing feats of strength.

That week, Gusti had plenty of time to write in his diary. He pondered over what he might put in the philtre to gain Freya's love, and he wondered who might help him. He considered whether it was right to use a philtre at all. Could love that was gained by a trick be real? In the end, he decided that the philtre should contain pure water. What else, he thought, is so close to love? It may be taken cold or hot, it is clear and insubstantial, it refreshes, but when it is consumed it is gone. And most important, there is more of it in the world than anything else.

Here you must bear with me, because the diaries end, and so I have had to reconstruct what actually happened. My aunt Thora, whose mother was there, says that Gusti went to Vigdis Thorarinsdottir and told her of his trouble. She led him to a clearing in the bush where she comforted him in her own way and promised to slip the contents of the philtre into Freya's coffe on the morning of the wedding day. That morning, Freya chose Gusti and they were married and had thirteen children. Ketil Hallgrimsson was so sad that he drowned himself in the lake that same day.

My aunt Lara, Thora's sister, agrees with the story, but claims that Vigdis drank the water herself. That morning, Freya chose Ketil Hallgrimsson and he did not drown for twenty years. By that time, he had fathered all the children whose descendants now live in Arborg. Vigdis left her husband and went to live with Gusti and they had thirteen children, though they never married. All their descendants now live in Riverton.

The people from Arnes tell a story very much like the story of Gusti, but in their version, a marvellous stranger dressed all in silver appeared on a magnificent boat and claimed Freya for his bride. They moved to Wynyard and had thirteen children and all the Icelanders in Saskatchewan are descended from them.

My cousin Villi, who is only six years older than me, but who speaks better Icelandic, says that the family is trying to hide something. He has overheard whispers, and he believes that Freya chose both Gusti and Ketil, that the three of them raised thirteen children and no one ever knew who was the father. He says the whole thing about the fish is just made up so people will think it is only a fairy tale and not enquire any further. After all, our uncle is the mayor, and any scandal might go bad for him in the next election.

I have my own ideas. If I were making up this story, I would tell you that, yes, Gusti did go to see Vigdis and tell her his troubles, and yes, she did comfort him in her own way, telling him of the secret love she had always felt for him and begging him to forget Freya. If it were my story, I could tell you that Gusti was not a flexible man, that he had made the faithful Vigdis pour the water into Freya's coffee, that she had chosen Gusti and they had married. Then, because I would want a happy ending, I would show you how Freya's bad temper and wicked tongue drove Gusti away, so that he married the faithful Vigdis, while Freya chose the hapless Ketil, who, for all his feats of strength, could never get the better of her. I would say they each had thirteen children, and all the people of Gimli are descended from them.

But I would go even further, because a story needs a proper ending, and I would do something about the fish. I would let Gusti catch him once more in a net and when the fish began all that nonsense about the end of the world, I would have

There Can Never Be Enough

Gusti take him home to Vigdis, who would boil him and feed him to the thirteen children. So there you are.

The Naiads

After my father quit fishing because he got seasick every time he went out on the lake, I didn't spend much time on the water. My father spent even less. He opened a garage and sold Kaiser and Frazer cars. This was in 1952, and I don't suppose many of you, even those who can remember 1952, will remember Kaisers and Frazers, and I'm pretty sure you'll have forgotten the Henry J. Why, a few short years after a war with Germany, would anyone have named a car "Kaiser" and expected to sell it? Actually, my father sold quite a few of them. They were beautiful cars and ran well, but like most failures they were ahead of their time. After that he sold Fords and Mercuries, but his heart wasn't in it. Finally, he discovered that he had a real talent for supervising the building of sewers, and so he devoted the rest of his life to that art.

I worked in the garage, changing tires and pumping gas, and later I worked in the sewers as well, though I never quite caught my father's enthusiasm for that life. I began to dream of the lake: not mere fantasies about the fisherman's life, but real dreams at night from which I would wake with such a powerful sense of the feel of cold water and slimy fish that I would be shaking and covered with sweat.

Still, I didn't return to the water. There really wasn't time for it. The sewers had convinced me so strongly of the need for an education that every minute not spent studying was spent working to guarantee that I would have enough money to continue studying. I suppose, in a way, I emulated my father. I went underground. I worked in the labyrinthine network of ideas of people like Heidegger and Claude Lévi-Strauss. When, one day, I surfaced, I discovered that I had earned a Ph.D. and was teaching philosophy in a small university whose name doesn't matter. I was forty-two years old. Somewhere along the way I'd picked up and lost a family consisting of a wife and three daughters. I'd hardly even learned their names before they were gone.

I remembered, when I surfaced, the smell of water. By now I'd spent too much time at philosophy to do anything directly, so I went out and bought some books about sailing. After six months of study, during which I developed a considerable technical vocabulary but had not yet looked at a body of water larger than one of those little cesspools they put in fancy housing developments and call lakes, I bought myself a sailboat. This I did over the most strenuous objections of my father, who had fished from skiffs with outboard motors and believed that, by their very nature, sailboats were designed to capsize and sink. I explained something about the history of sailing and the unreliability of outboard motors but I might as well have been talking of medieval plumbing procedures for all the effect I had. He even went out and bought me my own plot in the cemetery our family frequents. This might have worked, except for my training in philosophy. I knew enough about cause and effect and enough about necessary relationships not to be fooled by this false paradigm.

The Naiads

In case I haven't made it clear, I intended to sail on Lake Winnipeg. You might not know that Lake Winnipeg is one of the most dangerous bodies of water in the world. It's nearly three hundred miles long and in some places it's eighty miles wide. What makes it so dangerous is that it's also shallow, and so it builds huge waves that are very close together. During the winter, while I waited for the ice to disappear so that I could launch the MS *Daimon*, my father regaled me with tales of violent storms and sudden death, bodies found bloated or rotting in the nets. He brought out maps and showed me dangerous reefs and hidden rocks. He explained that it was impossible to sail in the middle of the lake because of the storms and impossible to sail near the shore because of the rocks. Still, I am my father's son, and I stuck to my guns. When the ice broke from the lake in early May, I launched the MS *Daimon*, all twenty-five feet of her, at the dock at Hnausa. For my father's sake I carried a five-horse Johnson outboard which, as it turned out, carried my boat more often than the wind. The external world is much less malleable than the world of ideas, and the eloquent gestures of sailing that I had rehearsed in my mind turned to clumsy graspings when I actually tried them.

By early August, though, I had satisfied myself that I was something of a sailor. I had sailed alone every day, even in the roughest water, and I was confident that my boat was not going to sink. I had learned, too, that I liked solitude. The only book I took on the boat was Roger Tory Peterson's *A Field Guide to the Birds*, and I vowed that it was the only book I would ever permit aboard.

I was happy. I suppose, though, there's something in human nature that is never satisfied by mere happiness. I began to dream of Well's Harbour. When I was eleven years old, my father had taken me moose hunting with him at Grindstone Point. He was still a fisherman then, and we had gone by boat. In spite of my father's seasickness, there was no other way. The nearest road stopped fourteen miles short. We camped on Fox Island, and on the way back, we stopped at Well's Harbour. It was a half-mile crescent of the whitest sand I have ever seen. We had hunted in early October, and the morning we spent at Well's Harbour was grey, with sleet and a bitter wind from the northwest. Now, I could only think of it as a tropical paradise, a south seas island in the northern prairies.

When I announced that I was spending all of August camped at Well's Harbour on my sailboat, my father was nearly cataleptic with rage. Then he decided he was coming too. I told him that I refused to have a septuagenarian vomiting on the boat, and threatened to put him in an old folks' home. He wheedled and threatened but I was firm. No septuagenarians.

I left on the first day of August, a Sunday. A gentle breeze from the south let me sail up the lake on a broad reach, and by evening I was there. It was exactly as I had dreamed it, a curve of white sand backed by a riot of green trees. The only jarring note in my dream of perfection come true was a blaze-orange nylon tent and a small green canoe on the east shore of the bay. I dropped anchor, furled sail, and, as my sailboat swung gently about, I went down to get my binoculars.

Back on deck, I could see there were three figures swimming, or rather, sporting, in the water, splashing each other and diving. When I searched them out in my binoculars they resolved into three young women, entirely naked. I can see I'm going to have some trouble with this. I nearly said nude, and they certainly weren't nude. I want you to believe me when I tell you I was annoyed that they were there, though of course I didn't put away my binoculars until they waved

to me, an indication either of friendliness or defiance. It was
my first encounter with the naiads, as I came to think of them,
and I resolved to pay no attention to them. In the morning,
they would pack up their tent, get into their green canoe and
be gone.

They were not gone in the morning. My first indication of
this continued presence occurred when I was wakened by the
sailboat's sudden lurch, the sound of feet pattering above my
head, and a voice shouting, "Anybody home?"

I slipped into my trunks and clambered up through the
companionway. There, still dripping from the lake and as
naked as the day she was born, was one of the naiads. She had
long red hair and the kind of complexion that is only available
to redheads.

"Can we borrow a cup of sugar?" she asked, and before I
realized the lunacy of the request I was halfway down to the
galley to get it.

"Sorry," she said with a laugh, "but I had to say something,
didn't I? Can I have a towel?"

I got her a towel, grateful for some release from having
to stare at her, but she only used it to dry herself and then
sat on it. The only response I could think of was to pretend
that there was nothing out of the ordinary, that naked young
women climbed aboard my boat every morning. I offered her
a cup of coffee, but she refused.

"This is a really nice boat," she said, and I agreed, beginning to point out its better features: the thrusting bowsprit,
the fine entry at the water line, the gleaming bright work top-
sides, the snug cockpit. I stuttered into silence as I realized
that she wasn't remotely interested, and beyond that, the language of sailing, I suddenly became aware, was full of lascivious suggestion.

"My name's Diane."

"Jack," I said, and we shook hands with lunatic formality.

"My friends are still sleeping," she said, "Laura and Becky." Then, seeing my confusion, she added, "We're camping here for the whole month. We agreed not to wear any clothes until we leave, which is why..." and she made a gesture my eyes couldn't help following, "anyway, it's perfectly natural."

"Yes," I agreed.

"Anyway, you're invited over for a drink at four o'clock." She stepped to the edge of the boat, stood there a second in an awkward balance, then dived smoothly into the water and started swimming for shore, her white buttocks flashing in the sunlight.

I don't have to tell you that the rest of the day was spent in fantasy. Dreams of possession. I cleaned and polished my boat as if I were engaged in some rite of purification, and, yes, I know all about the symbolic value of that. I'm something of an expert on symbols. By a quarter to four, I was so convinced of the imminent direction of my future, I was shaking like a leaf. I had cleaned myself until I shone with an even greater lustre than my boat. Choosing a costume was a difficult matter, but in the end I decided that a simple black bathing suit would seem neither overdressed nor overeager. I inflated my little two-man raft, assembled my plastic two-piece paddles, and launched myself in the direction of Camp Paradise.

I was formally introduced to Becky and Laura by my red-haired visitor of the morning. They were, if such a thing is possible, even more naked than she was. Becky had long dark hair, Laura had long blonde hair. Except for the colour of their hair, the three were interchangeable, or else my eye was too undiscriminating to notice subtle differences. A black-and-white-checked tablecloth was spread over what I guessed was an old fish box, and four small logs were arranged around it.

The Naiads

In the centre of the table were a bottle of red wine of the sort that is named after water fowl, and four plastic wine glasses.

After the usual formalities, awkward banter and the exchange of general information about employment and background, we sat down to the table. It wasn't quite what I'd expected. Becky, who seemed to be the leader, convened a council of war. She had divided the harbour into three sections, and prepared a timetable indicating at what hours of the day each area would be available to me. The timetable, which ran until the end of the month, would guarantee that we would not encounter one another again. There was, she pointed out, room for negotiation. Two o'clock might be exchanged for three o'clock, or Wednesday for Friday, but it was clear that orgies had not been planned, and there was little room for the development of lasting friendships.

I acceded, of course, negotiating only for a proper share of the blueberries that grew along the edge of the tree line. It seemed to me that Diane, the red-haired one, looked a little wistful, and might have permitted a less rigorous routine, but she maintained solidarity, and so, after a few minutes, there was nothing for me to do but to wish them good luck and paddle back to my lonely boat. Later that night, I woke out of a dream in which Heidegger and I were working on a sewer.

When I finally did get up, the sun was high in the sky. It must have been ten o'clock. I turned my binoculars to the girls' camp, but there was no movement. They were obviously late sleepers.

I poached myself an egg and made a pot of coffee. The boat was still immaculate from yesterday's cleaning, but today I was free from lust, and so I left the dishes, climbed out onto the deck with Peterson's *A Field Guide to the Birds*, fourth edition, and settled down to work on the tan I intended to bring back to the college in the fall as a gift to my students.

There are, as you probably know, very few tanned philosophy professors.

I began with *Colaptesauratus*, the Yellow-shafted Flicker, but the reference in the first line to the "conspicuous white rump" distracted me, so I flipped over to page 230, the *Paradidae*, or Wood Warblers. I was in the early stages of a bird-watching career and had decided with the meticulous thoroughness that had carried me through a Ph.D. that I would memorize the field marks of every bird found in this area before I did any actual field work. This kind of memorizing, like the conjugation of verbs in a language you do not speak, is very difficult, and requires intense concentration. I had worked my way down to *Dendroica magnolia*, the Magnolia Warble, when I heard the sound of an outboard motor.

I decided to ignore it, but it is impossible to memorize one thing when ignoring another, so I shifted up onto one elbow to see what was going on. A skiff was coming directly at me, towing a water skier. The skiff shot by, my grey-haired septuagenarian father waved to me, and rolling in the wash, I recognized the skier by her red crown patch, conspicuous white rump and rufous undertail coverts.

Every paradise has its snake, and in this particular paradise, the snake was my own father. I remembered that as a child I had come across the phrase *in loco parentis* and had translated it as "with crazy parents." It seemed now prophetic. I had a *loco* parent, who in defiance of all the rules of good sense, not to mention doctor's orders, had manifested himself like some Walt Disney version of Hamlet's father, and was about to make my life unbearable.

I climbed into my rubber raft, reassembled the plastic paddles and rowed, with majestic deliberation, in the direction of the girls' camp. I wasn't sure whom I was most angry at, the girls, whose cavorting on water skis seemed a deliberate betrayal after the ascetic ritual separation I had agreed to not twenty-four hours earlier, or my father, who seemed bent on suffering his heart attack at the very edge of the wilderness. At any rate, I knew I had right on my side. When I had first gone to Camp Paradise I had arrived as a kind of blushing voyeur full of lust and so an easy mark for moral defeat. This time, all decency and morality was with me in my rubber raft.

Becky and Laura met me as I touched the shore. Diane was still skiing on the far side of the bay. "So," I shouted, beaching my boat in sand.

"So what?" Becky asked.

"What are you doing with my father?"

"He's sweet," Laura answered. "He came by and offered to take us water skiing. What's wrong with that?"

"He's not sweet. He's a wicked old man with a bad heart and he has to go home. He has no right to be here."

"I thought we had an agreement," Becky answered coolly. "You have the other side of the bay and you agreed not to come here."

"The agreement did not include the debauching of my father," I told her, feeling myself go red in the face. "The agreement did not include water skiing."

"We simply will not talk to you if you're going to act like that," Becky said, and she flounced off down the beach, followed, at a little distance, by Laura. I'm not sure whether the word I want is "flounced" or "bounced." At any rate they left. You're always at a disadvantage talking to naked people, even when you're angry, because your inability to look them in the eye makes you seem shifty and evasive.

By this time the skiff had completed the circuit of the bay and was heading for shore at much too great a speed. My father turned the boat at the very last minute, and the skier came straight at me. Her skis hit the shore, she popped out of them and flew straight into my arms, bowling me over onto the sand. We disentangled ourselves, more slowly, I think, than was necessary, and she cried out breathlessly, "That was great. Are you going to give it a try?"

"No. This is the end of the water skiing. He's going home right now." This was truer than I realized at the moment. When I looked up, expecting to see my father reluctantly landing, I saw instead the skiff rounding the point out of sight.

"Where is he camped?" I asked, but the girls didn't seem to know, and even when I invoked my poor worried mother waiting up nights for his return, they couldn't help. Finally, there was nothing to do but return to my boat.

I devoted the day to Peterson, working my way through the sparrows, whose bewildering similarity to each other seemed scarcely to justify distinguishing one from the other. I found myself increasingly annoyed by Peterson's style. It has about it a frantic cheerfulness that the world will not support. "One of the handsomest of sparrows," he says of *Zenotrickialeucophrys*. *Aimophiliaaestivalis* he sees as shy, inclining to play hide-and-seek. I liked only *Ammodiamushenslowii*, a secretive sparrow, easily overlooked. I liked him despite his song, "a hiccupping tsilick" which Peterson calls "a poor vocal effort." Peterson is a man of strong feelings, and sometimes his prejudices show through his ostensibly objective approach. I checked for my father a couple of times but saw only the girls sprawled on the rocks, sunning themselves like turtles.

The next three days passed in that kind of idyllic haze that can only be put together out of sun and water. I checked on the girls regularly, and discovered that they too had binoculars and were checking on me. I walked my allotted section of the beach during my allotted hours. I picked a few blueberries and some wild raspberries, and discovered a kind of sour cherry that grows close to the ground. And of course I brooded on my father. I most certainly did not want him spying on me, but on the other hand I did not want to discover his remains on some distant beach. When he didn't show up again, I decided he must have gone home. For all his frailties, he has always seemed to me indestructible.

On the fourth day, I took a couple of pots and paddled over to the blueberry patch to lay in a supply. It was very early, just after the sun had popped, blood-red, above the horizon, and I was worried about bears. I remembered from the days of my moose hunting that there were bears in the area, and I wondered whether I should go over and warn the girls. No, I decided, it would be interpreted as a hostile move, an attempt to frighten them. Besides, they seemed to be able to take care of themselves quite well.

There's a theory that an infinite number of alternate universes co-exist, and anything that can happen is in fact happening in one of them right now. I think sometimes that the lines of distinction get blurred. That's the only thing that could account for what happened next. I had no sooner worked my way up into the deeper bush, fearing a bear, than I heard a rustling a few yards away. My heart thumped, and for a moment I froze with terror. I took a step and heard a branch crack right beside me. With a roar that might have been an attempt to frighten the bear, or might merely have been sheer panic, I hurtled myself out of the bush and onto the beach, into the stunning early morning silence.

Out in the sunlight, my fear of bears seemed ridiculous.

Nevertheless, I began to move cautiously in the direction of my rubber raft. Then, in the green of the shrubbery along the beach, I caught a flash of white. I lunged into the bushes and pulled out a squealing redhead.

She fought fiercely, but I refused to let her go until she had settled down. Then in the sternest voice I could muster,

I told her, "That was a stupid thing to do. I nearly had a heart attack. I thought you were a bear."

She laughed. "You were really funny, standing there shivering. I thought men were supposed to be big and brave. When you yelled, you made a little squeal, just like a pig." She giggled again, until I made her understand the seriousness of the situation. Then we formally shook hands and agreed that no serious damage had been done. I offered her a blueberry from the pot now spilled on the beach. She accepted it as a token of forgiveness.

We sat together on the beach, watching the sun climb slowly up from the water. She told me that in real life she was a psychiatric nurse, and the other girls were teachers. They'd all been friends in high school, but really hadn't seen much of one another until this trip. They'd planned it for years. I told her about the MS *Daimon*, extolling its virtues and the freedom of life at sea. Finally, she asked, "If you like the boat so much, how come you never sail it? You just keep it anchored and lie on top of it looking through your binoculars."

"I do not. I only look through them to check that things are all right. I'm going sailing right now. Do you want to come?"

"No. Yes. What the hell. It's just too boring lying around sunning myself all day long. We've already done all the reminiscing I care to."

We got into my two-man raft and rowed out to the sailboat. I hoisted the sails, broke anchor, and a steady breeze let us run easily out of the bay. I noticed, as we left, that the other two girls were waving from the camp, obviously shouting something, and flapping towels. Diane didn't notice, and I failed to bring it to her attention.

There's not much to tell about that day. The breeze was gentle, and we ghosted softly around the islands in that part of the lake. Out of pity for me, Diane slipped on my tee shirt, a gesture so inflammatory that I had to warn her that she was a great deal safer in a state of nature. I was coming to understand the argument made by the directors of nudist colonies that after a very short while you begin to accept nudity as normal, and lascivious thoughts disappear. If the tee shirt was any indication, I was going to have to exercise a steely self-control when I returned to civilization and saw women fully dressed.

And so, nothing happened except we sailed and chatted and ate little crackers with that kind of cheese you squeeze out of a tube. It was dark when we got back, and I offered to lend Diane my rubber raft, but she refused. She gave me a peck on the cheek and dived into the water. For a couple of minutes I could hear her splashing. Then there was nothing but me and the boat and the starless, moonless sky.

I went to bed almost immediately, pleased with the day, but also suffering from a vague sense of failure. Surely, if a naked girl comes sailing with you, there is some sort of implicit invitation, and I should have done something about it, if not out of lust, then just to keep my self-respect and confidence. I drifted into a dream about labyrinthine sewers, where I sailed my boat through giant pipes. I was awakened by a cold wet girl crawling into my bed. She seemed to be weeping.

"What are you doing?" I asked, though the answer seemed apparent.

"They threw me out," she said. "I broke the rules, so they won't let me stay with them."

"What do you mean?"

"The rule was that we were to have nothing to do with men during the trip. I went sailing with you, so they won't let me come back."

"What are you going to do?"

"I'm throwing myself on your mercy." She snuggled against me, and cold and wet as she was, I hadn't the heart to send her away. The problem, it seemed to me, could be settled in the morning. Meanwhile, there were more pressing concerns.

I woke the next morning with the feeling that I was being suffocated, which was in part true since an arm had been thrown over my head and a breast had effectively stifled my breathing apparatus. The pillow beside me was red with hair. I slipped out of bed as gently as I could, apparently without waking the sleeping intruder. I cooked bacon and eggs, and then, in a moment of inspiration, opened a bottle of champagne I had intended to use at the launching of the MS *Daimon*, but had forgotten. I awakened the naiad in my bed, whispering softly, "Breakfast."

She wrinkled her nose, said, "You're disgusting," and rolled over.

I left her breakfast beside her and went up on the deck to consult Peterson. He usually has something to say for every occasion. I opened the book at random, as you're supposed to do with the Bibles you find in hotel rooms, and pointed to the middle of page 136. It said, "Breeding females are gray above with a patch of rufous on the neck and a white throat." It wasn't an exact description, but perhaps I had an immature here, and the grey would come in time.

A few minutes later Diane crawled onto the deck, a wine glass full of champagne in her hand. Her hair seemed to have got even redder overnight, though that might have been the effect of the sun.

"You weren't very coherent last night," I told her. "Do you think you could explain the situation a little more clearly?"

"Are you married?"

"Yes," I told her. "I'm expecting my wife and seven

children on the four o'clock plane." Then, seeing the expression of dismay on her face, I corrected my statement.

"No, actually, I have been married on occasion, but at the present moment I am entirely unencumbered. Am I to consider this a proposal?"

"No," she said, "not yet. I'll have to try you out a little more. It always works out that way. Any of the men who are any good are already married."

"I'm not married," I pointed out, perhaps a bit resentfully.

"No, but you're probably a bundle of neuroses. Wake up screaming in the night, go into a rage if someone leaves the cap off the toothpaste, that sort of thing. If you were any good, someone else would have got you by now."

"Nobody else has had the slightest chance," I practically roared. The conversation was clearly out of my control.

"Well, we'll see," she said. "Now, we'd better go over and get my stuff. They've probably torn all my clothes to pieces."

"Just a second. I haven't invited you yet. I hardly even know you."

"You don't have any choice. You seduced me, and now it's your responsibility. You have to take care of me."

"Who seduced who? I was calmly sleeping in my bed when you crawled in and seduced me. You're the one who's completely at fault."

"It was a trap," she said. "You inveigled me onto your boat, then when my resistance was lowered, you callously debauched me. If you'd had any decency in you, you would have found me my own bed, tucked me in and kept watch overnight. Besides, you're old enough to be my father."

There was a semi-truth to this last statement, but not a truth I was eager to acknowledge. I'd have had to start my sexual career a lot younger than I actually had in order to be the father of a woman in her early twenties. At any rate, I lunged at her, with what intent in mind I'm not sure. She slipped away and dived into the water. I dived after her, but it was soon clear that she was a much better swimmer than I was. Defeated, I agreed to take her ashore in the rubber raft to get her things, but only on the condition that we sign a contract regarding behaviour on the sailboat.

When we got to the camp, there was no sign of the other naiads. Diane's clothes had been packed into a cardboard box and placed by the water's edge. She looked into the box, and then said, "That's not good enough. I paid for one-third of the food, and I'm taking it." I explained that I had plenty of food on board, and moreover, no place to put extra food, but she was adamant. "It's my food, and I'm taking it." It took a full hour for her to gather up her share. She even divided the salt and pepper into three parts, and took her third, mixing it into a bag that already contained sugar and flour.

When we got back to the sailboat, there was a note wedged in the companionway door. It said, in a crabbed hand, "I saw what you did to that poor innocent girl. Now you have to marry her to keep the reputation of your family." There was a little puddle of vomit on the deck, which I cleaned up with a paper towel.

Diane laughed when she saw the note. "Shall we have a large wedding or just a small family affair? Of course, the shotgun will have to be tastefully decorated, small bows, I imagine. And an ambulance at the church door in case I have to be rushed to the hospital to give birth."

"It's not funny," I said. "It's my father. He is hiding somewhere and spying on us. I'm going to have to find him and tie him up and take him home. Other people have fathers who disown them and they never see them for years at a time. Why did I have to get one like this?"

"Don't worry," she said, "he'll be OK. He didn't get to be as old as he is without knowing how to take care of himself."

The Naiads

"I suppose," I answered, worrying less about his ability to take care of himself than this unasked-for invasion of my privacy.

"Look," Diane said, "I'm going to give you another chance. Last night wasn't a very good test. You'd just woken up and you were all groggy, so you weren't at your best."

"What do you mean?" I asked, suspecting I knew exactly what she did mean.

"Well, you know, it was just one of those occasions where the world failed to move. Not to worry, though, I'm sure you can do better."

"That wasn't entirely my fault, you know," I said, humiliation and rage beginning to seep through my body. "You were all wet and cold. You were slippery. It was like making love to a frozen jellyfish."

"I know, I know," she cooed. "You had all kinds of excuses. The question is, how well can you do under better circumstances."

"Well, you're not going to find out," I told her, and stormed off to consult Peterson. She did find out though, a couple of hours later, and pronounced it a great improvement. "You're just out of practice," she said. "A man of your age has to keep in shape."

Over the next couple of days I got in quite a bit of practice. We sailed over to Goose Island and collected fossils. We picked far more blueberries than we had any use for and we explored some old abandoned fishing stations.

Still, the whereabouts of my father troubled me. We'd sailed along the shore looking for him but had seen nothing. The next bay, however, was fed by a shallow creek, and I suspected he'd travelled a couple of hundred yards up the creek where he could remain out of sight. I couldn't get the sailboat anywhere near the creek, so we paddled over in the two-man raft. The camp was there all right, but there was no sign of my father or his skiff. Pinned to the door of his tent was a sign that read, "Leave my scotch alone." I turned the note over and scribbled on the back, "This means war." I wasn't sure what else I could do other than destroy his camp, and that seemed excessive.

By the time we got back to the sailboat, the sun was low in the sky. On the deck, eating a bowl of blueberries, was a naked blonde. So, I had another defector. Diane saw her a moment after I did, and she whispered, "She can't stay. She's got to go back. I won't have her on the boat."

"Welcome aboard," Laura announced as we scrambled onto the sailboat. She had a cardboard box full of clothes and groceries mixed indiscriminately together, and it was clear she intended to remain.

"What are you doing here?" Diane asked her. "Where's Becky?" Laura pointed to the shore. "She's at the camp. We had an argument and she gave me an ultimatum. Either do what she said or get out. So I got out. And here I am."

The green canoe was tied to the sailboat. I could see that whatever discussion was about to take place it was not a discussion I wanted to enter, so I said, "I'd better return the canoe." I stepped into the raft, attached the canoe and started paddling to shore. Laura and Diane had disappeared into the cabin by the time I looked back.

When I reached the shore with the canoe, Becky was there to meet me. "I guess you really think you're something, don't you?" she greeted me. "Everything was perfect until you came along. Why couldn't you go someplace else?" and she burst into tears. It's always difficult to know what to say to people who are weeping. The natural tendency is to comfort them, to take them in your arms and stroke their hair and say, "There, there, don't worry, everything is going to be OK."

This I did, and for a minute it appeared that it was going to work. She was a small woman and she fit amazingly well into my arms.

Suddenly, she pulled away and shouted, "Get out of here. Go back to your stupid boat." And she ran into the orange tent. I followed her, trying to explain my innocence. I was, after all, the victim of circumstances beyond my control, and I didn't want to be seen as the villain.

Inside the tent, she had rolled herself up in a sleeping bag. "They took all the food," she said. "All I've got left is macaroni and powdered eggs, and I don't even like macaroni." She burst into tears again. This time my attempt to comfort her was less successful.

"No you don't!" she screamed, pushing me out of the door of the tent. "You might have seduced them, but you're not seducing me. Get out of here and don't come back."

I stood bewildered outside the tent for a moment, but there didn't seem anything else I could do. Finally, I got into the rubber dinghy and rowed back to the sailboat. Diane and Laura were both dressed in tee shirts and shorts. Somehow, they looked smaller than they did naked. "What's this?" I asked, "is this some sort of new regime?"

Laura answered, "We just decided we'd wear clothes on the boat."

Diane didn't say a word. The binoculars hung around her neck, and she had an odd expression on her face. As I climbed up the ladder, she put a foot on my chest and pushed me into the water. I swam back to the ladder, but she'd taken a winch handle from the deck, and every time I came near she swung at my head. "What's this all about?" I shouted, keeping well away from the boat.

"You know damn well what it's about," Diane answered. "I

saw that cuddle on the beach and I saw you go into the tent." In the meantime Laura had hauled the rubber raft aboard.

"I can explain everything," I told them. "Just let me on board."

They refused all explanations, and when I tested their seriousness by swimming close to the ladder, I got a sharp blow on the ear for my pains. I pointed out how serious the penalty for mutiny was, but they were unimpressed. I explained that I wasn't a good swimmer, and I'd never make shore.

"Then you'll drown," Laura told me, "and it will serve you right. Maybe Becky will swim out and save you."

And in fact she did save me, not by swimming, but by paddling out in the green canoe just as I was going down for the third time. By that time I was shivering with cold. It's amazing how much energy you expend in a quarter-mile if you're not a good swimmer, and my stroke was a sort of modified dog paddle. Becky wrapped me in her sleeping bag and fed me macaroni and scrambled powdered eggs. It was a dreadful meal.

I plotted ways of sneaking aboard in the dead of night and reclaiming my sailboat from the mutineers. I had no irons to clap them in, but I could tie them up with rope and sail them to the nearest police station. A near drowning has a way of making you less generous than you might be in other circumstances. Becky agreed that she would help in exchange for food. We decided that four o'clock in the morning would be the best time for the raid and we sat down to wait. It was a cold night, so I offered Becky a share of the sleeping bag. When I woke up it was long past four o'clock, the sun was shining brightly, and I was zipped tightly into the sleeping bag. Just below my chin was a mass of black hair, and all of my potential arguments from the position of wounded innocence were shot.

I groaned aloud and woke my sleeping partner. She smiled and curled her head into my chest.

"No," I told her, "this is irresponsible. We've got to get up. I've got to get my sailboat back." I fumbled with the zipper, unable to get my arms outside the sleeping bag. The slide came free in my hands, and the zipper refused to move. We struggled to allow one or the other of us to slip out, but it was futile, and after a few minutes of struggling, neither of us wanted to get out. Sometime later I pointed out the irony of starving to death locked in a sleeping bag, when there was all the macaroni and powdered eggs anyone could want just a few feet away. I quoted both Sartre and Camus on the subject.

I might have quoted others on the fundamental absurdity of the universe had not the sound of an outboard motor distracted me. My father pulled into the shore right beside us, and without pausing to vomit, began his imitation of an Old Testament patriarch.

"So," he said, "is this what I've raised? A reckless libertine. A son completely without a shred of decency in his body. I've already phoned your mom and she was making preparations for the wedding. Now what am I going to tell her?"

"Just tell her to go ahead," said Becky. "It will all work out."

"Well, what about the red-haired one?" my father asked. "She had him first."

"I've got him now," Becky pointed out.

"Could you stop discussing me in the third person?" I asked as reasonably as I could, "and get us out of here? The stupid zipper is stuck."

"Don't let him out," Becky said. "Go get the others and we'll hold a conference."

"Oh, no you don't!" I shouted. "I'm getting out of here," and struggled to free myself.

"Oh, don't," Becky said, "not with your own father

watching." I gave up at that point, curled into a ball and, taking Heidegger's advice, contemplated my final passing. Becky cooed to me sympathetically all the while my father was gone out to the sailboat to get the others, but I refused to answer. When Laura and Diane arrived, they gazed down at me as if I were some kind of curious larvae. "It's disgusting," Diane said. "Some people are completely without morals."

Laura agreed.

"He's not very good, is he?" Diane said to Becky.

"He's fine," Becky replied. "He just needs practice. The raw material is all there."

My father and the girls discussed the problem. They decided that it was time the holiday was over. They would load the green canoe on the sailboat, and I could sail the girls back to the Hnausa dock. My father would go ahead on his outboard and have a car ready for us when we got there.

He leapt into his boat and took off around the point. Becky unzipped the sleeping bag. "It always sticks like that," she said.

It didn't take long to load up the tent and the remaining supplies. Two-thirds were already on board the MS *Daimon*. With Becky now dressed, my naiads looked like any collection of girls out for a day at the beach. Somehow, in clothes, they looked a lot different, but that might just be because I had become accustomed to seeing them through binoculars.

I lashed the canoe carefully to the deck. Already, the sky, which had been unremittingly sunny since my arrival, had begun to cloud over. A sharp wind was whipping up from the northwest. I brooded over nature's simple-minded adherence to the rules of romantic literature, but there it was, clouds, wind, and a spattering of rain.

We cleared the point, and I set a course that would take me wide of the Hecla reef, one of the dangers my father had pointed out to me when I first started thinking about buying a sailboat. "It's tricky," he'd told me. "There's no landmarks, so you think you're around it and then, pow, you're dead." The girls had scattered themselves as widely as they could and still be on the same boat. Diane was leaning over the prow in imitation of one of those carved figures on Viking boats. Becky was sitting in the centre of the deck, pondering the mysteries of *A Field Guide to the Birds,* glancing at me every so often with a look that was smug and critical at the same time. Laura had taken a seat beside me at the tiller and seemed genuinely interested in the way the sailboat functioned, though she seemed to share some of my father's reservations about its seaworthiness.

"What if we tip over?" she asked. The boat was leaning in the strong wind, and I have to admit, I was showing off just a little.

"It can't tip over," I told her. "The keel is weighted with three tons of lead. It's just like a child's tippy toy. The centre of balance is so low that it has to right itself."

She asked me a lot of questions about myself, one of my favourite topics, and I suppose I gave her a pretty accurate survey. I may have exaggerated the importance of the paper I gave in Milwaukee in 1993, but other than that I was, I think, measured and fair. I even admitted my compulsion to see that the caps were back on the toothpaste and the shampoo.

"Two out of three," she said. "That's not bad for a man when the consensus has it that he is not one of the world's great lovers."

"Prejudiced testimony," I argued. "The circumstances were bad. No wine, no soft music." I even offered, under Becky's by now baleful eye, to demonstrate the falsehood of previous reports.

"I think not," Laura said. "I'm inclined to trust consumers' reports, and you look to me like a bad buy."

Just then, Becky decided to join us. She was troubled by Peterson's advice that one should flush Rail by dragging a rope over a marsh. It sounded to her like cruelty to animals. At any rate, her arrival was sufficient to flush Laura, who disappeared below deck.

"As to this impending marriage, "Becky asked me, "how much do you think you can get for this sailboat?"

The time had clearly come for me to take a stand, and I did. I explained that I had already demonstrated my inability to sustain a serious relationship. I quoted whoever it was who said that a second marriage was a triumph of hope over experience. I announced my absolute commitment to sailing.

"It looks pretty dismal," she agreed, "but cheer up. Even a wasted life can be redeemed. On the surface you look pretty hopeless, but there's a kind of refreshing naivety about you that gives me hope."

And just at that moment, the impossible happened. With a sickening crunch, we struck a rock. The boat lurched and heeled over, but when it worked free, the tiller swung freely in my hand. The pintles, the hinges on which the rudder swings, had been forced out of the gudgeons, leaving them useless. I was surrounded by women in an instant, and the air was filled with what I imagine must be the sound of Capistrano at the time of the annual swallow migration.

"It's nothing," I lied. "I'll have it fixed in no time."

I had an extra tiller, I'm cautious enough for that, but repair was impossible. We were in heavy seas and force of winds, and, as I may have pointed out, I am not a first-rate swimmer. Even diving with a rope around myself, I had to be revived by mouth-to-mouth resuscitation twice.

The Naiads

Laura was the only one who knew the technique, and she was so enthusiastic about it that both times I was in an embarrassing state by the time I came to. Then, the girls took turns trying to make the repairs. They came to no grief, but they couldn't figure out what it was they were supposed to do once they were in position. Storm clouds had been mounting in the northwest and the wind was beginning to whip up whitecaps.

Finally, I lowered the anchor, explaining to the girls that we'd just have to ride out the storm. There is a lot of boat traffic in the area, and sooner or later someone would rescue us. I watched the yellow anchor line uncoil until with a final little flip it disappeared entirely into the lake.

"Who untied the anchor rope?" I screamed.

"Oh," said Diane, "was that the anchor rope? It was all balled up in the front there so it was terribly uncomfortable to sit. I just unclipped it and moved it over. You're the one who threw it out of the boat."

"Well, we're all going to drown now," I said, "and it's all because of you. We'll crash on the reef and that will be the end of us."

"I knew this thing wasn't seaworthy," Laura piped in. "We should have gone with the old man. He knew what he was doing."

I realized then that as captain it was my job to prevent panic, not to spread it.

"Everybody put on a life jacket," I told them. "With luck, we won't hit any rocks or reefs. We'll just drift to shore some place. In the meantime, we'll lower the sails."

They responded manfully, all three, and in a few minutes the sails were down, the hatches, such as they are, were battened, and each of us was tied to the deck so that we wouldn't be swept off if the storm got worse.

For a long time the storm maintained its intensity. We drifted under bare poles before the wind, and, the wind having veered around to the north, it seemed that our course was going to take us within a mile or two of our destination at Hnausa harbour. We all thought of word games we'd played as children travelling on long trips in cars, and we played them for hours.

Then, just as it got dark and we could make out lights on the shore, the rain and lightning began. In a few minutes it was impossible to see anything. Waves seemed to come at us from every direction, and only the ropes we'd tied to ourselves kept us from being swept away. Between the screams of fear whenever a particularly large wave struck us and the gentle sobbing in between, there was nothing to do but to cling together and hope. Then, with a lurch, the boat heeled on its side and lay grounded on a reef, to be pounded by waves. The mast carried away and drifted. Not far off we could see a sand bar, but the waves were so fierce it was clear that it would do us no good. It was only a matter of minutes before the boat would break up, and we would drift off in our separate directions.

And then, over the roar of the wind and the waves came another roar, more high-pitched and steady. A moment later, a skiff bumped against the wreck of the MS *Daimon*, and an old man with a green face and white hair leaped up to his waist in the water and started loading the girls into the skiff. For a mad moment I considered staying with the ship out of defiance, but at the last second, I too clambered in. Then we bucked out blindly into the storm. It was impossible to hear anything over the sound of the waves and the outboard motor, but I could see that my father's face was full of glee, and I think I could make out the words "I told you so."

You can see how it ends. We got back to shore safely. After

a brief and conventional courtship, held mostly in Chinese restaurants, I married Laura. Neither Becky nor Diane was invited to our wedding, though occasionally I catch a glimpse of one or the other in a crowded department store at Christmas. Laura and I have three sons. My abilities as a lover must have improved. At least, Laura no longer believes I need much practice. I've got a little thirteen-foot sailboat now, but I never take it very far out on the lake. I'm happy, I guess.

The day after the storm, I scoured the beach looking for salvage from the MS *Daimon*. All I found was a water-logged copy of Roger Tory Peterson's *A Field Guide to the Birds*, fourth edition. It was open at page 90, and I read, "Some birds may remain a mystery even to the expert until the specimen is in hand." Not some birds, Roger. All.

Sons and Fathers, Fathers and Sons

There is something about fathers and sons that could do with an explanation a little less mechanical than Freud's. Anybody who is both a father and a son will know what I mean. It's a devious business, this sending your genes out into the world in a body over which you no longer have control. It calls for extreme measures, and any relationship between a father and a son is organized around extremes. Nothing is unfair.

Let me begin. I was born in a real, honest-to-goodness tar-paper shack. In that sense, my proletarian credentials are impeccable. To be perfectly honest, I was actually born in a quite up-to-date hospital, attended by a doctor who, though inclined to forgetfulness, nevertheless had all his papers. I went directly from the hospital to the shack, where I spent the next three months until my father completed the house he was building. You see, I'm trying to be honest with you, though I'm not sure that's always the best policy. That shack, however little time I spent in it, is a metaphor of my beginnings.

My son, on the other hand, was born, at least relatively, into the lap of luxury. He moved directly into a basement suite. It was a natural childbirth, not that it was intended to be. He merely came too fast for the doctor to use any of the arcane methods modern doctors prefer. He was already in this world complaining about it before they even got his mother into the delivery room. He was saved the indignity that I faced, hauled into the world by a pair of forceps, my head squeezed so out of shape that in baby pictures I look vaguely hydrocephalic.

I was by all accounts a clumsy child. I never learned how to crawl, and though I learned to walk relatively early, my first use of this newly discovered talent was to hurl myself down the basement stairs, landing fortunately on the dog, a large yellow mongrel named Bruno. Bruno, for his services in saving my infant neck, demanded his pound of flesh. He bit me in the leg, leaving me with a fear of dogs that is in no way diminished today.

My father was what in those days was called a jack of all trades, and my clumsiness troubled him sorely. He had been a champion hockey player and a champion baseball player. It was clear to him by the time I was a year old that I was not going to be a champion anything. Later, when I went to university, I proved him wrong by becoming a champion ping-pong player, a sport which he had always loathed for its effeminacy. He congratulated me, but his congratulations came from a constricted throat and a puckered mouth.

My son, as you've probably guessed by now, is a first-rate athlete. He is the one chosen first for all teams. He plays games with a kind of easy abandon that makes difficult manoeuvres look like simple acts of nature. He has also a disquieting interest in the mechanical and the scientific, just the right qualifications for a jack of all trades. He takes difficult things apart, things like clocks and cameras, and he puts them back together so that they continue to function. I remember my father's disgust at my own lack of coordination, the thumbs struck by hammers or caught in car doors, the machinery put hopelessly out of adjustment by my ministrations. The workings of hydraulic brakes or power steering systems remain profoundly mysterious to me, however often my father explained that only a fool could fail to see at first glance how they function.

Not that my father was really much better coordinated than I am. He bent nails. His chisel slipped, and there was always something slightly askew in the kitchen cupboards he made. He hit fairly well-placed grounders that would never have got him to first base in a slightly better league, but were enough to make him a star in the leagues he played in. He did everything with a dogged intensity that carried his world before him. In me, he was looking for grace, but all he got was his own slight case of butterfingers without the will to overcome it.

He envies me my son who is everything he wanted me to be, everything he wanted to be himself. My son who can even sing in tune. I come from a family of tone-deaf bellowers. People often ask us what we are trying to say when we are in full song, which is even worse than being accused of being a bad singer. They can't even tell that we're trying to sing. We all own pianos and guitars and drawers full of mouth organs that none of us can play.

What is worst for my father is the knowledge that none of my son's graceful genes come from him. My son is tall and lithe, with wide shoulders and narrow hips, like the men of my wife's family, like the women of my wife's family for that. My father and his four brothers are middle-sized men with chests like barrels and short, thick, powerful legs. The women out of that mould make spectacular teenage girls, but go to fat early. My wife's family, on the other hand, call to mind greyhounds or thoroughbred horses. Thankfully, they are lazy and shiftless, as my father succinctly puts it, or else they would be unbearable.

I bear, unfortunately, a stunning resemblance to my father. At forty-five, I'm grey and balding, five-foot-eight and barrel-chested. I'm a successful psychiatrist, though I look as if I should be moving mattresses, and in fact, whenever I dare to dress casually, I am mistaken for janitors and repairmen. I've tried wearing a large gold ring with diamonds in it to prevent this, but it doesn't help.

Oddly, it bothers my son that he bears no resemblance to me. He likes it when lying aunts point out some mysterious similarity in our eyes or our jawbones. There is none. All he has inherited from me is a kind of desperate insecurity and bottomless desire for praise, which I got from my father, and he, I suppose, got from his, and so on back to some frightened paleolithic cave-son stalking a mammoth, in order to satisfy the unspoken demands of his cave-father.

How do you praise a son to whom everything is easy? He is always winning something. Our house is littered with trophies, his jacket is heavy with crests. He reports all his successes, or he used to report them until he discovered they made me uncomfortable. Now he hides them, and the neighbours tell me. It is not even possible to praise his effort, because he seems to put in no effort, though of course that can't be true. I suspect that I am only able to accept as honest effort those attempts that lead you to tears of frustration.

And that, of course, brings me to our moose hunt. Don't worry, no moose will die in this story. Not a shot will be fired in anger. The entire debacle was my own fault, and though I didn't admit it then, I admit it now. The flaw was reminiscence. My father used to take me hunting when I was young, and in the cold light of day I can remember how painful those trips were: hours of huddled crouching in marshes or in frozen bushes, shivering and wet, hoping that nothing living would stray into my range so that I would have to shoot at it. Miles of walking through deep and nearly impenetrable bush carrying heavy packs full of supplies. Yet, one evening, telling my son about my youth, I seemed only to be able to remember sitting around campfires late at night, the taste of bacon and eggs and coffee cooked over an open fire, sunrise over a lake so clear it was a perfect mirror. When my son, taken in by my poetic raptures, suggested that we go hunting moose, I was as excited as he was. We sat up late making our plans.

By the next morning I had come to my senses, though not quickly enough to avoid some sort of gesture at a hunting trip. I decided to go out to Anderson Point. There had been moose there when I was young, and it had the added advantage of being thoroughly in the wilderness and yet accessible by boat, so there would be no need to carry equipment or to slug through marshes. There was an old abandoned fishing camp that would allow a roof over our heads in case of rain. I was absolutely certain of bad weather.

I tried my best to conceal the trip from my father. When he heard about it via the women, he hinted broadly that he should be invited. I resisted, and when he was forced finally to ask if he could come, I refused, explaining that the trip was being undertaken to allow me some private moments with my son, and pointing out to my father that his seventy years would not be helpful in case of trouble. He had given up hunting himself some ten years ago, and I suggested that his retirement should not be interrupted. He in turn pointed out his greater experience, his knack at fixing outboard motors that broke down, his superior knowledge of the shoals and reefs that surrounded Anderson Point. I referred him to his recent electrocardiogram which hinted at a heart murmur, and refused to take responsibility for his demise. That left us at a standoff, and though over the next few weeks he continued to fish for an invitation, he did not press the point.

On September 22, my son Greg and I launched the eighteen-foot fibreglass boat I had rented for the occasion into the chilly waters of Washow Creek. The sixty-five-horse Mercury outboard started as smoothly as a Cadillac and the little ten-horse spare I had brought along out of my general mistrust of machinery lay comfortably in the bow. We had enough equipment and supplies to last for a month, though we intended to be gone for only three days. All my life I've been over-prepared, a backup ready for any contingency.

We left at noon on a bright sunny day with a slight breeze from the north. I wound my way through the gentle curves of the creek while my son practised making moose calls with a tin can and a piece of string that he drew through the bottom. He'd read about making moose calls in some hunting magazine and, of course, his worked perfectly. It sounded much more authentic than the actual calls of moose on the tape recorder I had brought along.

When we came out of the creek into Blind Bay, the breeze had risen, and the water was getting choppy. By the time we'd crossed the four miles of the bay out into the lake itself, there were rolling swells. And by the time we reached Crow Duck Creek, whitecaps were tossing the tiny canoe that hurried out to intercept us. When we pulled my father on board, he was soaked to the skin and the canoe was half filled with water.

"I didn't decide to come until the last minute," he told us. "Good thing I didn't miss you."

"Yes," I told him, not without a little sarcasm, "that was

certainly a good thing. You might have drowned or had a heart attack."

My son, on the other hand, was delighted. He pulled the canoe across the boat and strapped it on, welcoming his grandfather with unrestrained pleasure. He made the old man take off his clothes and offered him some of his own. Standing there in the boat, naked and shivering, my father looked like a figure of the damned out of a Jehovah's Witnesses' handout, but a moment later, clothed in my son's jeans and a rugby shirt, he looked almost maliciously jaunty. The only item of his own apparel that he kept was his old Minerva Gophers baseball cap that he had been threatening for years to give to the town museum. The museum had been less keen on that artifact than my father was, and so it had remained in his possession.

My father proved his necessity by pointing out hidden shoals and disguised rocks. I had no way of knowing whether these were real or imaginary, but I avoided them anyway. As a result, we arrived a couple of hours later than I had expected, and it was dark when we reached Anderson Point. I, frankly, could see nothing, but my father claimed he could tell where we were by the sound of the breakers, and my son actually said he could see a low line of buildings against the uniformly black shore. I followed their directions, and the boat crunched onto gravel right at the fishing camp.

We landed, walked the boat around a small point of land to a pier my father remembered and which was miraculously still there after twenty-five years of abandonment. We emptied the boat, dragged my overload of supplies into what had once been the main bunkhouse, and spread out our sleeping bags on the floor. My father brought out a mickey of rye, which seemed to be the only supplies he had brought, and we each had a throat-scalding swallow. My father and my son were both eager to talk, my father to conjure the death of ancient moose, my son to predict the downfall of future moose. I exerted authority both ways, turned out the flashlight, and insisted on silence.

During the night, I awoke briefly to the patter of rain and the sound of waves crashing on the shore. It was a lulling sound, and I was only briefly apprehensive. When I awoke to the grey light of a feeble dawn, the sleeping bags on either side of me were empty. I clambered into my chilly clothes and went outside. The whitecaps on the lake made it clear that we would be going nowhere in the boat that day. My father was huddled over a small fire, a frying pan in his hands and a coffee pot balanced on a stick.

"Breakfast in ten minutes," he called, as cheerfully and matter-of-factly as if he had a right to be there.

I muttered an okay and went in search of my son. I found him in a filleting shed, studying the graffiti on the walls as if they were Egyptian hieroglyphs.

"Look at this," he said. "June fifteenth, 1947." The wonder in his voice made that date sound inconceivably ancient. "It says J.T. loves M.P. I wonder who they could be?"

J.T. was Jimmy Tomlinson. His father had run this camp, and Jimmy, a classmate of mine, had left school a month early each year to go out here, because his mother was the cook. M.P. would have been Marlene Perkins, my son's mother and my wife. This evidence of an almost prehistoric passion stirred me strangely. Jimmy would have been nine years old at the time of this declaration. I wondered whether his love might have been reciprocated. Marlene was a grade behind us and, frankly, I had been only marginally aware of her existence until I had returned from university one summer, found her working in a drugstore and married her. I knew she had had other lovers, of whom

I was retrospectively jealous, but I hadn't known my emotions could go so far back in time.

"I don't know," I told my son. "A lot of fishermen worked here. It could be almost anyone." Jimmy Tomlinson was now an alcoholic, sunk so deep in dissipation that there was little hope for recovery. Still, he was one more scaler of my castle, one more ghost to brood about in the irrational moments just before sleep. "Come on," I said, "Grandpa's got breakfast ready."

The breakfast was delicious, marred only by my father's habit of breaking the yolks of eggs when he cooked them. It was an old family feud, and I stood firmly with my mother on the issue. The yolks of eggs should not be broken. My son, who had never eaten camp-fire cooking, pronounced the meal the best he had ever tasted.

Our plan had been to raid some of the small islands around Anderson point: Fox Island, Goose Island, Little Punk Island. Moose will swim for miles in the mating season, and there was a very good chance that, with little effort, we might find our quarry. My father explained that the canoe would come in handy because moose liked to feed in the mouths of the dozen small creeks just around the point. I put a damper on the plans by announcing that the weather made it impossible. We would wait until it calmed down. If the waves were smaller in the afternoon, we might try then. My son, who was eager and knew nothing of water, found me unconvincing. My father, who knew better, but who also knew that my conservatism would prevail, argued there was no danger. We stayed.

After that, conversation died. My son took a compass and announced he was going to go into the bush to find birch bark to make more moose calls. The Indians, he explained, always made moose calls out of birch bark. My father, who, since his retirement, had got out of the habit of early rising, announced he was going back to bed. I cautioned my son against the dangers of getting lost in the bush, but having squelched one set of plans, I couldn't garner enough moral force to stop another, and he disappeared into the yellowing bush.

Left alone, I went in search of further evidence of my wife's ghostly presence in the camp. I found it carved in the walls of the slumping outhouse. J.T. loves M.P. June, 1951. It argued a persistent attraction, but left Jimmy at thirteen, not yet old enough to be considered a danger. There had been four Tomlinson boys, all of whom I had considered sullen and introspective. Here on the walls, however, was astonishing evidence of their capacity for love. They had linked their initials with most of the alphabetic possibilities, making that lonely outhouse a monument to passion.

They had also been great makers of birthday cards for their mother. These were posted in the kitchen, and I was examining them for some consistent image when my son returned, interrupting my archeological speculation.

"I got lost," he said, almost proudly. "I checked the compass and it said I was going north. I checked it again about thirty seconds later and it said I was going south."

"You got turned around," I told him. "It's easy to do."

"I didn't believe the compass," he said. "I knew I couldn't have turned around in that short a time. So, since we're on a point, I figured if I went at right angles to the north-south line, I'd have to hit the lake, and I did, and I'm here."

A small thrill of horror ran down my spine. In the line of sons, unfortunately, I have no backups, no second chances. Anderson Point is quite large enough and quite wild enough for one to be lost and not be found. I determined then that my son would not leave my sight again during the trip.

By mid-afternoon, the clouds had cleared. The whitecaps

had turned into large rolling swells, and the sun, though it gave no warmth, made everything look bright and clean. We decided to go over to Fox Island, a trip of about three miles. The motor started with a sweet purr, though I turned the key convinced that it could never start. We idled slowly, because I was taking no chances with the swells, which seemed a lot larger as soon as we got around the point. Fox Island loomed ahead, a gigantic rock with sheer cliffs on the face. Around the other side, I knew, there was a gentle sloping shore, but we were making for another abandoned fish camp on the face side. There, a floating dock took you to a set of stairs carved into the cliff, and near the top was a filleting shed set into a niche so that it seemed a part of the cliff face itself. I remembered the view from there as spectacular, and it seemed the kind of reminiscence I might share with my son, recollecting it in twenty years for some future grandson.

The landing was uneventful. We tied up the boat and made our way up the stairs to the filleting shed. My son and I went into the shed to look at the view, and my father continued up the stairs to the top. The view was magnificent. We could see across Anderson Point to Washow Bay on the far side and pick out four or five other small islands. I heard a strange scuffling noise, as if someone were walking on the roof, then a thump, and suddenly my father appeared before us, looking in the window from outside. He seemed to hover a second, as if he had something he wanted to say, and then he was gone with a splash into the water below. I froze with horror, but my son was out the door in a second. I followed, and the last thing I saw was the bottom of his shoes as he dived forty feet down to the lake below.

By the time I made my way down to the bottom of the cliff, my son had dragged his grandfather up onto the floating dock and was administering mouth-to-mouth resuscitation.

The old man came to, choking and spluttering and cursing, as much horrified by the touch of male lips on his, I suspect, as by his near encounter with death. I was in a rage, wanting someone to blame besides myself, and knowing there was no one. I ordered them both into the boat and started the motor. It churned into life and I headed back to Anderson Point a lot faster than I knew I should. About a hundred yards from the dock, the motor coughed and stopped. I turned the key and heard a whining hum.

Details bore me, and they'd bore you too. I could describe my soaking father, hardly out of death's kingdom and already tinkering with the motor, my modest heroic son, eager to please, helping him. I'm not going to describe that, nor am I going to describe my churlish self, bad-tempered and clumsy, getting in the way, giving orders that had no possibility of being carried out. All I can tell you is that something happened in the water, some conjunction between the two that excluded me. They looked at each other like new lovers, they spoke to each other with shy politeness, they sidestepped me like you might sidestep an aggressive puppy.

And so it went for the rest of the trip. They fixed the motor. Back at camp, they prepared supper and talked eagerly of the next day's hunt. They ignored my pleas for darkness and sat up until late, polishing off the now sacramental mickey of rye whiskey. The next day, the two of them took the canoe and hunted in the creek mouths, my decision to keep my son in sight overridden by their desire. I pleaded a headache and stayed at the camp, reconstructing the history of the Tomlinson family, *père, mère* and *fils*. I grew to like them for their unreserved ability to carve their feelings into trees and walls. In a moment of inspiration I went back to the outhouse, obliterated Jimmy Tomlinson's initials from the heart that also contained my wife, and replaced them with my own. A petty act, you say, a futile attempt to change history which can't be changed? We'll see.

By the time I'd prepared supper my heart was brimful of love for both my father and my son. I had determined that I would wrest forgiveness from them if I had to wrestle them to ground to get it. Even when darkness came and they had still not returned I was confident. Even after I had launched the boat, rounded the point and come on the empty floating canoe, I felt no despair. I willed them onto land, chose Little Grindstone Point a mile away as the spot I would find them, waving from the shore. I went directly there, swept the shore with my powerful flashlight, and picked them out standing on the rocky beach where they had to be. I leaped from the boat before it even grounded on the shore, churned my way through the splashing waves and seized them both in a bear hug. We swirled, the three of us in a little dance of joy and love.

I refused all explanations and apologies, refused to explain how I knew where they were until we had made our way back to camp and we had finished the meal I had prepared. Then I opened the bottle of Scotch I had brought and poured us each a large ceremonial drink. I began with my version of events, a carefully embroidered version in which heroism and comic humiliation played a large part. Then my father, taking his cue, added another layer to the evolving myth. My son wound our versions together and opened new possibilities. We sat around that fire until dawn, telling and retelling what had happened, until we had a single version that belonged to us all, carved in the wordless night. To my surprise, I came out at the centre, not at the margins as I had thought I would. There was no need to forgive or ask forgiveness. The story did that for us all.

Just one postscript. The trip back was uneventful, except

that the motor refused to start again, and this time we had to use the backup ten-horse. As we were driving back along the old highway, a gigantic moose stepped out of the bush and stood on the road watching us, gleaming black as if it were wet. After a brief flurry of excitement as we reached for guns, we decided that the hunt had been too much of a success to ruin it now by killing a moose. And when I got home and asked my wife about Jimmy Tomlinson, she couldn't even remember who he was.

The Happiest Man in the World

Watch it," I told Sharon. She was bending over my leg, the needle, blackened by a candle, in her hand. Her dress hung open at the neck and I could see a nipple.

"Don't be a baby." They always say that, the women, as they begin their excavation.

"It's a boil," I told her. "You're supposed to leave boils alone. They get better by themselves."

"You don't get boils on the bottom of your feet." She was getting down to work now, poking the needle in and tearing the flesh. "There," she said, "it's open. Now I'll just squeeze out the pus." Suddenly, it really was painful. I winced.

"Don't move your foot." She was beautiful. The dim light in the kitchen softened the brown curls of her hair.

"It's a sliver," she said, triumphant, showing me a thin slice of wood. "It was all infected." She dabbed my foot with rubbing alcohol poured on a piece of Kleenex. I reached my hand under her dress and slid it up her thigh. She tightened her legs and caught it there.

"Remove it," she said, "or the needle goes back in your foot."

I removed it. She was never responsive when she was being professional. There was a spider web over the sink. A spider was working, making it a better web. Pure professionalism.

"There," she said, stretching up and reaching onto the counter for a band-aid. "Just about finished." She stuck the band-aid on, holding it by the little strips. "A boil is an infected hair follicle. There are no hairs on the bottom of your foot."

The foot felt better, there was no denying that. I limped a little, so as not to lose the sympathy I had built up.

"Men are such babies," she told me, picking up her book. She was reading *The Little Drummer Girl*. She hated it, but all her friends had read it. "I can't see why people read this," she said.

"Don't," I said. "You don't have to read books. If you don't like them, you can just put them down. This isn't school. They can't test you on it."

"No," she answered, "I've read this far, and I'm not going to waste all the time I've already spent."

It was hopeless. She always finished things she started. I had to be careful to head her off so she didn't start projects that involved a lot of work for me. Like stripping wallpaper or cleaning basements. She believed marriage was a fifty-fifty proposition, and she kept accounts. I had to do exactly fifty percent. I tried to explain that the person who started a project was responsible for it, and if the other person didn't want to do it, he shouldn't have to.

I couldn't convince her. Once, back in the city, I got a load of gravel for the driveway. I shovelled half of it before supper. After supper, she went out to shovel her half. I couldn't make her stop, and she wouldn't let me help. She shovelled until one o'clock in the morning, while I sat on the steps drinking

Scotch. All the neighbours walked by and looked at me with disgust.

"She wants to do it," I shouted at them, but it was clear they didn't believe me. When she came to bed, she was too tired to make love, which was probably just as well, because I was too drunk. I asked anyway, to build up credit for next time. We were each allowed a maximum of two consecutive refusals.

The band-aid came off my foot the next day when we were swimming. I showed Sharon my foot which was almost healed.

"All my family are great healers," I explained. "I had an uncle once who cut off his finger. He poured horse liniment on it and it was completely healed in a week."

"You just make up those stories," she said. "I don't believe you."

Some of them I did make up, but most of them were true. I do have an uncle who cures everything with horse liniment. He might have cut off his finger, and if he had, he would have cured it in a week with horse liniment.

Sharon was doing the backstroke. She's an excellent swimmer. I like to watch her do the backstroke, because she has large breasts, and they point at the sky when she swims on her back. I dived under her and came up on the other side.

"You sound like a hippopotamus," she said. "And you've got snot in your beard. Wipe it off."

"You've never seen a hippopotamus," I told her, wiping my beard with the back of my hand.

"I saw one on Jacques Cousteau," she said. "It looked just like you when it swam."

"Jacques Cousteau explores oceans," I explained. "There are no hippopotamuses in the ocean. You made that up."

"I did not. Once he explored this river, and it was full of hippopotamuses."

She was still doing the backstroke and I was swimming beside her doing a breaststroke. She turned over and swam away from me with a crawl. I can do the crawl OK until I have to breathe, so anything over twenty feet is a fair distance for me. I decided to go back to shore.

We were having guests. I love guests. They're always so happy when they arrive, their faces shining, bottles of white wine under their arms and sometimes even strawberry flans or chicken casseroles wrapped in aluminum foil. The children are already dressed in their bathing suits, and they carry brightly coloured towels. The teenagers hang back sulkily, but in a few minutes they are swimming too, shouting like the smaller kids. I love guests, standing on the deck in the little pools of water that drip from their bathing suits, holding their rum and Cokes in their hands and saying, "It sure is hot in the city."

Sharon doesn't like guests as much as I do. They always forget towels and bathing suits and the baby's colic medicine, and then she has to return these things. They sit on the furniture with wet bathing suits and when she sits down in her new white dress she gets a stain on it. She prefers rainy days when there are waves on the lake. Then she sits looking out the window, editing medical textbooks. She looks up words in her big medical dictionary and glues little pieces of yellow paper with questions on them into the manuscript. This is the source of her medical knowledge. If she wanted to, she could remove your appendix or your spleen, though of course she never does that, because it's against the law. She does repair guests when they suffer minor wounds, and she prescribes a number of non-prescription drugs.

Today's guests were late, like you're supposed to be when

you go to a cottage at the lake. Sharon had already dried off, and was sitting on the deck in a lawn chair, editing a monograph on the liver. I was reading a South American novel. All the poor people had taken over some land from a wealthy landlord and were building shacks on it. The politicians were trying to decide what to do. I was on the side of the poor people, who were all prostitutes and petty thieves, but who seemed to have a lot of fun. Then a little blue Escort drove into the driveway. The doors opened and poured people onto the lawn. There were six altogether, including the two little girls. My guests had brought guests of their own.

I pretended I was a cowboy, and welcomed them all in a Texas accent. I didn't carry it on for very long, because sooner or later all my accents turn into an Irish accent. My guest's guest was a famous writer. I had read all his books except the last one. I explained that I was trying to finish all the South American novels that had been translated, and that I would read his as soon as I was done. The writer said that he had been to South America and had got drunk with many of the writers. I wanted to ask him about the brothels, but his wife, who was a well-known actress, was also there, and I thought it might not be the best question to ask in her presence.

My own guest was my neighbour in the city, but he was also a poet in his spare time. You couldn't buy his books in any of the stores, but every so often he would show me reviews that said he was in the forefront of contemporary poetry. His poems wandered all over the page and had quite a lot of dirty words in them, but he himself was very neat. He wore newly pressed cream pants and brown sweaters. When he wasn't writing poetry, he was an archivist. His wife was a social worker who specialized in poor people and drug addicts. She was incredibly beautiful and always well dressed. I sometimes wondered how she managed to get along with the poverty-stricken drug addicts. She must have looked like something out of a magazine to them.

I ran to mix rum and Cokes while Sharon explained to them about the liver. Apparently it's an amazing organ, capable of renewing itself after incredible abuse. I was pleased to hear that. I've worried about my own from time to time. I added a slice of lime to each drink, turning them into Cuba Libres, and we made jokes about belonging to the Cuban Liberation Army. Then the guests all went swimming and I put some coals on the barbecue. I was barbecuing a crown roast of lamb from a recipe in *Gourmet* magazine.

My guests' daughters both looked like the little girl who used to carry the candle in the ad for Fisk tires. They were identical, except that one was bigger than the other. I warned them about swimming out over their heads, and promised them lemonade when they were through. All my guests were frolicking in the water, leaping like porpoises and laughing. The grackles had discovered an old dish of dog-food and were carrying bits of kibble to feed to their babies in a nest just behind the cottage.

The dinner turned out just fine. The lamb was a bit rare, but it's supposed to be. The writer told funny stories about South America and about doing a reading at the Central Institute for English in Hyderabad in India, where he was arrested as a communist agitator and the ambassador had to come and get him out of jail. His wife told about doing a topless role in a radio play. The director wasn't happy about what she was doing until finally she tore off her blouse and brassiere and read her part bare-chested. Sharon told some funny stories about the pancreas. I poured everybody big glasses of brandy. Then we put the two little girls in the spare bedroom, and we all sat around and played canasta until one o'clock. The men won both games, though there were some accusations about talking across the table. Sharon got into the white wine, and when the guests left she was starting to get a little tough. When she drinks white wine she talks out of the corner of her mouth like Edward G. Robinson.

We walked the guests out to the car, helped load the sleeping children, and waved as they drove away with a spurt of gravel. We went back into the house and started to wash dishes. Sharon was dangerously silent, and she broke a glass, a sure sign of trouble ahead. It was one of those little flowered glasses my mom had given me for my birthday, but I didn't say a word. I knew I'd have to provoke her soon, but I didn't want to for a while. I love washing dishes. The water is soft and warm on your hands, and the glasses sparkle when you rinse them. When you get the cupboards wiped off and the elements out of the stove cleaned, everything looks inviting and new.

When we were finished I said to Sharon, "All right, out with it. Let's have it."

"You don't have any guests due until three o'clock tomorrow," she said. "How are you going to survive the morning?"

I could see it was going to be OK. When she starts with sarcasm, the wound isn't very deep. "They're your guests," I reminded her. "You invited today's batch and tomorrow's." Sharon loves guests too, though she says she doesn't, but sometimes, especially if she gets into the white wine, she gets tired.

"God," she said, "you're such a swine."

I suggested we go for a walk instead of having a fight. She agreed, and we walked down the beach as far as the big rock. On the way, I told her a story about an Arab prince who had five hundred wives. He loved them all deeply, and couldn't bear to be out of their presence. They loved him too and were all faithful. He got to thinking about how bad it was for them that they could only spend one night with him every year and a half. Because he was fair minded, he decided he would release all but one of them. He drew lots and kept the one whose number came up. The rest of them he married off to wealthy sultans and other princes. For a little while he was happy, until he discovered that his wife was being unfaithful to him. When he confronted her, she told him she was sick of him and bored with her life. She said she felt suffocated by always being at his beck and call. The next day, she poisoned him. She inherited his entire kingdom, and the first thing she did was marry five hundred husbands.

Sharon wanted to know what the story meant, but I told her that it was just a story and it didn't mean anything. A warm breeze had sprung up as we walked, and small waves splashed at our feet. A full moon glinted yellow off the lake. We rolled up our jeans and walked in the little waves all the way back to the cottage. Then we took off all our clothes and went skinny dipping. We decided that a little later we would make love.

Some day it will be winter. The lake will be frozen and the leaves will all have fallen from the trees. A cold wind will sweep in from the north, and we will wake up in the morning to discover our hair has turned white. But just now, it is summer, early August, when the warmth of July still lingers. The trees are still lush, and every morning the sun rises like an orange out of the lake.

"Hurry," I told Sharon as we ran out of the lake, naked and dripping, over the beach and into our cottage and bed. "Hurry," I said again.

A Girl's Story

You've wondered what it would be like to be a character in a story, to sort of slip out of your ordinary self and into some other character. Well, I'm offering you the opportunity. I've been trying to think of a heroine for this story, and frankly, it hasn't been going too well. A writer's life isn't easy, especially if, like me, he's got a tendency sometimes to drink a little bit too much. Yesterday, I went for a beer with Dennis and Ken (they're real-life friends of mine) and we stayed a little longer than we should have. Then I came home and quickly mixed a drink and starting drinking it so my wife would think the liquor on my breath came from the drink I was drinking and not from the drinks I had had earlier. I wasn't going to tell her about those drinks. Anyway, Wayne dropped over in the evening and I had some more drinks, and this morning my head isn't working very well.

To be absolutely frank about it, I always have trouble getting characters, even when I'm stone cold sober. I can think of plots; plots are really easy. If you can't think of one, you just pick up a book, and sure enough, there's a plot. You just move a few things around and nobody knows you stole the idea. Characters are the problem. It doesn't matter how good the plot is if your characters are dull. You can steal characters too, and put them into different plots. I've done that. I stole Eustacia Vye from Hardy and gave her another name. The problem was that she turned out a lot sulkier than I remembered and the plot I put her in was a light comedy. Now nobody wants to publish the story. I'm still sending it out, though. If you send a story to enough publishers, no matter how bad it is, somebody will ultimately publish it.

For this story I need a beautiful girl. You probably don't think you're beautiful enough, but I can fix that. I can do all kinds of retouching once I've got the basic material, and if I miss anything, Karl (he's my editor) will find it. So I'm going to make you fairly tall, about five-foot eight-and-a-quarter in your stocking feet. I'm going to give you long blonde hair because long blonde hair is sexy and virtuous. Black hair can be sexy too, but it doesn't go with virtue. I've got to deal with a whole literary tradition where black-haired women are basically evil. If I were feeling better I might be able to do it in an ironic way, then black hair would be okay, but I don't think I'm up to it this morning. If you're going to use irony, you've got to be really careful about tone. I could make you a redhead, but redheads have a way of turning out pixieish, and that would wreck my plot.

So you've got long blonde hair and you're this tall slender girl with amazingly blue eyes. Your face is narrow and your nose is straight and thin. I could have turned up the nose a little, but that would have made you cute, and I really need a beautiful girl. I'm going to put a tiny black mole on your cheek. It's traditional. If you want your character to be really beautiful there has to be some minor defect.

Now, I'm going to sit you on the bank of a river. I'm not

much for setting. I've read so many things where you get great long descriptions of the setting, and mostly it's just boring. When my last book came out, one of the reviewers suggested that the reason I don't do settings is that I'm not very good at them. That's just silly. I'm writing a different kind of story, not that old realist stuff. If you think I can't do setting, just watch.

There's a curl in the river just below the old dam where the water seems to make a broad sweep. That flatness is deceptive, though. Under the innocent sheen of the mirroring surface, the current is treacherous. The water swirls, stabs, takes sharp angles and dangerous vectors. The trees that lean from the bank shimmer with the multi-hued greenness of elm, oak, maple and aspen. The leaves turn in the gentle breeze, showing their paler green undersides. The undergrowth, too, is thick and green, hiding the poison ivy, the poison sumac and the thorns. On a patch of grass that slopes gently to the water, the only clear part of the bank on that side of the river, a girl sits, a girl with long blonde hair. She has slipped a ring from her finger and seems to be holding it toward the light.

You see? I could do a lot more of that, but you wouldn't like it. I slipped a lot of details in there and provided all those hints about strange and dangerous things under the surface. That's called foreshadowing. I put in the ring at the end there so that you'd wonder what was going to happen. That's to create suspense. You're supposed to ask yourself what the ring means. Obviously it has something to do with love, rings always do, and since she's taken it off, obviously something has gone wrong in the love relationship. Now I just have to hold off answering that question for as long as I can, and I've got my story. I've got a friend who's also a writer who says never tell the buggers anything until they absolutely have to know.

I'm going to have trouble with the feminists about this story. I can see that already. I've got that river that's calm on the surface and boiling underneath, and I've got those trees that are gentle and beautiful with poisonous and dangerous undergrowth. Obviously, the girl is going to be like that, calm on the surface but passionate underneath. The feminists are going to say that I'm perpetuating stereotypes, that by giving the impression the girl is full of hidden passion I'm encouraging rapists. That's crazy. I'm just using a literary convention. Most of the world's great books are about the conflict between reason and passion. If you take that away, what's left to write about?

So I've got you sitting on the riverbank, twirling your ring. I forgot the birds. The trees are full of singing birds. There are meadowlarks and vireos and even Blackburnian warblers. I know a lot about birds but I'm not going to put in too many. You've got to be careful not to overdo things. In a minute I'm going to enter your mind and reveal what you're thinking. I'm going to do this in the third person. Using the first person is sometimes more effective, but I'm always afraid to do a female character in the first person. It seems wrong to me, like putting on a woman's dress.

Your name is Linda. I had to be careful not to give you a biblical name like Judith or Rachel. I don't want any symbolism in this story. Symbolism makes me sick, especially biblical symbolism. You always end up with some crazy moral argument that you don't believe and none of the readers believe. Then you lose control of your characters, because they've got to be like the biblical characters. You've got this terrific episode you'd like to use, but you can't because Rachel or Judith or whoever wouldn't do it. I think of stories with a lot of symbolism in them as sticky.

Here goes.

Linda held the ring up toward the light. The diamond flashed rainbow colours. It was a small diamond, and Linda reflected that it was probably a perfect symbol of her relationship with Greg. Everything Greg did was on a small scale. He was careful with his money and just as careful with his emotions. In one week they would have a small wedding and then move into a small apartment. She supposed that she ought to be happy. Greg was very handsome, and she did love him. Why did it seem that she was walking into a trap?

That sounds kind of distant, but it's supposed to be distant. I'm using indirect quotation because the reader has just met Linda, and we don't want to get too intimate right away. Besides, I've got to get a lot of explaining done quickly, and if you can do it with the character's thoughts, then that's best.

Linda twirled the ring again, then with a suddenness that surprised her, she stood up and threw it into the river. She was immediately struck by a feeling of panic. For a moment she almost decided to dive into the river to try to recover it. Then, suddenly, she felt free. It was now impossible to marry Greg. He would not forgive her for throwing the ring away. Greg would say he'd had enough of her theatrics for one lifetime. He always accused her of being a romantic. She'd never had the courage to admit that he was correct, and that she intended to continue being a romantic. She was sitting alone by the river in a long blue dress because it was a romantic pose. Anyway, she thought a little wryly, you're only likely to find romance if you look for it in romantic places and dress for the occasion.

Suddenly, she heard a rustling in the bush, the sound of someone coming down the narrow path from the road above.

I had to do that, you see. I'd used up all the potential in the relationship with Greg, and the plot would have started to flag if I hadn't introduced a new character. The man who is coming down the path is tall and athletic with wavy brown hair. He has dark brown eyes that crinkle when he smiles, and he looks kind. His skin is tanned, as if he spends a lot of time outdoors, and he moves gracefully. He is smoking a pipe. I don't want to give too many details. I'm not absolutely sure what features women find attractive in men these days, but what I've described seems safe enough. I got all of it from stories written by women, and I assume they must know. I could give him a chiselled jaw, but that's about as far as I'll go.

The man stepped into the clearing. He carried an old-fashioned wicker fishing creel and a telescoped fishing rod. Linda remained sitting on the grass, her blue dress spread out around her. The man noticed her and apologized.

"I'm sorry, I always come here to fish on Saturday afternoons and I've never encountered anyone here before." His voice was low with something of an amused tone in it.

"Don't worry," Linda replied. "I'll only be here for a little while. Go ahead and fish. I won't make any noise." In some way she couldn't understand, the man looked familiar to her. She felt she knew him. She thought she might have seen him on television or in a movie, but of course she knew that movie and television stars do not spend every Saturday afternoon fishing on the banks of small, muddy rivers.

"You can make all the noise you want," he told her. "The fish in this river are almost entirely deaf. Besides, I don't care if I catch any. I only like the act of fishing. If I catch them, then I have to take them home and clean them. Then I've got to cook them and eat them. I don't even like fish that much, and the fish you catch here all taste of mud."

"Why do you bother fishing then?" Linda asked him. "Why don't you just come and sit on the riverbank?"

"It's not that easy," he told her. "A beautiful girl in a blue dress may go and sit on a riverbank any time she wants. But a

man can only sit on a riverbank if he has a very good reason.
Because I fish, I am a man with a hobby. After a hard week of
work, I deserve some relaxation. But if I just came and sat on
the riverbank, I would be a romantic fool. People would make
fun of me. They would think I was irresponsible, and before
long I would be a failure." As he spoke, he attached a lure to
his line, untelescoped his fishing pole and cast his line into
the water.

You may object that this would not have happened in real
life, that the conversation would have been awkward, that
Linda would have been a bit frightened by the man. Well,
why don't you just run out to the grocery store and buy a bottle of milk and a loaf of bread? The grocer will give you your
change without even looking at you. That's what happens in
real life, and if that's what you're after, why are you reading
a book?

I'm sorry. I shouldn't have got upset. But it's not easy, you
know. Dialogue is about the hardest stuff to write. You've got
all those "he said"s and "she said"s and "he replied"s. And
you've got to remember the quotation marks and whether the
comma is inside or outside the quotation marks. Sometimes
you can leave out the "he said"s and the "she said"s but then
the reader gets confused and can't figure out who's talking.
Hemingway is bad for that. Sometimes you can read an entire
chapter without figuring out who is on what side.

Anyway, something must have been in the air that afternoon. Linda felt free and open.

Did I mention that it was warm and the sun was shining?

She chattered away, telling the stranger all about her life,
what she had done when she was a little girl, the time her
dad had taken the whole family to Hawaii and she got such a
bad sunburn that she was peeling in February, how she was
a better water skier than Greg and how mad he got when she

beat him at tennis. The man, whose name was Michael (you can use biblical names for men as long as you avoid Joshua or Isaac), told her he was a doctor, but had always wanted to be a cowboy. He told her about the time he skinned his knee when he fell off his bicycle and had to spend two weeks in the hospital because of infection. In short, they did what people who are falling in love always do. They unfolded their brightest and happiest memories and gave them to each other as gifts.

Then Michael took a bottle of wine and a Klik sandwich out of his wicker creel and invited Linda to join him in a picnic. He had forgotten his corkscrew and he had to push the cork down into the bottle with his filleting knife. They drank wine and laughed and spat out little pieces of cork. Michael reeled in his line, and to his amazement discovered a diamond ring on his hook. Linda didn't dare tell him where the ring had come from. Then Michael took Linda's hand, and slipped the ring onto her finger. In a comic-solemn voice, he asked her to marry him. With the same kind of comic solemnity, she agreed. Then they kissed, a first gentle kiss with their lips barely brushing and without touching each other.

Now I've got to bring this to some kind of ending. You think writers know how stories end before they write them, but that's not true. We're wracked with confusion and guilt about how things are going to end. And just as you're playing the role of Linda in this story, Michael is my alter ego. He even looks a little like me and he smokes the same kind of pipe. We all want this to end happily. If I were going to be realistic about this, I suppose I'd have to let them make love. Then, shaken with guilt and horror, Linda would go back and marry Greg, and the doctor would go back to his practice. But I'm not going to do that. In the story from which I stole the plot, Michael turned out not to be a doctor at all, but a returned soldier who had always been in love with Linda.

She recognized him as they kissed, because they had kissed as children, and even though they had grown up and changed, she recognized the flavour of wintergreen on his breath. That's no good. It brings in too many unexplained facts at the last minute.

I'm going to end it right here at the moment of the kiss. You can do what you want with the rest of it, except you can't make him a returned soldier, and you can't have them make love then separate forever. I've eliminated those options. In fact, I think I'll eliminate all options. This is where the story ends, at the moment of the kiss. It goes on and on forever while cities burn, nations rise and fall, galaxies are born and die, and the universe snuffs out the stars one by one. It goes on, the story, the brush of a kiss.

Prelude to America

She shouldn't have done it. She shouldn't have lain with him there in the sweet meadow, the sun low in the sky, the music still ringing in her ears. So what if he had played on the violin while everyone danced, so what if he sang like an angel? She was only seventeen and he was the father of five children, so what if her blood had flooded her body like a disease, she should have said no, I can find my own way home, thank you. She should have said I am sorry, sir, what you ask is impossible. The nineteenth century had tipped on its fulcrum and they were sliding towards a new century, but there was still plenty of time. She could have said no.

But she didn't. It's a curse on the whole family. We can't say no. When somebody invites us to pleasure, we forget what we were doing, we forget all our plans, and we're thrashing in the bedclothes or crushing the flowers in the sweet meadows. There was plenty of warning. The gulls were crying out danger, the terns were calling beware, beware. The heat of the blood is no excuse, but we make it our excuse again and again.

And that's what Thorunn did in the Icelandic dawn when the century was gathering itself for disaster. She forgot that she could recite whole sections of the Bible, that her father was the priest at Tjorn, that her mother had warned against such a moment. So this is love, she thought, and she slipped out of her dress as if it had no buttons, as if it had been designed to be thrown carelessly on the grass. Even the starlings were upset. They flew out over the fjord so that they would not have to watch, they flew right past the swans nesting near the mouth of the river, they flew north in the direction of the Arctic Circle that hovered just on the edge of the horizon.

Ah, but when it was over she was sorry, you want to say, she had learned her lesson, but it was nothing of the sort. It's a curse on the whole family, this inability to feel proper guilt, to learn from our mistakes. We should be wearing sackcloth and ashes, some of us should learn how to pray properly, somebody should ask for forgiveness. But we don't. At least Thorunn didn't. She danced home as happily as if she had won first prize in the confirmation class.

And she did it again. The very next night. She slipped out of doors when she should have been sleeping and lay with Arngrimmur again, just beyond the church in plain view of her father's bedroom, in plain view of her own grandmother's grave. And the next day, when she should have stayed in her room and begged the Lord's forgiveness, she told her sister everything, she told Petrina Soffia, who was only fifteen, how love happens, the mechanics of the thing. She said it all aloud in the barn when they were feeding the new calf, when anyone might have been listening.

It's a curse on the whole family. We can't keep anything to ourselves. We have to blab it all out, tell each other things that should never be spoken aloud. We have no secrets, none of us, and no shame. Don't tell us anything, we will tell everyone else, we don't even whisper. You may as well publish your secret in the newspaper as tell it to us.

And so by the end of the week everyone in the valley knew. Thorunn was so happy about being in love and so amazed with the simple dynamics of lovemaking she told everything to Petrina Soffia. And Petrina was so amazed at her sister's discovery that she told Nanna and Inga, and even their little brother Bjorn, who was only five years old. And Nanna told Disa and Inga told Margaret, and Bjorn thought about it and asked Thorunn, who kissed him and said not to worry, everything would be fine.

That's another problem. We all believe that everything can be cured with kisses. There's no use telling us kisses are part of the problem, that kisses might be the whole problem. We kiss each other when we meet and we kiss each other when we part, and we sometimes kiss perfect strangers. I'll tell you more about that later.

And of course everybody in the valley knew in no time. This is a valley that can't keep secrets. Secrets slide down the slopes of the mountains. Elves whisper the secrets to the cattle. The wind from the fjord blows nobody any good.

So by the time that Arngrimmur's wife found out, Thorunn's belly had begun to swell. The swans on the pond kept their dignity. They nodded their heads and looked at their reflections in the water. The glacier in the south end of the valley moved one more notch toward the fjord. Half the people in the valley packed their bags and moved to America. Arngrimmur bowed his head like a swan and stayed in his house.

Thorunn looked at her reflection in the water and she liked what she saw, the rounding of her belly. She was without shame. When Arngrimmur walked by on the road she waved to him, and she laughed a laugh that haunted him for nine years. He woke in the night in his bed, and the laugh rattled him so he couldn't sleep, and he had to get up in the dark and breathe deeply one hundred times before he could sleep again. For nine whole years.

Did I tell you that we're all plagued by ghosts? Every last one of us, even here in America. It's like this. There were so many ghosts in the valley, there wasn't room for them. And so many people left for America, there was nobody left for the ghosts, so they went to America, too, though not until 1883. One of them is always after me to move his bones. But that comes later. Remind me to tell you about it.

So while Arngrimmur was dealing with that ghost of a laugh, Thorunn's father was making arrangements. He could have sent her to America, but she didn't want to go, and he thought she might get into even more trouble there, in a place that wasn't an island, so you could go anywhere you wanted. And so he married her off to Jon Helgason.

Actually, it wasn't so easy. She didn't want to marry Jon Helgason, even though he had his own farm down the valley, just at the foot of the glacier where the river makes a turn and the bridge keeps falling down. Even though his wife had been dead for ten years, and even though he had his own house and his own sheep and he promised she could have her own horse. Even then she resisted. But then Bjorn drowned in the pond, and everything was too much for a while, and when things settled she was married and had a daughter.

It was a time when children often died, and Thorunn's daughter died, too, even though she did everything she could to keep her alive. It was the whooping cough that took her in the middle of the night, and none of Thorunn's prayers moved God to intervene. Arngrimmur was in sorrow, too, though he couldn't show it. When Thorunn cried at the funeral, her cry entered Arngrimmur's soul, and it haunted him for nine years. Every morning when he awoke, he was so sad he had to take one hundred deep breaths before he could get out of his bed.

Jon Helgason was old, there's no denying that. He was sixty-six when he married Thorunn, and they were married for four years before she shared his bed. Perhaps she was waiting for Arngrimmur, but after a while, there seemed no point in waiting. She had to make the best of things. That's a good thing about us. We all make the best of things. Life isn't always fair, and you have to take what you are given.

Thorunn had two sons with Jon, but they were both albinos with white hair and pink eyes. Jon was so old that his seed had gone bad, and it wasn't strong enough to make a child who could live. Both boys died at the age of two, and Thorunn decided she would have no more children.

But then Arngrimmur's wife died, and he was left alone. His oldest daughter Nanna moved off to America, and the younger children went to live with other people, so he was all by himself. He decided to live his life as a hermit, but he was the only one in the valley who could play the violin, and he was the only one in the valley who could play the flute, and the people needed music, and so even though he was unhappy, he sang and he played, and even though he yearned for Thorunn, and woke in the night to her laugh and in the morning to her cry, he was caught by his life and he had to live it.

And so after a wedding where he had played and sung, he lay in the sweet meadow with another young woman. Only once, he swore, and only half willingly, because she had asked him to. It's a curse on the whole family. We are too polite to refuse, and so rather than hurt anyone's feelings, we popu-late the planet with the fruits of accidental love. Arngrimmur found himself the father of another daughter. I don't know what became of that daughter. I ought to know. It's written in a book, and I could look it up, but I don't want to. That's a different story, not the story I want to tell.

Here's what happened next. Jon Helgason was climbing onto the back of a horse. He put one foot in the stirrup and swung his leg over the horse. Only he didn't stop. He contin-ued right over the horse onto the ground on the other side, and when Thorunn came to help him up, he was dead.

They buried him right there on the farm, in the exact spot where he had died. And the grass had not even started to grow on his grave before Thorunn married Arngrimmur. Nobody in the valley spoke ill of them for that. Everyone knew they had been meant for each other from the start, and only bad luck had kept them apart. The day they married was nine years after Arngrimmur had heard Thorunn's laugh and his haunting had begun. She laughed again, the night of their wedding, and after that, Arngrimmur slept through the night. She cried the next morning for all their lost children, and Arngrimmur never heard her cry again.

The twentieth century was coming at them like an ava-lanche and they didn't have much time. They set to work and had four more children. The whole family is like that. When something needs to be done, we get right down to it and do it. Nobody in the valley was happier than Arngrimmur and Thorunn. Once, the new priest preached a sermon which everybody knew was aimed at them. It told a parable about the dangers of lying in the sweet meadows with people who you should not be lying with, but Arngrimmur and Thorunn were so happy that the story ended up with the wrong moral, and the priest never preached it again.

Their children were Nanna and Bjorn and Angantyr and Petrina Soffia, every one of them named for someone else, because that's one way of keeping the dead alive. And after a while Arngrimmur died. I don't like to talk about his death, but I've got a long story to tell and it's best to get the hard parts done early. It was pneumonia. He forgot his coat and walked home without it. A sudden storm brought sleet and rain off the ocean, and Arngrimmur got pneumonia and died.

So this is where the story begins, after Arngrimmur's death when the family had to go and live with relatives and there were twenty-two people living in one house. The story is about the second Petrina Soffia, daughter of Thorunn and Arngrimmur, who was beautiful and good and looked so much like her mother the people in the valley had trouble telling the difference. On her seventeenth birthday, an old farmer down the valley, a nephew of Jon Helgason, offered to marry Petrina Soffia. I told you that there were twenty-two people living in the house, so it was hard for her to refuse.

Petrina Soffia asked her mother what she should do.

Thorunn said only one word.

"America."

And so Petrina Soffia packed up everything she owned, all her clothes and her books, and she put them in her suitcase and she walked all the way to the harbour and boarded a boat and sailed for America. Nobody in Iceland ever heard from her again.

She brought more than her clothes and her books. She brought a memory of mountains and glaciers and fjords. She brought the taste of wild berries on mountain slopes and she carried in her lungs the freshest air in the world. She brought a thousand songs her father had taught her and she brought the memory of how to make *pönnökukurs* and *skyr* and how to knit sweaters and how to keep a dying lamb alive. She gathered up all the lonely and abandoned ghosts in Iceland and brought them with her. She brought sweet meadows and the cry of gulls.

And when the boat finally landed in Quebec, she stepped right off into America and into the twentieth century and she never looked back.

Lucky for us.

The Drunk Woman Is Singing in My Office

The drunk woman is singing in my office. Nobody knows who she is or how she got there. There are secretaries whose job it is to keep other people out of my office, secretaries who smile and say, "No, Dr. Arnason is not in," even though I sit behind my oak door at my oak desk, twisting paper clips and throwing them into the wastebasket. They know how to tell people who telephone, "No, Dr. Arnason is with someone just now. Leave your name and number and he'll get back to you." And now, somehow, a drunk woman has got beyond all the secretaries and is in my office singing.

She is singing a mournful love song in a deep, breathy voice. There is a refrain that goes, "Come back to me my sweet," which she pronounces as "shweet," with the slurred "s" of the drinker. Her voice is not unpleasant, though there is something hard in it that I don't completely like. I have gathered the secretaries into another office to ask how the drunk woman got into my office. They inform me that no one has come past them. They suggest that she might have come in through the window, but I remind them that we are on the

147

sixth floor, so this is unlikely. They suggest that she has been there all along, singing, but I reject this suggestion. I would surely have noticed before now.

I have sent the youngest secretary to spy on the drunk woman from behind the potted plants by the door. From there, she can see into my office. The potted plants are supplied on lease by a small firm which grows them in a nursery on the third floor of an old warehouse. Once a week the two women who own the plants come over to water them and to feed them small white tablets. The plant ladies are imperfectly beautiful, and so they have been abandoned by their husbands, who recognize the danger of imperfect beauty. The dark woman has a mole on her cheek, a small furry mouse, that is only a bit too large to be attractive. The blonde woman has high, perfect breasts, but her waist is only slightly too thick. Their husbands, who were both psychiatrists, know that such women can never be faithful and so they have cut their losses, choosing instead firm peasant girls with smaller aspirations.

The youngest secretary has come back to tell me that the drunk woman is dancing now. She is swirling around the room, dipping and rising to her own song. The youngest secretary does an imitation of the dance, balancing on the edge of falling, exaggerating all her motions. I have never noticed before that the youngest secretary is beautiful, but she has never danced for me before. I will have to see that she is transferred. I have work to do, and I cannot sit in my office thinking about the youngest secretary and her lovers, bearded lawyers who talk to her of torts, and young, blue-jeaned truck drivers who handle her roughly.

I have told the secretaries that the drunk woman in my office must be removed. I have authorized the calling of security guards, and if that fails, then the police. I have informed them that I will be gone for the day, but I have also whispered to the oldest secretary that in case of emergency I may be reached in the cocktail lounge of the Downtowner Hotel. There are never emergencies; ours is not the sort of operation that has emergencies, but it is a ritual we have evolved. The oldest secretary is very good at her job, but she needs someone she can call in case of emergency. If I did not provide this, she would leave and get a job with someone who does have emergencies. She told me once that she had wanted to be a nurse.

And now, in my dark corner of the cocktail lounge in the Downtowner Hotel, I sip on my glass of John Jameson Irish whiskey. I prefer Old Bushmills, but I have recently discovered it is made in the north of Ireland while John Jameson is made in the south, and in Irish matters I am a Republican. I think of the drunk woman in my office, and I am sad. Moments of truth and beauty are so rare in the world, and once more I have missed my chance. I might have gone into my office and sung with her. We might have crooned lullabies about lost love and riversides. She might have cradled me in her arms and stroked my hair. We might have cradled and sung, cradled and sung.

Or I might have gone in and danced with her. There is a radio in my office, and we could have found suitable music. We might have whirled and dipped, spinning around the room until we were both laughing and dizzy. Then we might have collapsed, still laughing, onto the couch, she might have cradled my head and stroked my hair, cradled and stroked. She might even have said she loved me.

Instead, I am alone in a bar in the middle of the afternoon, and already the security guards or the police are speaking to her in firm, stern voices. They may even be laying their hands on her to drag her out of my office. I am no fool. I know grace when I see it. I have chosen to sit in this bar drinking John Jameson with ice and water, feeling my joints and muscles relax. I have made my choices.

Square Dancers

Do square dancers, when they vote, wonder "Will this government be good for square dancing?" Do they brood on the injustice of a world that fails to take their art with sufficient seriousness? Are there grants or scholarships for young square dancers of brilliant promise? When they are together, do they tell tales of unremitting dedication that took one dancer to the top, while another dissipated his talent in drink or tragic love? Is there even a top one can get to, some final dance-off after all the local competitions, called, probably, the "North-Americans"?

In the spring, they flood the campuses of North America, the men in colourful shirts and little western string ties, the women in billowing skirts, buoyed out by massive crinolines. Where do they get those crinolines? Is there a company that specializes in producing crinolines for female square dancers? You never see those crinolines in stores, so there must be some other arrangement for selling them, mail order, perhaps, or special square-dance clothing parties, where everybody comes and tries them on. Maybe there are pro shops, like the golfers have.

They like the campuses, because the gyms are large. You can see them sitting in squares at the tables in their bright costumes. Most of them seem to be about fifty, but every so often you see a younger couple. Almost always, the male has a thin, dark moustache, and the female has a bouffant hairdo. Sometimes, there will even be a very young couple with the open faces you see in the crowd waiting to go in to a revival meeting.

Something about them reminds me of robins, though I can't quite say what. For all his red breast, the robin is a little drab, and there is something just a little drab about a gathering of square dancers, no matter how bright their clothes. The interesting thing about them is that when they change into their street clothes, you can't tell them from anybody else. You could walk past dozens of square dancers in a Target store, and never know it.

How do they get started? Do they discover the vocation, like a priest does, or are they enlisted by friends, who say to them after a barbecue, "Have you ever given any thought to square dancing?" Is there a missionary spirit among the committed? Do they hold membership drives? Can anyone join, or are there selection committees who ponder each candidate's rightness for admission? Is there an oath? A secret handshake?

Golfers are different. You can sometimes know golfers, even be friends with them, but unless you are a square dancer yourself, you will not know square dancers. And yet they have children, brothers, sisters. Somebody must know them. Do their families sometimes tell them, "This is madness, you can't dance your way around the continent. You're ruining your life with this obsession." Do they sometimes hire professionals to try to steal back their loved ones from the square dancers? Must they be deprogrammed?

Is there a special language? Something besides do-si-do, allemande left and promenade? All special groups have their own argot, and so square dancers must, but why have we never heard them? We see them sitting in the university cafeterias waiting for the next competition, but when we try to eavesdrop, all we hear is a deep murmur, like water under a bridge, and the odd burst of embarrassed laughter.

Why didn't we know this was happening? Suddenly, one day they were there, thousands upon thousands of square dancers with their checked shirts, their string ties, their crinolines and their bandanas. There must have been a beginning, some period when there were only a few scattered groups. And how did it all begin? Was there some individual who decided, "It's high time there was a square dancing revival, and by gum, I'm the man to start it?" Or was it in the air, some obscure compulsion that moved individuals almost without their knowing it? Does it start as a desire to tap the foot, then perhaps a little hop on the way to the bathroom, when suddenly your arm crooks into the arm of someone with a similar compulsion, and suddenly you're dancing?

They love order, these square dancers. Their costumes match. Their squares are perfect, and they move in time to the music. When the caller cries, "Swing your corner lady," they swing, they over-and-under on command. And who is the mysterious caller, the partnerless man who orchestrates the tight patterns, what is in this for him? Is it enough just to be able to make such order with human bodies, human wills? Or is he a highly paid professional chosen for some quality of voice, some exquisite sense of timing that the rest of us can't recognize?

Only this much is known. Somewhere, outside, people

are dying in El Salvador and Chile, the stockpile of bombs is rising, the lakes are dying and the sea is out of control. Inside, they bow to their partners, they take their places in the square, and when the caller's voice begins its old familiar cry, they dance, never missing a beat.

The Circus Performers' Bar

I am the first of our group here tonight, alone at our table in the corner of the Circus Performers' Bar on Latayefsky Street. I walked here along the canal in a fog that turned the streetlamps into blurs of gold and my fellow canal walkers into ghosts. It's an unusual winter in St. Petersburg, nearly the end of January and still no snow. Every day it rains, drizzle out of a grey sky.

Here in the Circus Performers' Bar, a fire blazes in the fireplace and the smell of fresh bread makes me think of my mother's kitchen in Vilnya. Perhaps this winter I will go back to visit the old folks, but I have been promising myself to make that journey for three years now, and always, something comes up to make it impossible. I'm sure it would be the same as it always is. First, there would be feasting and rejoicing over the return of the prodigal son, hugs and kisses everywhere, beer and sausages and sauerkraut. Then in a few days, their narrow peasant minds, filled with superstition and fear and petty malice, would begin to weigh on me. I would say something wrong, suggest perhaps that the Jew on the corner was as much a victim as they, and we would begin the inevitable argument, the argument that drove me from home when I was fifteen. My father would shake his fist and curse me, and I would ride the dreadful train back to St. Petersburg, shaking with rage.

I am normally the last to arrive. I like to step into gaiety and good companionship after it is already ripe. I like to be a little less drunk than the others, the receiver rather than the giver of confidences. And I like to be the one who is responsible at the end to see that the others are got safely home with the correct scarves and mitts and hats. The others count on me to be the sober caretaker.

But tonight some heaviness of the spirit drove me from my room on Svetlana Street. All afternoon I felt restless, neither my beloved Shakespeare nor my equally beloved Flaubert could settle me. I, who love so much to be alone, could not bear my solitary company, and I fled into the street. I should have gone to the performance of the Boukevenian dancers at the Palace of the Arts. Afterwards, I might have joined them for supper, plied some savage mountain girl with vodka and wit, and taken her back to my room. We could have made love intensely; I am not an acrobat for nothing.

That's what I should have done. Instead, I sat on the bridge near the railway station, watching the thick dirty water curl beneath me until I was chilled and hurried here. Now I sit, sipping my Pernod and watching my fellow performers straggle in. Leuba Romanovna, our fat lady, sits in her special chair, where she stays all day long, drinking oceans of beer and eating tiny dainty sandwiches. She lives in a room at the back of the bar, and every day she spreads herself out by the window to watch the people walk past. Sometimes the prostitutes from the street come in to join her for a few minutes, just to get warm, but most of the time she is silent and alone.

At the next table, Pyotr Petrovich drinks in his bitter rage. No one ever sits with him. Sometimes, he hires a prostitute and is gone for an hour or so, but this is not very often, because the prostitutes know him. He beats them, and they demand very high pay for his pleasure. He is a mean and hurtful man, but the children love him in his clown's costume with his bright red nose. Then he is all sunshine and warmth. It's as if the goodness in him were drained from his body by his performances, leaving only rage.

The animal handlers have already gathered at their table, telling coarse jokes and complaining because they must care for the animals in the winter, while the rest of us live our ordinary lives. There are always a few gawkers, hoping to get a bit of a free show, but they are always disappointed because in ordinary street clothing even the freaks look like anybody else. Ilya the Fish Man has covered his scales with a black suit and looks like a butcher's boy with a bad complexion. Mitka the Three-Legged Man looks like any other cripple.

But now, look, the door has swung open and in comes Taras Zarnytsyn, the Captain, with his broad chest and his cavalry officer's beard. "Let the revels begin!" he shouts, and he throws his dwarf's body forward in a high, arching flip that lands him in the centre of the room. The gawkers applaud. This is what they came to see. The Captain claps his hands. "Marfa, Dounia, bring me wine, bring me sausage, bring me the blood of princes. Tonight the Captain celebrates."

"A song, Captain," somebody shouts, and the others take it up. "A song, Captain, give us a song." With a bound, the Captain is up on a table, and the room fills with his rich baritone. He sings a song of love, a song of spring. Deep in the mountains a maiden weeps for her lover, a dashing cavalry officer. On a distant plain, the ravens peck the eyes from a dead soldier. Every eye in the room fills with tears, weeping for lost love and the inevitability of death. Then, suddenly, the cavalry officer comes back to claim the maiden. It was not he who lay dead on the plain, but his enemy. The room fills with laughter and shouts. The Captain might have been an opera singer, one of the finest in all Russia. But the people who go to operas will not listen to a dwarf, and so he is an acrobat in the Circus of the Western Region. The crowd cries for more. No one likes a fine performance more than a circus performer does, but the Captain bows graciously and joins me at our table.

"Ah, Dmitri," he teases, "you are early. Come to negotiate with the prostitutes before they raise their fees for the evening?"

I feel my face redden. Like everyone else, I feel inferior when alone with the Captain. His energy and good will are so intense that it seems like some special favour he bestows when he directs his attention to you.

"I have sent my proof of Fermat's theorem to Paris," I tell him, feeling like a schoolboy. I have a letter from *Le Journal des Mathématiques Spéciales*, and if the mathematicians of Paris cannot find a flaw, they will publish it.

"Good, good," he says, not understanding the importance of what I have told him. I know too that I have just broken the unwritten rule of the troupe. We may speak of our lusts and desires, our inner fears, but we may not speak of our talent. The Captain will not tell me of his humiliations at the opera house. I know he still goes to auditions, though he is never chosen. I should not tell him of my mathematics, or at least I should only tell him of success, and the letter, while encouraging, is not yet success.

Before we can begin again, this time keeping the conversation at the level of banter where it belongs, Ivan, Lev and Carl arrive, and they have in tow a young girl. Ivan, with a sweeping bow, introduces her as Sonia. She has the whitest skin I have ever seen, and her hair is jet black. Hers is the kind of beauty you never get to study, but only see passing quickly on a crowded street. I can see that Ivan, Lev and Carl are already in love with her, and I know that in a very few minutes I will be too. I groan aloud, foreseeing weeks of hopeless yearning, futile attempts to turn myself into something that might attract her, knowing even at this moment when I haven't yet fallen in love that there is no magic in this world strong enough to transform me into what I would have to become.

Lev, the poet among us, runs to the kitchen, calling for Marva and Dounia. I can hear him telling them that no, sausage will not do, she must have a chicken. Lev has had many of his poems published in journals, though he has never met another writer or an editor. His poems are strange tales of giants, men from some remote tribe in the Urals who are kind to their children and wives, and who defeat their enemies. Lev is a Jew.

Sonia leans across the table to Ivan telling him, no, no, it is too much, there is no need. He answers her, putting on the Moscow accent of his youth, that she need not worry, it is but a trifle. Ivan is an engineer and he constructs his sentences like bridges. He is the only one of us who was not driven from his home by an angry father, who was never beaten. He need not be an acrobat. He could work with his father in Moscow, the father who loves him, who comes to see our performances and weeps.

Carl whispers to me that they found her on the outskirts of the city. She had been wandering lost in the forest. A hunter had discovered her and out of pity was taking her home, but he had feared that his wife would not understand, and so had asked for their help. They know nothing of her except that her lover has been imprisoned by the czar. She was going to meet him, to live outside the camp and visit him on Sundays, but she had no money. The conductor of the train had let her ride as long as he dared, but she had to leave when the soldiers came. She had lost her way then, and wandered for hours until the hunter found her. Carl wants to paint her. He will pay her to model for him until she has enough money to buy another ticket, and who knows, maybe she will forget about her lover in his prison.

We are done for, all of us, I can see that now. The street girls, the prostitutes, the lonely farm girls just arrived in the city were some compensation for the brutal joke played on us by nature and our fathers. But this girl of blood and milk with her black hair, black eyes, white skin and red lips will teach us what we are: stunted inadequate parodies of men leaping up to try to touch the moon. Lev is back with the chicken and a goblet of white wine, and we try to counterfeit a gaiety that will disguise the yearning that hangs heavy over our table at the Circus Performers' Bar.

The Captain is teasing her now, telling her that she must join the circus. He tells her that he will buy her six white horses, the most beautiful horses in all of Russia. She will dance on the backs of the horses as they circle round and round the ring, and the crowd will cheer and cry, "Sonia, Sonia." She laughs, and her laughter tinkles like bells. Her black eyes sparkle as she teases him back, saying she would be happier with one small pony she could ride in a lonely field. We glow with her approval.

And now suddenly I see that Nikolai and Rodya are in the room, slipping from table to table whispering something that turns each table to excited conversation. Rodya is our carpenter. When his hands touch wood it takes on the shape he desires. All our clubs and hoops, our bars and horses come from his hands. It is strange that he and Nikolai should be the closest friends, because they are so different. Nikolai is our leader, the disciplinarian who designs our pyramids, who coaches us through the endless hours of practice, tumbling and juggling until our routine is perfect. He is an anarchist, and in every village of the Western Region he attends secret, mysterious meetings.

Now they are at our table, bursting with such excitement that they scarcely notice Sonia. Never mind, there will be plenty of time for that.

"Gentlemen," Nikolai cries, "the new age is dawning. The shackles of the old are forever gone. The revolution has begun. The troops fired on Father Gapon and a hundred people are dead. Now the citizens are out in the streets in Moscow and soon the entire country will be in a fire that will burn away the old. This Sunday of blood will live forever." We stare at him in amazed disbelief. "Think of it," he goes on, "you, Dmitri, will teach at the University. The Captain will sing at the State Opera. Carl, your paintings will hang on every wall."

"And the prisoners," Sonia asks him, "what will become of the prisoners?"

"Already they are being freed everywhere. The new Russia will have no need of prisons."

Nikolai leans over to talk intensely with Sonia. Her cheeks are flushed with excitement. Whatever shape the new world takes, there will be room in it for her. However it is made, it will need princesses. But after this hour, nothing will ever make it whole for me. Here I sit, burning with love, aching with desire, stunted, dwarfed, and out in the street, already, the guns are beginning.

The Girl of Milk and Blood

Giorgio

The cold dry bora is blowing again, down from the east beyond the mountains. My face is cracked, like the clay bottoms of the stream beds after the fall rains have run off into the valley below. Each crack is a tiny portion of agony, and the relentless wind fills them with dust. The women rub their faces with butter to keep them smooth, and that is good enough for a walk to the well, or over to the neighbour's place to gossip in the afternoon, but it is of no help for a day spent on the side of the mountain. The cattle are always thirsty, as if the dryness of the wind had sucked the very moisture from their bodies.

It is on days like this that I think of my boyhood further east in the underground caves and streams of the karst. Deep in the limestone caves, there was only one season, a cool, dark season of crystal water and candlelight at noon. When I joined the brotherhood, I never dreamed of this godforsaken mountain with its impoverished valley below. I knew nothing of the disastrous rains that can wipe out a village in an hour, or the kind of stubborn people who would gather up their surviving relatives and rebuild their village in the path of the same murderous flood. I never thought of snow ten metres deep, or this devil of a drying wind.

There is beauty here, all right, but it is a spare, cramped beauty, the beauty of twisted dwarf juniper and green alder and stunted rhododendron. In the spring, the snowdrops peep out from the melting snow, and later there are gentian and saxifrage, rock jasmine, campion and primrose. If your eyes are keen, you might see rabbits or partridges or grouse and, once in a very long time, a golden eagle or a mountain roe. For the rest, you must satisfy yourself with vipers, salamanders and newts. And this is fitting, I suppose, because this is a community without forgiveness. Here, no wrong is ever forgotten, no insult ever properly redressed, even by death. Revenge seeps up from the valley below like a poisonous fog, and it dries our souls as surely as the bora dries our skin.

Bellemondo is the name of our village, a name left over from some hopeful past, though it is nothing but an irony now. Our sister villages are Pontebba and Comegliano, but no one ever goes to them. Once in a while some enterprising villager will take the mountain roads down to Udine and catch the train to Trieste, perhaps to buy a wedding dress for a daughter or to present a government official with some bewildering request. In this village we speak Friulan, and in the valley below the farmers speak Slovene. Italian is a foreign language, spoken only by the odd official who blunders into our village, and by our mayor, who is mayor only because he can speak Italian. We of the brotherhood speak it, of course, but we are considered outsiders, though all seven of us have spent most of our lives here. In this village you can be an outsider for generations.

Our village sits at the foot of an old castle, where once a baron ruled in feudal splendour, though there has been no baron here for over a century. Now, the castle belongs to the Americans, who repaired the high walls that surround it, and who, for a couple of weeks each summer, arrive in their four-wheel-drive vehicles and disappear behind the wall. They bring everything they need, so that they never have to speak to a villager. Or they used to. Now the Germans have taken over, though they are almost as distant as the Americans. Every few days a military vehicle drives through the town and down the winding road to Udine.

All we know of the war is that the Germans are in the castle. We of the brotherhood have a radio, and we follow the strange course of the war as if it were some extended game whose rules aren't clear, even to the players. But perhaps today we will learn more of it. Antonio, whose duty it is to listen to the radio, told me this morning that Marshall Badoglio has declared war on Germany. That means that the Germans, who were our friends, are now our enemies, and the mysterious people in the castle are now an occupying force. We are all encouraged to join the resistance, though so far there has been nothing to resist. We are told that the Germans are brutal, that they rape women and murder little children. Our women in their black shawls and black dresses with their rotten teeth are no great incitement to rape. They even tie handkerchiefs around their knees so that the sight of so much flesh will not unduly excite their husbands. Still, there are enough children around, though I sometimes wonder whether the joys of the flesh or the need for another hand in the fields is the chief inducement to lust in our village.

This year, I am in charge of the cattle. Each morning, I drive them high into the mountains to feed on the sparse grasses, and at night I return them to their shed, which, as in every other house in our village, is directly below our living quarters. I look forward to the snows, when the cattle will have to stay in, and I will only have to throw them their hay and milk them. Then, through the long dark winter days I will play chess with Mario or Emilio, or one of the others whose work will not take him from the house. Last year I was the fisher and could spend my time in the cool of the forest under the beeches, the larch and the towering Norwegian spruces. I was clever at that, and I caught more trout and eels than we seven could eat. Sometimes I would even catch a sturgeon, and though the old ones speak of a time when sturgeon were plentiful, they are rare enough now. Next year I will be the carpenter, and though my hands are not good with wood, it will be better than sitting on the side of this mountain in the dry, cold wind that never, even for a moment, lets up.

Sandro

Giorgio tells me that something is happening at the castle. From the pasture in the mountains he can see over the walls into the courtyard. There is now a large black limousine parked with the army trucks. Someone very important has come, though there is no gossip in the village. Whoever it is must have arrived at night with the convoy of trucks. He says he thinks he saw a woman in a white dress walk to the gate, then hurry back to the castle door, but he is a half mile away and it is unlikely he could have seen that. Herding the cattle is the worst job. There is nothing to do but sit, and sometimes the imagination takes over. When it was my turn, I too saw strange things.

I think I may have made a very bad mistake. One of the drivers stopped his jeep and asked me the way to the castle. Without thinking, I answered him in German. He seemed surprised, though he said nothing. It is difficult enough for a dwarf to escape notice without advertising his presence by speaking languages he should not speak. Gian Petro says that the time of our mission is near. I hope so. I have waited twenty years in this place, knowing only my own part of the mission and sworn not to tell or ask of the others' parts. On the day that Gian Petro gives the word that the mission must begin, then we shall all know. Now, even he knows only the signs that will release us to our acts.

Once again, the spring has failed. Gian Petro tells us that once this was the most fertile valley in all of Italy. In spring the vineyards on the slopes sprang into life and the air was so heavy with the fragrance of blossoms you were made dizzy by it. Then, he says, the cattle were fat and didn't have to be driven up into the mountains, because the grass was so lush that when they ate one blade, another leaped up to take its place.

Then, the air was heavy with bees, and a thousand different kinds of birds woke you with their singing every day. The peasants sang at their work, and there were festivals for every occasion, the Festival of the Spring Flowers, the Festival of the Jousting of the Queens, the Winemakers' Festival, the Festival of the Shoemakers' Guild and a hundred others.

Now, there are no festivals. The air itself seems to be poisoned. When the bora blows from the east, the leaves on trees shrivel and crack. When the clouds come in from the south, the rains wash away a whole summer's work. From the north come snows that bury us and untimely frost that kill the young buds. Only the west wind brings us hope, but the wind is almost never from the west.

I have tended the vines with immaculate care, tying them into hearts as my father taught me to do at home in the Moselle valley, but where there should be a riot of leaves there are now only a few sickly buds. At home the wine was amber and tasted like honey. Here, I will produce once more a wine that is pale and sour. Only the vegetables that hide underground can survive: turnips, potatoes, carrots and parsnips.

Perhaps the Germans know that, and that is why they are searching all the houses. Three more truckloads came in today. Large humourless men who surrounded all the houses in the village, then searched them from top to bottom. They found nothing, of course. The houses are all above ground. The few partisans we have are frightened young men who hide in the caves lower in the valley, and have no weapons to oppose the occupiers.

Antonio

Listen. Through the spit and crackle of the radio set you can hear all the voices of Babel: French, German, Italian, English, Russian, Spanish, Dutch, Arabic, so many languages, so many lies being told. After each battle, all sides proclaim themselves winners, so much destroyed, so many killed, bridges blown up, factories exploded. They taunt each other in each other's language, they urge the people at home to sacrifice for final victory, so many glorious countries, so much fighting to preserve civilization from the maddened hordes outside.

After a while, you know them all, all the languages. They say the same things in the same rhythms so that you learn that meaning is not in the words but in the patterns, some grammar common to them all for which the words are merely clothing. And somehow, somewhere in the gaps between what is said runs a thin line of truth, a delicate wavering line that breaks and rejoins, disappears into the welter of words, then reappears. This is the line I listen to, this thin band of silence that carries the current of events.

I have listened for so long now that I hardly need my other senses. I make my way home down the steep mountain path from my cave by the sound of the water rippling in a distant stream, the whistle of wind over rocks, the nodding and rustling of trees. I hear the earth's exhalations, the moisture in the earth being drawn upwards by the sun. As I approach the town, I hear the women roll over in their beds, I hear the men scratch themselves. I can hear the scurry of mice in attics, the spinning of spiders' webs, the grass growing and leaves unfurling. If I stand very still, I can hear into the hearts of atoms, the electrons swirling around their nuclei.

And so I know this war is nearly over. Through the radio's static I can hear the tanks moving upward from the south. Rome fell today, and I could hear the sounds of rejoicing in the streets. It will still be a while before the troops get this far north, and so we must be very careful. We are like a patient with an evil growth in the heart. We must be careful that the operation that removes that growth does not kill us all. I have warned the partisans to keep to their caves. Events larger than them are shaping history, and it is better they be alive to farm when this is over than some German car should be destroyed.

Someone is being held in the castle, someone who is more important than any single battle. Giorgio has seen her from the pasture above the castle, a woman in a white dress who is rarely allowed into the grounds. I believe I can hear her weeping as I circle the castle on my way home from the listening cave. Von Ribbentrop himself has been to see her several times. He comes in the dead of the night and is gone again by morning. I thought perhaps she was his daughter, but I no longer think so. The radio from the castle reports in a code I cannot understand. It sounds like the random static you hear when there are sunspots.

Guido

They splish and they splash, these trout, they dance on their tails. When the weather is good, they are eager for the net. They say to each other, "Look, Guido is here again, we will tease him with our dancing, then, when he is frantic with worry that he will catch nothing, we will swim into his net." The eels, they are another thing, the eels, they are evil. They glide so silently over the shallow beds of streams, they hide in the deep holes, they are like the snake that tempted poor Eve when she was all innocence and could not have known better. They eat birds, yes they do, those eels, they eat baby ducklings. The mother has a brood of ten, then in one silent swallow so that she does not even know it has happened, she has a brood of nine.

But worst of all is the dark one, Old Snapper, who hides in the depths of the deepest pools. Sometimes, you think you see a log, just below the surface, something darker than the darkness of deep water, but when you see him, it is already too late, because he always sees you first and is gone. The others are all proud because they caught sturgeon, but they never caught Old Snapper, and what is the good of catching any other? I have caught them too, sturgeon I mean, but I have let them go. The trout are fine because they know they are food, and they like to be caught, and the eels are fine because they are evil and deserve to be eaten, but a sturgeon is no good unless he is Old Snapper, because every mouthful you eat reminds you that Old Snapper is still there, at the bottom of some pool, laughing at you.

It is going to be harder to catch him, now that winter has come and the snow is piled along the banks of the streams. In some places, there is ice, but the ice is treacherous. A German soldier fell through the ice, and if Old Snapper has not eaten him, he is at the bottom of a pool. In the spring he will rise and be tumbled down the stream until his clothing catches on to a root or a twig, and we will find him and take him to the priest to bury.

Old Snapper and the German soldier will have to wait until another day. Today I must catch trout. Since the girl of milk and blood has come to live with us, I must see that we have fresh trout every day. It was me who found her, little Guido who everyone pats on the head because I am happy and I sing. I took her from the woodcutter, who is a good man but full of fear. He found her wandering under the larches in her white robe with three drops of blood on her breast. Her eyes are the palest blue, and her long hair is so white that it looks silver. Her complexion is the colour of milk. The woodcutter says she escaped from the castle. She was terrified and didn't want to go back. The wood-cutter didn't know what to do. If the people from the castle caught him with the girl, they would kill him, and so he brought her to us, to me, little Guido. I took her to a cave that only I know, and lit a fire. Then when it was dark, I went for the others, and we carried her home wrapped in a blanket. Gian Petro says it is the start of our mission. We must protect her until other things come clear. That night, I was given an extra portion of the evening rum, then I sang a song for them, a song about a little bird that is pierced by a thorn, but who sings so beautifully that all the animals of the forest weep, until their tears become a river and a golden boat floats down the river with a handsome prince who rescues the little bird, who is really a princess. When I was finished, the girl of milk and blood kissed me on the forehead, and since then I have been so filled with joy, my heart is ready to burst.

She is good, the girl of milk and blood, so good that think-ing of her goodness can bring any of us to tears. Her skin is so delicate that anything that touches it leaves a bruise. She says she must do her part in our household, and so she mends our clothes. Last night, a needle pricked her thumb and splattered three drops of blood onto her white robe, so that she was just as I found her. She fainted, and when she awoke, she could remember nothing, only that she is terrified of the castle. Gian Petro says it is a warning of danger. He says we must go about our business as if nothing had happened, and he has cautioned the girl of milk and blood not to open the door to any knock. I think if I could catch Old Snapper, the dark one, everything would work out right. I have mentioned this to the others, but they tell me that is nonsense. Still, I think I know how it can be done, not with a net, but with a line, and a lure made from a piece of cloth with three drops of blood.

Rico

Today my hands shake, the chisel turns and twists, making gouges in the wood. Gian Petro says I can have no day of rest, but must continue making sabots. We are in terrible danger, he says, and so we must go on as if nothing had happened or else our mission will be lost. I think it is lost already with the loss of the girl. We should never have tried to live our ordinary lives. We should have taken her to the deepest cave and hidden her away until it was safe. We have supplies sufficient for a year, and if the war still raged, we might spirit her away to the south, to freedom.

Now the house is still with an awful silence. All that joy that bubbled through the house these last three months is gone. The walls seem still to hold the echo of her songs, and the ripple of her laugh hovers in the corner of the room. And still we have no idea who she was, no more idea than she had herself. She was like, not a newborn child, but a newborn

172

woman. Her innocence was amazing, a purity so great that it was palpable. Her hands were so delicate she could never have done a stitch of work in her life. And yet she learned, she learned quickly. We would have done everything for her, but Gian Petro said, no, she was not a plaything. She would have to work for her keep like the rest of us.

And work she did. She darned our clothes and washed them cleaner than they had ever been. She swept the floor and made the beds and cooked our meals. At first, she had to be shown how to do the simplest things, how to thread a needle, how to hold a broom, how to start a fire. But once she had learned, she made us feel awkward and clumsy just watching her grace.

Her skin was so delicate that anything might bruise it, and she cut herself often. Then she would bleed, though never more than a few drops. Her cuts would heal miraculously in a day, but the bruises lasted for weeks, tingeing the whiteness of her skin with blue. She cooked the most wonderful meals, but would eat nothing herself except a little milk and, occasionally, to please Guido, a mouthful of trout. She was frightened of the eels and refused to touch them. When Gian Petro insisted she cook them, I took a few moments away from my chisels and cooked them for her. It was a small deception.

The plants in our house are starting to droop, mourning for her, though I water them every day. When she arrived, they burst into a profusion of leaves, as if it were already spring. She spoke to them, encouraged the tiny buds, called white flowers out of plants that had never flowered before, white flowers with a touch of scarlet at the centre.

I wept while I made the coffin, staining the glass with my tears. Giorgio wept in the cattle shed, and the cattle wept with him. Sandro and Mario wept over their game of chess, and Antonio says he could hear nothing over the radio but the sound of distant weeping. Only Gian Petro did not weep, but his eyes were tense and bewildered, full of fear in a way I have never seen before. He brought me the glass, from where I do not know, and he told me my craft would be tested as never before. In spite of my grief, I was proud when we laid her in the coffin of glass. Every detail was perfect, the glass cut and fitted and sealed so there was no sign of joining, no hint of workmanship, no evidence of the craft that was behind the art. The coffin was as perfect as any jewel, as impervious to the elements as any rock.

Someone is responsible, and I fear it may be me. We were warned never to leave her alone, even for a second, and she was warned never to open the door to any knock. I had gone to the cattle shed for a moment to speak with Giorgio. Sandro and Mario left their game of chess for a moment to bring her an icicle from the roof because she had teased them into getting it for her. She loved to suck on icicles like a child with a frozen treat. Antonio was at his listening post and Guido was fishing in his frozen stream. Gian Petro was in the village as usual. There was a knock, there must have been a knock, she opened the door, she must have opened it herself against all the warnings, and when I returned she was dead, a piece of apple lodged in her throat. The rest of the apple sat on the table, its skin as red as blood, its flesh as white as milk.

Gian Petro was in a rage when he returned a few moments later. I could tell him nothing, only confess my lack of responsibility, my failure. Sandro and Mario, from their position on the roof, saw a flapping of black rags in the street, like a giant crow, but thought it was only one of the crones of the village passing. A sudden cold wind nearly blew them from the roof, and they had to cling to the chimney until it passed.

Then, that terrible night, the coldest night of the year, we carried her in her coffin up into the mountain. Gian Petro broke the trail through the deep snow, and we six struggled behind him, stumbling on our tiny legs, though the coffin with its treasure inside weighed no more than a bird. It was both the lightest and the heaviest load I have ever had to bear.

And now what are we to do? There is no longer any point to the making of sabots or the catching of eels, no point to the raising of cattle or the making of wine, no point to the working of metal or to listening to the reports of a war about which I no longer care. My heart tells me that this war will never end, that spring will never come again. We shall only have war and winter, winter and war.

Mario
This place is full of fear and pain. In the darkness of this dungeon we replay a medieval battle of light against darkness, good against evil. Throughout history, this castle has been the head of the valley, the centre from which wisdom and morality spread to the sprawling body of the community, but now there is a cancer working here, a foreign body that has seized control and whose evil seeps outward, infecting the whole.

The villagers led the Nazis to our door, and who can blame them, full of fear and superstition, trying to save themselves at any cost. They have allied themselves with a failing demon, though they cannot know that. They clustered around the soldiers who dragged us from our beds, they jeered and shouted and their faces were filled with hate, our weakness as hateful to them as the Nazis' strength.

The war will be over in a few days, but that will be too late for us. We are in the coils of a dying but still-dangerous monster. At dawn the firing squad, they have told us, after our week of pain. And so our mission fails, or else we have done our part in some larger plan that has no further use for us. The girl was innocence itself, she loved and mothered us, and her death, I think, is the death of innocence and goodness in this world. Perhaps the Nazis will be replaced with some even larger evil, though it is hard to think what evil might be greater.

We have been tortured and mutilated beyond anything I thought the human body could bear. And they used the tools of my trade, the metalworker's tools, pincers and tongs and fire. They have slowly removed our fingernails, crushed our arms and legs, set fire to our hair and carved their hateful symbol in our flesh with a burning poker. We have told them nothing, though there is nothing to tell but the location of a mountain grave, a glass coffin and a body they might defile but could not offer pain. Tomorrow they will ask us one more time, then they will pour the hot lead of bullets into our bodies, whatever our answer.

I am almost eager for that death. See us for what we were, what we are. Our bodies stunted and deformed, half men always on the lookout for the kick, the beating that the others must give because we affront them by wrapping desire in such awkward flesh. We are comic at a distance, terrifying when we're near, conjuring in every man the dwarf within.

And though I am eager, I am sick with loss. I yearn for one more taste of the water from a cool stream, for the scent of roses on a heavy summer day, for the scratch of wool on my skin. I want to see clouds low over the mountains, to hear Guido sing a song full of joy. I ache for the world that will end in the morning.

Here in this tiny dark cell we seven are huddled as if we were one flesh. We cannot tell whose moan we hear, even when it is our own. The warm blood we feel is ours communally, the fear we share one common fear. Only Gian Petro has hope and his soft voice is murmuring words of comfort, but it is too late. Hope is the final torture, the last delusion. We have given our lives to a mission that is probably a failure, may even have been a chimera from the start.

Now, the first rays of dawn will be spreading from the east. The soldiers will be oiling their guns and preparing the blind-folds. There will be one large grave waiting in the courtyard, a bag of quicklime beside it. They will be so intent on their task that perhaps they will not hear the soft thunder of the bombs that rock even our cell below the castle, the distant rumbling of the guns.

Gian Petro

This is a spring that takes itself seriously, that believes in the history of transformations and is not satisfied with the simple mechanics of budding and flowering. When the bomb landed on the castle, opening the cocoon of our cell, I stepped across the broken bricks of the wall into a blazing dawn. The clouds had curled themselves into balls of cumulus and were dreaming along the horizon to the south. I looked for the others, Giorgio, Sandro, Antonio, Guido, Rico, Mario, but they had disappeared. I reached my long arms into the air, stretched my long legs, felt the strength ripple through my body. Then I heard the voices inside me. Little Guido, whispering to me, told me where to look for Old Snapper, the dark one. Giorgio told me where the cattle liked to feed, Rico sent a message to my fingers telling me the exact pressure of a chisel on wood, Mario sent a vision of a bracelet wound from gold chains, and Antonio let me hear the whistle of crickets in a distant stream.

And then I knew that the first miracle had occurred. In the crucible of that exploding bomb, our mass of deformed dwarf flesh had separated into atoms, then reformed into molecules. The molecules had re-knit themselves into amino acids and proteins, shaped themselves into complex chains, twisted and curled into the only possible body. The accidental electricity of that explosion had charged that body with life and filled each neuron and synapse of the brain with seven memories. It had concentrated all the ghosts of the castle, all thoughts that had been thought there, all the passions that had seeped into the stone walls of the castle and delivered them to us, to me. I realized that I had been born that second, and so I named myself. Gian Petro.

When Gian Petro stepped into the courtyard, out of the ruins of the castle, he saw that thousands of mushrooms had sprung up during the night. They formed a soft bed, like velvet, and as he strode across them, crushing them, they exuded a delicate milky substance that smelled, not unpleasantly, like bleach. Beyond the gates of the castle, the open field that led to the village was filled with snow-white flowers, each with a core of crimson. Along the wall that separated field from road, the vines were covered with mauve trumpet flowers that whispered to him softly. There were bees everywhere, humming ecstatically.

The village was full of music. People were singing and dancing in the streets. An old man played a violin, dancing as he played, and a young man accompanied him on an accordion. The villagers had shed their winter black and were dressed in bright reds and yellows and blues. A pretty girl swirled by, her red dress so bright it seemed in flames. Her lover wore a white shirt, open at the neck, with a brilliant red bandanna. "Baron," they called to Gian Petro, "the war is over. The war is over." He smiled at his people's joy, but he kept walking through the village, past the tables heaped with food and wine, past the donkeys with garlands around their necks, down the winding path into the valley.

The grass was so lush along the pathway that sometimes

it was hard to tell where it wound. The vineyards along the slope were a riot of leaves, and the grapes, though not yet ripe, seemed ready to burst with sweetness. Underground, the roots were burying themselves deep, searching for water. They passed underground messages up through the sap to the highest leaves of the trees. Brilliant birds flashed yellow and red in the blur of green.

The baron continued onward, down through the valley into the forest. Under the pine and spruce, it was cool, and sunlight dappled the carpet of needles. He came to a small, fast-running stream and followed it to a pool deep in the heart of the forest. There, the body of the drowned soldier had surfaced. It was surrounded by a mass of white water lilies, and water lilies seemed to be growing out of the flesh. Gian Petro pulled the body from the pool and laid it gently on the grassy shore. Then he drew a line and hook from his pocket and baited the hook with the white root of a small willow. He tossed out his line into the pool, and the dark one rose to the bait. Gian Petro pulled him in without effort and laid him on the bank beside the dead soldier. They were exactly the same size, and from a small distance, it was impossible to tell them apart.

Gian Petro followed the stream a little further, until it turned, then he continued up the mountain on the other side of the valley. The trees soon became sparser and were replaced with gentian and saxifrage and rock jasmine. When he reached the very top of the mountain where the glass coffin lay, he saw that it was surrounded by snowdrops and tiny red blood flowers.

He strode across the carpet of flowers, not caring how the sap bled from the tiny plants he crushed. He opened the lid of the glass coffin, picked up the girl and laid her down in the flowers. The piece of apple that had stuck in her throat came free, and she breathed. Her pale white cheeks turned red with life as he took her in his arms. He spoke to her of love in his seven voices, and as they loved, the discreet sun hid his face behind a cloud. Every living thing reached up eagerly to the gentle rain that followed.

Tansy from My Garden

Put tansy in my coffin," she said. "When I die, put tansy in my coffin, and bury me with my head to the north so I can face the sun."

"Why tansy?" I asked her. "Why not rosemary? Why not rue?"

"Tansy for immortality," she said. "Tansy for sprained ankles, tansy for varicose veins, tansy to remove freckles. Once I was freckled. Did you know that? A poultice of tansy and all the freckles went away."

"Why not rue?" I insisted. "Why not the herb of grace that I stole from my neighbour's garden?"

"Too dangerous for pregnant women," she answered. "But it keeps away fleas and flies."

"But so is tansy," I told her. "Tansy is also dangerous for pregnant women. Though you are not pregnant. What do you say about that?"

"Rue for snakebite," she said. "Rue to keep away the plague, though to tell you the truth, I don't much fear the plague, what with penicillin and all."

I went out to the garden. The tansy was spreading its green ferns, but it was only mid-June and the yellow flowers had not yet appeared. The rue was healthy, but still small. Its yellow flowers hadn't appeared either. The rue was next to the rosemary, but sage and savoury and sorrel separated it from the tansy. I had planted the herbs alphabetically this year, in case I forgot one of the names. Then I could just check the index of my book on herbs, and I could figure out the name of whatever I had missed. Last year I planted by the colour of flowers, and the rue and the tansy were in the yellow garden, along with the chamomile, the calendula and the sweet bay. I even tried growing dandelions and wormwood for the colours of the flowers, but they weren't successful.

In the field behind the house, a bobolink trills his unfaithful melody. He's keeping a harem, a half dozen nests with wives tending to his indiscriminate progeny. No wonder his warble is so sweet. The bobolink is white above and black below, as if someone had explained camouflage to him, and he'd got it backwards. He was thinking of all that wooing he had to do, and so he wasn't paying attention.

"You still have freckles," I told her when I came in from the garden. "You've always had freckles. A saddle of freckles across your nose."

"I'll need another poultice," she said. "Fresh tansy from the garden. I'll take care of it next Thursday."

"Next Thursday you are going to Düsseldorf," I reminded her. "And just when the basil will be ready."

"Wednesday, then. Wednesday, I'll take care of the freckles."

"And I will have to make the pesto myself," I told her, unable to hide a note of bitterness in my voice. "I will have to pick the tender leaves and grind the garlic and shred the cheese and pour the olive oil. And we have no pine nuts. Did you know that we were completely out of pine nuts?"

"I have wide eyes," she said. "My face is five eyes' width. And my eyes are hazel. Both are said to be signs of beauty."

"Yes," I agreed. "You are beautiful, freckles and all, though your eyes are blue. Tell me again why you are going to Düsseldorf."

"Windows," she said. "It has to do with windows. Sand-blasted and sculptured glass. Glass that has been stained with colours. Glass so clear you cannot know it is there. Glass that is impervious to bugs and spiders and the unfortunate droppings of birds. And doors. Doors with glass in them. Windows and doors. And walnuts will work just as well as pine nuts. We have all the walnuts your heart could desire."

"It's not a question of expediency," I told her. "I know we have walnuts. We also have hazelnuts and almonds. It's a matter of principle. If you do not have pine nuts, can you really claim to have pesto?"

"Walnuts have an even richer history as regards pesto than pine nuts," she said. "Tradition counts for something."

In the shower Thursday morning, I sang in my rich baritone, "See the pyramids along the Nile." You remember the song. It has a bittersweet, rueful tang to it, and since I am not an early riser, I often find myself a touch melancholy in the shower.

"Was that meant for me?" she asked, when I came out of the shower, smelling masculine and pure from the strong soap I habitually use. "Are you sending me subliminal musical messages from the bathroom while I am preparing for a gruelling business trip in Europe?"

"Nothing of the sort," I told her. "In the shower, my heart is entirely pure. Later in the day, you might have to deal with some mild duplicity, but in the morning I am incapable of subtlety."

Her freckles had disappeared. Her face was entirely clear. "I prefer the freckles," I told her. "They make you look wholesome and healthy. The daughter of a farmer. Someone close to nature."

"Good," she said. "Plant another row of tansy."

"That business about tansy in your coffin," I asked. "Was that modish *fin de siècle* morbidity, or are you worried about flying across the Atlantic?"

"You always miss the point," she said. And I drove her to the airport and waited in the parking lot until her plane left the ground without incident and turned its nose towards Europe. Nasturtium is the nose twister.

"Remember me," I crooned in the shower, "when the nights are cold and lonely." The water pressure was low and that meant I'd have to go down into the basement and adjust the pump again. "Remember me, when you're by the riverside." I think I may have made up the second line myself. I've never heard anyone else sing it.

Rosemary for remembrance. By now she would have arrived in Düsseldorf. She would have unpacked her bags and discovered the sachet of rosemary I sent along. "Oh, Rosemarie, I love you," I sang. Sea mist. The old queen of Hungary made so beautiful by rosemary that she was still receiving proposals on her deathbed.

The radio announced that a jet had crashed on landing at the Düsseldorf airport. A minor crash, only seven dead. No mention of Canadians among them. The telephone rang. I bruised my shin on the way to answer it. They were concerned about my rugs. They wanted to wash them with a new patented method that would remove the deep-down dirt.

"No," I said. "Thank you. I have other things on my mind."

"Your plantain leaf is excellent for that," Romeo told Benvolio, "for your broken shin." I limped all morning as I telephoned numbers for information.

"There is no information," they told me. "It was a domestic Lufthansa flight from Frankfurt to Düsseldorf. There is no report of Canadians aboard."

"If it was a domestic flight," I said, "they might not know whether or not there were Canadians aboard."

"Yes," they agreed. It was possible the authorities might not know.

Bitter gall and wormwood. The idea of the lover's death is more horrible than the idea of your own passing. Wormwood grows everywhere. On moonlit nights it shimmers silver in the fields. We call it wild sage in these parts. I could brew myself absinthe, and die like a French artist, earless perhaps, or simply rotting in Marseille. The monks put wormwood in their ink to poison it so that mice would not eat their precious words. Even language has its dangers.

I would have to intervene with the gods, I knew that. There was no point in trusting to earthbound authorities. If a phone call came and announced that she was dead, then she would be dead, and nothing could recover her. The earthbound authorities live in a world where there is only one possibility at any given time. The gods are more flexible.

Ganymede, the cupbearer to Zeus, was transformed by a potion from a mortal to a god. The key ingredient was tansy. I gathered tansy from my garden, lavender for the flavour, lovage for emotion, sweet bay for protection, and anise as good measure to protect me from my own brew. Tansy, I am told, contains thujone, a relative of the THC that makes marijuana so delightful, but a misplaced molecule or two converts it into a deadly poison. Still, if you are going to talk with the gods, you have to take some chances.

I brewed my tea, adding just a scant teaspoon of sugar to take off the edge, and if I must confess, yes, I also added Scotch, a single malt I had been saving for some unimaginably important event. I drank and slept, and I suppose I must have intervened with the gods while I slept, because the telephone awakened me.

It's always one thing or the other. The news is good or bad. You have won or lost. It was she on the telephone, safe in Düsseldorf, exhausted by the flight and by a day of meetings, but somehow strangely exhilarated. She felt, she said, reborn.

I asked her about the crash, and she said I had it all wrong. The plane had crashed at Dortmund, not at Düsseldorf. Seven were injured, but no one had died. The glass-makers of Düsseldorf, those masters of windows and doors, were as good as they had promised. Their glass was clean and clear.

"Have the freckles returned?" I asked her.

She said they had.

"I have plucked all the tansy from my garden," I told her. "Not a leaf remains. You will have to put up with freckles for another season." I did not tell her of my intervention with the gods. Some things are best left unsaid.

"I think I may be pregnant," she said. "I have no symptoms, but I am irrationally convinced that I am."

"Good," I answered. "Then I'll pluck out all the rue as well."

Bad Girl

O nce upon a time, in a small town just near the Saskatch-ewan border, there lived a very disobedient girl. Her name was Ellen, and she was in grade twelve. She wanted to go to university to study music and become a famous singer, but her mother wanted her to get a job in town as a clerk in the Co-op store, and her father wanted her to stay on the farm and help her mother with the milking and the chickens. They were both deeply religious people, and they were afraid that if Ellen went out into the wide world, she would lose her reli-gion and come to harm.

"I don't know how many times I've told you," her mother would say, "but I'm telling you again. If you wear your skirts as short as you do, you are asking for trouble."

"Don't talk back to me, young woman," her father said almost every day. "And don't flash your eyes at me. I know insolence when I see it, and I won't tolerate it, do you understand?"

Ellen knew she was disobedient. She was supposed to pray in a soft voice at the beginning of each class, but she hadn't done so for years, and nothing had happened to her. She had sneaked off and gone to a movie with the other kids, and God had not struck her dead. She'd even had a glass of rye whisky with some of the boys at a dance to which she had been forbidden to go, and she had not got drunk and the police had not caught her.

In fact, it seemed that the only bad things that ever happened to her were delivered by her own parents. Ellen's mother liked to slap her when she didn't work hard enough. Her father beat her whenever he found out that she'd done something he didn't like. But everybody else in town was good to her, and they all loved to hear her sing. They said things like, "You've got the voice of an angel. You should study and become an opera singer."

Her parents warned her that God watched her every move, and that he would not be mocked. He would deliver pain for disobedience.

"If that's the case," Ellen said to herself, "then my parents must be working off a lifetime of disobedience."

And that seemed as if it might be true. Her father went to church every Sunday, but the bank was threatening to take away the farm, and he'd broken his leg when he rolled the tractor, and now he walked with a painful limp. Her mother had varicose veins and some sort of stomach disease that made her breath smell so bad that nobody wanted to sit next to her, not even in church. If they were God's chosen, Ellen decided, then she'd just as soon escape his notice.

Ellen got straight A's in grade twelve. School work came easy to her, and she liked the classroom, where everyone was polite to each other, and where you really did seem to get what you deserved. If you worked hard, you got an A. If you didn't, you got a B or a C. If you didn't do anything at all, you failed.

Bad Girl

Ellen's biggest disobedience was the secret bank account she kept. She was working part-time at the Co-op and saving up to go to university. If she won a couple of scholarships, she was sure that she could do it. Her greatest fear was that her parents might find out about her bank account and seize it. It would be a month until she turned eighteen, and she wasn't sure whether her parents could steal her money or not. The one thing she was certain about was that if they found out, religious or not, they would take her money from her.

The other problem was Larry. Larry was madly in love with Ellen and he wanted to marry her. Ellen knew that her parents would forbid the marriage at first, but she was pretty certain that they'd finally give in. It was the one place that she was hoping for their rigidity. If she married Larry, then she would never be a famous singer. She would be a farm wife just like her mother, and she would become dry and mean and get varicose veins and bad breath.

About a month earlier, Larry had become so insistent about marrying her that the only way she could convince him not to go to her father and ask for her hand was to sleep with him. Or not so much sleep with as have sex with in the back seat of his Chevy. Ellen had been worried that she would get pregnant, and her mother had warned her so often about sex that she assumed it would be a painful and horrible experience.

It turned out to be the most fun she'd ever had. She couldn't believe how nice it was, and after the first time, she walked around like Marco Polo must have when he discovered China. She could hardly think about anything else, and for a couple of weeks, she didn't do anything to anger either of her parents. She almost agreed to marry Larry.

Her father noticed her change of mood and became very watchful. He drove his pickup into town and spied on Ellen when she went for lunch to the Chinese café, and he insisted that she come right home from school and not go out in the evening. Ellen didn't care. She had sex with Larry standing up in the janitor's room during study period.

Ellen's father talked to Ellen's mother, and Ellen's mother took her aside and talked to her about sex. Ellen could barely stand the smell of her mother's breath, but she listened.

"I just want you to be careful," her mother said. "If you lose your reputation, then nobody will want to marry you. Your father and I would just die if you got pregnant. We couldn't hold up our heads in church. And don't think it's any great deal. It's something a woman has to suffer, and there's no point to starting suffering any sooner than you need. And you are the church organist. Remember that."

Ellen did not forget that she was the church organist. It was the single good thing that she could say about the church. Her father would never have let her continue to take lessons if it weren't that it made him look good at church. Sometimes, when she was playing a hymn and she saw her father standing in the first pew, singing off-key in his whiny voice, she imagined him keeling over with a heart attack. She wouldn't even stop playing. She'd switch into something joyful and triumphant with great crescendos.

Ellen felt that the best way to avoid suspicion was to be as disobedient as her parents wanted. So she didn't do the dishes she was supposed to do, and she didn't feed the calves, and her mother slapped her. She took the car without permission on a Sunday afternoon and made love to Larry in a haystack, and got back late for supper. Her father beat her with his belt, and made her pray on her knees for two hours, but he stopped following her around and spying on her with his binoculars.

When the school year came to an end, the principal told her father that she'd won a thousand-dollar scholarship.

"Good," her father said. "She can buy herself a couple of

calves and raise them over winter." The principal told him that she could only use the money to go to the university.

"How about Bible college?" her father asked.

"Well, yes, I suppose," the principal answered. "But I thought she wanted to study music."

"Got her heart set on Bible college," her father said, and he went home and announced to Ellen that she would be attending Thorncrest Pentecostal Bible College.

"Got your heart set on an education. Well, this is the only education that really counts," he told her. "It'll teach you a little about authority and discipline."

Ellen felt that she would sooner go to prison than to Bible college. She would sooner work in the Co-op or help around the farm. But it gave her an excuse to apply to the university.

You had to be accepted at the university to get into Thorncrest, she would tell her parents if they asked. She had applied for several bursaries and a government loan, and when the letters of reply came from the university, she managed to sneak the answers by her father by getting to the mailbox first and hiding the responses in her room.

In the meanwhile, Larry was nearly frantic about her going away to the city to study at Bible college. He wanted her to stay home and marry him, and when she told him that she wasn't ready to make that sort of commitment and maybe they could just be friends, he wept and then raged, and told her that she'd be married to him by fall, just you wait and see.

Things came to a crisis the day before her birthday. Larry caught her on the way back from the Co-op, and announced that he couldn't live without her, and that if she didn't agree to marry him, he was going to kill her and commit suicide. He showed her the shotgun he had bought for the occasion. Ellen agreed to marry him, of course, but she convinced him not to tell her parents until the morning of her birthday. He agreed to wait a day, but no longer.

When she got home, her father was waiting for her. He waved a sheaf of papers at her. "I've been in your room," he said. "Checking for drugs because you've been acting so strange. And I found these."

"Those are my applications for Thorncrest College."

"It doesn't say Thorncrest College. It says university."

Ellen wasn't sure how much her father knew about the application process, but her only hope was to bluff. "It has to say university. First you get accepted to the university. Then when you get there, you fill out a form for Thorncrest College."

"Well, it don't explain this," he said, waving her bankbook in the air. "It don't explain how you got four thousand dollars in the bank."

"I earned it, working at the Co-op and babysitting. It's my money." Ellen's heart sank as she saw her hopes for escape dimming. Even Larry suddenly loomed as hope.

"Stole it, you mean," her father said. "You've been eating my food and living in my house with all that money in the bank and me nearly crazy trying to find a way to feed you. You owe me that for room and board."

"Your father's right," her mother chimed in. "That's properly our money."

"And we're going straight down to the bank to get it," her father added, and he caught Ellen by the wrist and dragged her out to the pickup. When they got to town, he hauled her from the truck and dragged her to the door.

"Now you get that money and bring it directly out," her father said.

Ellen reached out her hand and pulled the door handle. It wouldn't open. The tellers in the bank were all at their stations, counting their change, but she could see that the clock on the wall read one minute after three.

"It's locked," she said. "It closes at three on Mondays. We'll have to wait until tomorrow."

"We're getting it now," her father shouted, and he began to hammer on the door of the bank. At first there was no answer. Finally, the manager came to the door and spoke to them through an electronic box.

"We're closed," he said in a tinny electronic voice.

"Well, open. We got some banking to do."

"I'm sorry. You'll have to wait until tomorrow."

"Open that door. We're coming in now." Ellen's father was livid with rage. The manager, on the other side of the glass door, seemed equally livid.

"I'm calling the police," he said. "The teller has already called them. You can't force a bank to open when it's closed."

"Call them, then," Ellen's father shouted at the door. "They can take away this thieving slut until I get my money back from her." And he turned to glare at the spot where Ellen had been standing only a moment before. There was nobody there, and the pickup was gone.

Ellen drove home as fast as she could, skidding on the gravel of the driveway as she rounded the corner. Her mother was out in the barn, or perhaps in the chicken house. At least she wasn't in the house, and Ellen was grateful for that. She tossed clothes at random into a suitcase, and collected all her papers with their acceptances and bursaries and put them in too. Then she put on her shortest skirt and walked to the highway and stuck out her thumb. The first car that came along picked her up and gave her a ride all the way to the city. She stopped at the first bank she came to and used her bank card to withdraw three hundred dollars. Then she spent her first night away from home in a Holiday Inn. She swam in the pool, and she ordered breakfast in bed for the next morning. She felt no guilt. She felt only a sense of peace that she had always known was waiting for her somewhere.

Her father disowned her, as she had hoped he would. He put a message in the local paper saying that he was no longer responsible for her debts, and she read it in the university library. But he didn't pursue her any farther, and no police came to her door. Larry disappeared into the past as if he had been erased from a sheet of paper. After the second day, she could hardly remember his face. Ellen moved in with a medical student who thought he was poor, but he paid the rent and he was a decent lover.

Ellen did not see Larry or either of her parents after that final day, and she didn't think she ever would. There was, however, one brief electronic moment when they were together. Ellen's parents had gone to the Legion to play bingo. Larry was the caller. At intermission, he turned on the big television at the front of the hall. Ellen appeared on the screen in the role of Carmen. She was dressed in a revealing cotton dress and was sitting on a low stool. Her rich voice filled the hall for just one second before Larry turned the switch and put on the hockey game.

Ellen perched carefully on the side of the bed so as not to awaken her lover. From the window of the villa, she could see the sun glint on the Mediterranean waves. Ellen's parents straightened their cards. Larry's voice began, "Under the B, six."

Fifth Gait

The horses of Iceland have a fifth gait, the *tölt*. They can walk, trot, gallop and pace as well. When they use the *tölt*, only one leg at a time touches the ground, and the noise they make is a rapid tattoo. The gait is so smooth that you can drink a glass of whisky without spilling a drop. And the *tölt* can be faster than the gallop.

In 1983, I sat in a farmhouse in Iceland a few miles from the Arctic Circle, drinking Scotch. A horizontal sun poured golden light into the room. A herd of Icelandic horses galloped by the window. The golden light caught in their flying manes, and for a moment, time paused and I could see every detail, the flecks of saliva on their mouths, the individual hairs of their coats, even the disturbance of the air they breathed. Then they thundered by. I was drinking Scotch. I didn't spill a drop.

When Grettir Asmundson was made an outlaw, he lived on the island of Drangey. When his fire went out, he swam a full mile to the mainland, and then swam back with a basket full of coals. He didn't drop a single coal into the freezing arctic sea. So much is a matter of balance.

That was a long time ago, and when my grandfather told me the story, I thought it had happened in Canada, on the shores of Lake Winnipeg. I thought the island was Hecla Island. In 1993, I stood where Grettir had stood, and looked over to Drangey Island. I could never swim that far. At least I know that much.

The Icelandic horse is short, only about thirteen hands, but it is stocky and can carry a much heavier load than most horses. You may not call it a pony. It travels over the treeless, black, volcanic plains using the *tölt*, as smooth and seamless as a glass of Scotch.

If you are climbing alone in the mountains, especially if you are a child, you must beware of Nökkur. He is the most beautiful of horses, and he wants you to ride him, but if you do, he will carry you off to a lake high in the mountains, and he will take you under that lake to where he lives. Everyone will think you have drowned. You can recognize him because his hoofs are on backwards.

About two hours north of Reykjavik, someone has restored an old sod farmhouse, though it looks not so much like something restored as like something that has always been there. Next door is a church. When I went to look at the church, a tourist doing what tourists do, there was a funeral going on. Several hundred people had gathered, more than the church could hold, and they milled around the building in their elegant dress. The next day we checked the obituary pages in the local paper. A great horseman had died. He had eight obituaries. The next day he had five and the third day he had four. A man of many friends.

My wife is out this very minute learning how to ride Icelandic horses. She came to riding late, and so takes it more seriously than a young girl might. She wants to get it right, and she takes lessons and studies books about the correct posture, about finding the right seat. She can walk, trot, gallop and pace, and now she is looking for the fifth gait, looking for perfect balance.

When I was a child, horses were everywhere. The T. Eaton Company delivered its catalogue orders throughout Winnipeg in elegant blue carriages pulled by perfectly matched teams of horses. At my grandmother's farm, a herd of horses galloped dangerously through the yard every night just at dusk. They had been there when my grandfather died, and my grandmother continued to feed them for twenty years, though they were never harnessed. When she became ill and had to go to a nursing home, her sons caught them and sold them.

Once, on our way back from a glacier in Iceland, we were caught in a roundup of sheep. There was only one road, and we had to share it with hundreds of them, every shade available to sheep. Our Land Rover crawled by, directly into the setting sun. The sheep were being herded by young men on horseback. Every man had at least one child with him, blond and intense, sharing his saddle. The riders and horses were haloed by the light. Space explorers on a different planet couldn't have felt more alien than I did then.

I grew up with horses, but I never learned to love them. They were too large and too unpredictable, and my relationship with them was too formal. I had to harness them, hook their traces to the singletree of the rake or the doubletree of the hayrack and drive them out to the fields to work. I spent hours following Minnie and Betty, Princess and Tom. Sometimes, I would ride them, either to the fields or back, harnessed, usually, but sometimes bareback. I know I should have learned to care for them, but sometimes familiarity is not enough.

In California last winter, my wife went for a trail ride into a desert canyon. It was the first trip of the day, and she was the only customer. Her trail guide was a cowboy from Oklahoma. He was an Ian Tyson fan, and during the off-season he sang in bars in Los Angeles. He sang her love songs as they rode through the cacti and sand. He was leather-skinned and looked alcoholic, my wife told me. He showed her a cactus wren, but when she checked it later in the bird book, it was something else. And I could never hold a tune.

At the Moscow Circus, just before the failed coup when everything seemed possible, I watched an amazing narrative told entirely with men on horseback. The lights dimmed. The music came up. Something threatened a storm. A dozen riders swept into the ring, circling at an impossible speed. Suddenly at the edge of the ring a maiden was watching. The most daring of the riders plucked the red bandanna from his neck and threw it onto the ground. The next round, he leaned from his saddle and picked it up with his teeth. Then he picked up the girl and swept her onto his saddle behind him. They rode erotically in the gathering darkness of the ring until suddenly her brothers arrived, riding frantically and holding torches. Somehow, and I'm surprised that I can no longer remember how, the girl was killed and the brothers and the lover and his friends rode out to a sad funereal end.

The Icelandic saddle is different from either the English saddle or the western saddle. It is set further back on the horse for a different balance. It sets most of the weight over the back legs, and this, I am told, makes it easier for the horse to walk over the rough volcanic fields of the Icelandic interior. A horse with such a saddle can carry more weight than if saddled in the western way.

At Fort Steele, just outside Cranbrook, British Columbia, you can find the largest herd of black Clydesdales in the country. They are enormous, powerful horses, but the soft fall of white hair that covers their huge hoofs makes them somehow fragile, as if beauty were clumsily allied with strength.

My uncle was president of the Horseman's Benevolent Protective Association. He raised racehorses and ran them at the local racetrack. He always raised them from scratch rather than buying them. He liked to win, but since he always lost money, it couldn't have been winning that lured him to horseracing. I asked him about this once, and he told me there's something about the outside of a horse that's good for the inside of a man.

Odin's horse was faster than the wind. He was named Sleipnir and he had eight legs. Odin rode him into battle, when he led the Valkyries to choose the bravest of warriors to die and join him in the festivities at Valhalla. His feet were on the right way.

Not long ago, we spent some time in New Zealand, driving from motel to motel in our little rented Ford, trying to figure out what the extravagant amount of roadkill might mean. What were all those dead animals? Were New Zealanders more dangerous than other drivers? In the month we were there, we never ran over anything ourselves.

And my wife did notice that whenever we saw horses in the fields they were invariably covered with blankets. And yet it was February, only the end of summer, and both the days and nights were warm. We asked many people about the problem but nobody knew the answer. Yes, they said, they knew that horses wore blankets, but it had never occurred to them they might not.

I went to watch my niece compete in the finals of the Pony Club competition for the Canadian championship. She had won it before and was considered the one to watch. The young girls who were competing looked awkward and coltish when they were not in costume and seated on their horses. Most of the mothers were stage mothers, investing their whole lives in their daughters' talents. I stood with the fathers, mostly over-weight, distracted men with a lot of money who wanted to buy their daughters' dreams for them. My niece won again. When she rode, it was difficult to tell where the girl ended and the horse began.

For a couple of hours one September afternoon, I watched a horse roundup in a valley in the west of Iceland. From every direction, men on foot with dogs chased horses from high in the mountains down to a set of corrals at the centre of the valley. The horses were funnelled into a maze of fences and emerged in separate pastures where each horseman could gather his own. But I couldn't help wondering whether the herds from the mountains represented the same groupings of horses as the herds in the corrals. Had those horses, in the wildness of their summer, made new commitments, organized themselves into herds that served the interests of horses, not people? Was there something tragic in this separation? Some lack of balance?

In New Brunswick, I went to a heavy-horse hauling con-test at Burtt's Corner. The horses were working farm horses, most of them part something, part Belgian, part Clydesdale, part Percheron. Men hitched the horses to a flatbed loaded with concrete blocks, then measured how far the team could pull before it came to a stop. I remember a man and his five-year-old son watching together. Their stances were identical, one foot forward, hip thrust sideways, cap pulled low over the eyes. Each had a large trucker's wallet in his back pocket and each was chewing on a straw. There was something odd in such perfect reproduction.

Iceland banned the entry of horses other than the Icelan-dic horse in 1100. For nine hundred years no other kind of horse has been permitted. An Icelandic horse who leaves the country may never return, though the Icelanders are less fussy about their citizens. But then, dogs and cats were not permitted in cities or towns, and until recently, there was no television on Thursdays.

I grow old. It gets harder to find a balance. I sleep too late or I do not sleep at all. The things I believe are not much in favour these days, and I find it hard to read a newspaper. My wife is in love with horses. My children are scattered and gone. The phone rings and I don't answer it. The mail piles up on my desk. I need a rapid tattoo, a *tölt*, a fifth gait, some way of moving smoothly and swiftly across the surface of my life, my glass so carefully balanced I never spill a drop.

Once in a Small Bar in Odessa

Once, in a small bar in Odessa, we drank beer that came in one-gallon pickling jars, and ate salted fishes whole. We sat on nail kegs at inverted wooden barrels in the noonday dark of the bar whose walls and ceilings were a single arc. Ukrainian and Polish sailors drank with swarthy Georgians and Azerbaijanis. Gambrinus. The bar where Kuprine drank his way through a Russian winter and dreamed the story of a small bar in Odessa.

Later, in Denmark, we caught a train to the ferry at Rødby. We chatted with a black Jamaican woman named Ingrid, who had just come from visiting her Norwegian grandmother. She recited a few phrases of Norwegian in a sing-song West Indian accent. The train was named Gambrinus. Jan Primus. The patron saint of beer.

We were tourists, of course. Once you leave home you are always a tourist, however serious your business. They stared at us in the bar in Odessa, Lise, the only woman in the bar, dressed in a silver jumpsuit, her blonde hair tumbling over her shoulders like a waterfall. She might have been a space-age

Venus rising from the Black Sea. The sailors devoured her with their eyes.

"They will be robbed," Oleg said, gesturing in the direction of the Polish soldiers. "They are too eager for friends to drink with, too eager for someone who can speak Polish, someone who can help them to find love in Odessa."

The Black Sea rolls in with the power of any ocean. The waves crash so they seem heavier than water should be, black and more viscous. We waded in the cold water, the black water. Oleg stood disapproving at the limit of the waves. Lise went in too far, as she always does, raising her skirt nearly to her waist, but a wave caught her and she was drenched. The bored and nearly naked beauties of Odessa did not move where they lay on the sand, out of the bite of a crisp wind that had come from heaven knows where.

The driver of the mini-van would not let Lise enter his vehicle until I bribed him with a pack of Marlboros, the international medium of exchange. I don't smoke. Neither does he. Lord knows how many hands will hold this pack before somebody finally smokes it.

In the catacombs below the city, the hideouts of the heroic martyrs of the Second World War are waiting for tourists, but except for some local schoolchildren, we are the only ones there. Two Tanyas, one an expert on the catacombs, the other a speaker of English, lead us by the hidden machine guns to the rock beds where they slept, the deep dripped wax of their candles, these martyrs who did not see the light for two years, and then all they saw with the light they had dreamed of were the barrels of rifles.

In Kiev we had walked through the narrow catacombs holding before us the candles we had brought, down halls so narrow they brought me nearly to panic, past saint after shrunken saint blanketed in their tiny coffins. The catacombs of Odessa are higher, broader, wider, lit by electricity. If you straightened them out, they would run all the way to St. Petersburg. A wreath marks one black, unlit turning where a guide and a group of schoolchildren were lost.

"And never found?" we ask.

"Oh no!" the Tanyas tell us. "They were found. They must have been found. It could not have been otherwise."

At Gambrinus, the manager joins us for a beer. He is tall, thin and bald. He looks like a man who has failed at something higher and been reduced to this. A dancer, perhaps, or a poet. He was once a high government official, Oleg tells us. In some mysterious way he was disgraced, but since perestroika, he has hopes. The government seeks his advice, but he thinks in the brave new world that is coming, he will grow rich instead.

At the cottage in Denmark we learn about light. The yard is flooded with sunshine thick as marmalade. The trees and grass have tried out every shade of green, and the purple lilacs are seduced by the sunlight into releasing all their heavy fragrance into the air. In the forest beyond the garden, dappled light filters through the beeches, making the white blossoms of wild onions a crazy quilt. Small deer stare at us, wide-eyed and unafraid. At midnight we swim in the Baltic in absolute blackness, and the water is as cold as the Black Sea.

"Black as the grave in which my friend is laid," Lise says, and I think of Lowry drunk and brooding on the Pacific. Back at the cottage, we drink a bottle of Maltøl. It seems without alcohol, but Lise says it is an aphrodisiac.

Oleg tells us we must not stay too long at Gambrinus. The Black Sea sailors are famous for their violence, and it is true that they drink morosely and do not laugh. Kuprine must have sat at one of these tables, alone. I don't think the sailors would have joined him listening to the strains of a ghostly Jewish violin.

All this happens in late May, early June in the year of 199_. We leave Odessa for the small town of L———. Oleg introduces us to Stanislav, a poet who has walked from Washington to San Francisco without learning a word of English and with only his return ticket in his pocket. He did not spend a cent in America. His daughter Barbara, precocious and assured at nine years old, has several perfect English sentences. "How do you do? My name is Barbara. This is the town in which I live."

"I do not believe in the future," Stanislav tells us. "A Ukrainian who believes in the future is a fool. We are not meant to be free. We are meant to be brutalized and shot in the street like dogs."

"Stanislav believes in the future," Oleg says, after he has translated this. "He is a hopeless romantic."

"The coup has failed," Lise says. "The world is yours."

Stanislav wants to know what Lise has said. He has the trick of Ukrainian men of standing so close that he could kiss you in a moment if he wanted. Oleg translates, and Stanislav kisses Lise. He recites a poem at length. Oleg does not translate, but tells us that the poem is about a father's failure to return from the war. A son and a mother wait until all the returning soldiers have passed. When the father fails to arrive, the mother tells the son, "You are the father now."

"Yes," Barbara says. "He is my father."

It is my turn to recite a poem, but I know none of my own by heart. I can recite only British poems of Empire. "Horatio at the Bridge." "Tubal Cain." "Ozymandias." Stanislav wants me to recite Walt Whitman, but I can only tell him, that is another country.

Later that night at the Odessa Seaman's Club we drink Georgian cognac and play chess. I feel baroque and defensive. I play a King's Indian in the first game and we draw. As white, I play a Queen's Pawn Gambit, but Stanislav knows the game by Botvinnik, from which I have stolen it, and he beats me quickly. We are both drunk by the third game, and against his attack, I arrange my bishops in fianchetto. Full of contempt, he masses his forces in the centre and I pick off an errant knight. He cannot believe he has been so easily tricked. Oleg agrees. Stanislav would never allow such a thing to happen. Lise reminds them that he is playing with a capitalist and that he will have to spend the rest of his life looking over his shoulder for bishops.

And the next morning in the Hotel Krasnaya, the lobby is full of fat priests in black carrying wooden staves. Stanislav awakens us at seven, bringing sour buttermilk in triangular Swedish paper cartons. He recites another poem, but Oleg is not there to translate it. This time I am ready and I respond with Alden Nowlan's "God Sour the Milk of the Knacking Wench." Stanislav is moved to tears. He kisses me full on the lips and leaves.

I tell Lise that this is an unusual experience for me. I have not kissed men before.

"Good," she says. "Did you like it?"

I have to think. "There was nothing unpleasant about it," I tell her. "Though I don't think I would initiate a repeat performance."

The fat priests seem to be waiting for someone of real importance. A black Volvo is parked on the sidewalk in front of the hotel. From somewhere in a hallway outside the lobby, a whining American voice rises over the subdued murmur of Russian and Ukrainian. "I was a sinner like you before I was saved," it says. "Then our Lord made me his own."

"He's insane," I tell Lise. "That is the voice of the certifiably mad."

"Yes, but you can't tell in North America," she answers.

"The distinctions between sanity and madness are stretched so thin, you can never be sure. You have to come here to hear it."

Once, in the Fraserwood Hotel in Manitoba, the owner sat and drank with us on a dank October afternoon. The farmers in the bar all spoke to each other in Ukrainian. In the corner, an old man played a violin.

"We use six-row barley," the owner explained, "and we use a lot more corn. The barley makes it husky and the corn makes it sweet. That's the only difference between Canada and the States. Beer."

We drank toasts all afternoon, read our fortunes in the amber glasses, the sweet and husky beer. Jean the First invented the toast in the thirteenth century. Jean Primus. Gambrinus. The Flemish king of beer. The owner told us the story of a berry-picking expedition from Gimli to Grand Beach across Lake Winnipeg. Three pairs of lovers, the most beautiful and promising in the whole area in 1913, that last year of grace before the Great War. Their boat was swamped in a sudden summer storm, and they all drowned. They were found in couples clinging to each other in death. We toasted love.

In a small bar in Odessa we toast friendship. We eat salted fishes and drink the sweet and heavy Ukrainian beer that smells of new-mown hay. Oleg tells us that he will go to England soon as part of a group that is interested in peace. His way will be paid by the English, and they will give him forty pounds for his expenses. We toast England and peace.

The air in Gambrinus is heavy with the sweet scent of Russian tobacco. It drifts, a blue mist, above the heads of the drinking sailors. The ghost of Kuprine tilts his glass at me, and I tilt mine back. The sailors hum an eastern song, full of betrayal and loss, full of the sound of violins.

Once in a Small Bar in Odessa

"Will you drown with me?" I ask Lise. "Wrap your arms around me and drift down through the dark currents of the Black Sea?"

"No," she answers. "Not in the Black Sea. Not in the Baltic. Not even in Lake Winnipeg. We've had enough of drowning." I can see the reflection of her face in my tumbler of beer, but whether the gold is in the liquid or her hair is impossible to say.

At the Grave of Taras Shevchenko

They were painting the ceiling of the lobby in the Hotel Krasnaya. A man sat at the top of a stepladder about twenty feet high and by wobbling the legs of the ladder he was able to walk around and paint patches he couldn't otherwise reach. Lise said he looked like some kind of giant bird.

"It's ridiculously unsafe," Per told her. "If he falls off that, he's going to kill somebody." The lobby was filled with people who had to keep moving out of the painter's way as he wobbled his shaky ladder across the room. He seemed to be doing a sloppy job, and when Per handed in his key at the desk, he noticed that it was covered with drops of white paint. It was hard to tell whether the people in the lobby were also covered with paint. Per wiped his hand across his hair. Nothing. He must have escaped the universal paint-up.

Outside, the Chaika was waiting. It gleamed a malignant black among the grey and faded-blue Ladas and Skodas. Some party member's Volvo was the only competition, but it was a mere half the length of the Chaika, and the Chaika's driver gazed at the other driver with serene contempt. A pretty girl in a yellow dress with white polka dots rushed up to them.

"You are the delegation from Canada," she told them. "I am Natasha. I will be your guide today for the visit to the grave of Taras Shevchenko."

"We're not actually a delegation," Per told her. "We're just tourists."

"Yes," she said. "From Canada."

"Yes. And we thought maybe we wouldn't go anywhere today. Maybe we'll just walk around and do some shopping." The girl seemed confused, and her face darkened.

"My instructions are today at ten a.m. to take you to the grave of Taras Shevchenko."

"We'd sooner go shopping."

"You can't go shopping. It is necessary to have coupons to shop."

Per pulled a batch of coupons out of his pocket with a triumphant flourish. "You mean these?"

"How did you get those?"

"When I changed my money. The girl in the hotel gave them to me."

Natasha was even more confused now. Her face was flushed and she looked prettier than she had before. A little wisp of her dark hair curled into the corner of her mouth and she pushed it away with her tongue.

"This is very difficult," she said. Her accent was a delicate lilt, but it still resembled the fake accents of Boris and Natasha in the *Rocky and Bullwinkle Show*. "We have arranged to meet the deputy secretary of health for the Oblast. He is already waiting."

"Don't be difficult, Per," Lise said. "Let's go see Taras Shevchenko." She climbed into the back of the Chaika, and Per followed. Natasha stood outside and gave instructions to the driver.

"I think I'm falling in love," Per told Lise. "Did you notice those high cheekbones? Those black Slavic eyes?"

"Her eyes are blue," Lise said. "And she's not your type. Too imperious."

"I don't know. We could probably work it out. She could dress in leather and discipline me with small willow switches. We could buy a Doberman."

"Stick with open-faced blondes. I happen to know you don't like pain." Her blonde hair curled over her shoulders.

They drove through the streets of Kiev, past a demonstration at the central square where a couple of hundred men were waving their fists at a building across the street, past the golden domes of an ancient church and past the enormous figure of a worker that dominated the city. Natasha gave a running commentary that sounded as if it had been memorized in its entirety. She didn't even glance out the window as she described what they were passing.

Soon after they crossed the high bridge over the Dnieper, the Chaika pulled up at a bus stop and a short and very stocky man got into the car. He greeted them cheerfully and forcefully in Ukrainian. Natasha translated.

"He welcomes you to Ukraine. He hopes your journey has been happy and successful. His name is Vlodomir Domanski, but you may call him Vlodya. He is the deputy secretary of health for the Oblast, but he is also a poet. A lyric poet. He has published thirteen volumes of poetry. His subjects are love and nature. He would like you to tell him about your work."

"I write novels," Per said. "Detective novels and spy novels set in exotic locales."

"You do not," Lise said. "Don't believe him. He writes novels about young boys growing up on the farm, full of adolescent torment and sexual confusion. He's really good at sunsets and descriptions of geese flying south in the fall."

Natasha hesitated for a moment, then said something in Ukrainian.

"I have told him that you are a writer of prosaic," she said.

"That's right," Lise said. "That's him."

"When we get back to Canada," Per told Lise, "I am trading you in. I am going to send you back to Sweden and demand a replacement that is not defective in the areas of sympathy and simple human decency."

"You can't send me to Sweden," she answered. "My great-grandparents came over. My family has been Canadian longer than yours." She stuck her tongue out at him.

"The Swedes are famous for their warranties," Per said. "In a case as clear as this, I'm certain they'll stand behind the product."

They were out of the city now, past the airport and heading southeast. The road was lined with tall trees. The bottom of every tree was painted white. Per thought it looked like a scene near the beginning of Roman Polanski's film *Knife in the Water*, except that it had been misty and raining in the film, and now there was brilliant sunshine. The fields along the road were lush and green. The crops, whatever crops they were, seemed to be flourishing. There were fewer cars now. Most of the traffic was motorcycles with sidecars. There was never anybody in any of the sidecars. They seemed to be filled with produce or boards or rusty machine parts, as if they were tiny pickup trucks.

The health secretary poet was talking to the driver, who was driving even faster now than he had driven during the week they had spent in Kiev. In the city, everything got out of the Chaika's way, but country drivers seemed more stubborn, and several times they had met other vehicles while passing, so they were three abreast on the narrow road.

"He was five times the driving champion of Ukraine,"

Natasha explained of the driver. "Now he is seventy-nine, but he still drives very fast." Natasha said this as if she were proud of him.

They pulled off the main road onto an even narrower one that followed the Dnieper River. Here there were sand dunes and broad beaches. The river looked like a big blue lake, but there were no cottages and no pleasure boats. The fields were full of wild flowers, but there didn't seem to be any more crops. The vegetation had changed too. Now they passed evergreens and white trees that might have been poplars or birches.

They crossed the Dnieper again, and Per realized that they were passing over a hydroelectric dam. The broad stretch of water they had just followed was a lake created by the dam. They drove into a village at the far end of the dam, a large town actually, though the sign as they entered declared it a village. The streets of the village were crowded, and the people were all very well dressed. Many of them wore leather jackets and dresses. Pretty young women in miniskirts looked as if they were on their way to a party, though it was not yet noon.

"Why are Ukrainians so well dressed?" Lise asked Natasha. "I thought there were shortages. I thought you were supposed to be poor."

"There are shortages," Natasha answered. "We are poor. Yet everybody has fine clothes. That is our mystery."

"Yes, but how do you explain this mystery?"

"It cannot be explained. No one can explain it." The Chaika veered to the left and began to climb a steep gravel road so narrow that trees brushed against it. Vlodya began a long explanation of how difficult it was for a poet to have to be responsible for the health of twelve million people. Both of his subjects were denied him. He was too busy to fall in love, and he spent all his time in the city and did not get the opportunity to commune with nature. He hoped that this trip would allow him to write a poem.

"He must be planning on falling in love with you," Per whispered to Lise. "There won't be any nature at Taras Shevchenko's grave."

But there was nature. The grave itself was marked by an enormous statue of the poet, a monument about thirty feet high on a cliff overlooking the river. Red and yellow flowers outlined the borders, but they were almost swamped by the deep grass and wild flowers surrounding the area.

A small bald man arrived and shook their hands with considerable emotion. Natasha said that he had devoted his life to caring for Shevchenko's grave. He was always moved to meet great poets from other countries.

"Tell him I'm not a great poet," Per said. "Tell him I write detective novels."

Natasha conveyed the information, which brought tears to the little man's eyes. He spoke at some length and came over and wrung Per's hand again.

"He is very moved," she said. "Mickey Spillane is his favourite author, and he hopes that your works will also be translated into Ukrainian so that he might read them. We have so little crime that there are no detectives, and so no one in the Soviet Union can write detective novels. But we have hope. Since perestroika we have many criminals, and soon we will have detectives to catch them. Detective novels will surely follow. We have no great criminals like you have in the United States, only moneychangers and extortionists right now."

"Tell him I'm not from the United States. Tell him I'm from Canada."

"He will not understand. We believe that Canada is a part of the United States."

"But it isn't."

"Nevertheless, that is what we believe."

"Maybe someday they'll put up a statue like this for you," Lise said. "Maybe half the streets in Canada will be named for you someday." Lise had wandered over to the wall at the edge of the cliff and she returned now to where Per was standing with Natasha and the detective-novel fan. Vlodya stuck so close to her that Per wondered whether he might not actually have fallen in love with her.

"No chance of that," Per told her. "If you admit you're a writer in Canada, they won't honour your credit cards. You have to pay cash in advance for everything."

"How about George Bowering?" Lise asked. "Maybe they'll put up a statue to George Bowering." She had heard Bowering read in Winnipeg once. As a rule, she didn't like writers, though she liked reading. Per never brought writers home for her to meet.

"Not even George Bowering. Not even Margaret Atwood. Maybe Margaret Laurence."

"Well, there's some hope then."

The party had drifted towards a big white building that turned out to be a museum. A very large elderly woman with steel-grey hair was introduced to them. She announced that she would be their guide to the museum. She was wearing a pin that said El Paso Texas. She explained that the city of El Paso had once had a Taras Shevchenko festival, and she had been invited to attend. Her English had a slight Texan accent.

She led them through the museum, reciting a description of the pictures and drawings on the wall as if she were a tape recorder. Per kept drifting away from the lecture to look at Shevchenko's drawings. They were really very good. Every time he moved away, however, the Texan voice lapsed into frosty silence until he returned. The secretary of health stayed so close to Lise that she appeared to be leading him on a leash. They had a moment of freedom in a room full of tents and cooking equipment that looked as if it were meant to represent the Indians of western Canada, but was apparently a recreation of the conditions in Tashkent or someplace where Shevchenko had been banished.

Lise joined Per behind the largest tent. "I think he asked me to sleep with him," she said. "He keeps whispering Russian into my ear."

"That's Ukrainian," Per told her.

"Whatever. It's certainly meant to be romantic."

In each room of the museum an old woman with gold teeth sat in a chair and watched that they didn't touch anything. The women all wore headscarves and heavy woollen sweaters, though it was very warm. The woman beside them now appeared deeply offended that they were talking, and she coughed loudly. The Texan was poised to begin speaking again, so they followed her into the next room.

Taras Shevchenko seemed to have had a lot of difficulties in life, but he also seemed to have had a lot of fun. The czar kept banishing him, but he kept coming back and having all kinds of love affairs. He was under sentence of death but seemed to be able to travel freely and was loved by everyone in the country.

"They're hopelessly inefficient," Per said. "In Canada or the States, if the government didn't like a poet and sentenced him to death, they wouldn't let him wander around like that. They'd catch him and put an end to it."

"But the people loved him," Natasha explained.

"Well, they don't love poets in the New World."

"Are you endangered?" Natasha asked.

"Not endangered. Simply ignored." Vlodya was standing beside a full-length portrait of Taras Shevchenko, and Per suddenly realized that he looked exactly like the poet. There was the same dark hair, the same stocky build. From a side view, they both had small but significant pot-bellies. Lise, standing beside him, was almost the same height. Her blonde hair and ivory skin were the exact opposite of his dark swarthiness.

On the way back they stopped at the cafeteria of a small zoo where the cook miraculously produced a banquet, though neither Per nor Lise could identify a single dish. Vlodya made elaborate toasts and tried to fill them up with vodka. As soon as any glass was not entirely full, he filled it up. When it was finally clear that neither Per nor Lise was going to get drunk in the middle of the afternoon, he went off with the driver to try to hunt down enough gasoline to get them back to Kiev. They sat on the banks of the Dnieper by the little zoo and watched the barges drift by.

"Did you notice that he looked exactly like Taras Shevchenko?" Per asked Lise.

"Yes. Do you think he's a reincarnation?"

"Probably. What are you going to do about his fascination with you?"

"I'll break his heart. That's what always happened to Taras."

"I thought Taras was successful with the ladies."

"You weren't paying attention. His heart was always being broken."

And that's what happened. When they got back to the hotel at the corner of Taras Shevchenko and Pushkin streets, Natasha took Lise aside and delivered Vlodya's declaration of love. Per went up to their room alone so that no one would be embarrassed. Lise declined the kind offer, but thanked

Vlodya for the compliment, and he went away to try to mend his broken heart.

There was no hot water in the room, and Per was cursing from the bathroom, where he had just discovered this fact. "What can you say about a country that can't provide hot water in a luxury hotel?" he said.

"You can say that they love poets, that poets can be elected as leaders and that it is still possible to be a mad romantic," Lise answered.

"Right," Per answered, walking into the room, his naked body dripping cold water. "Next week, Odessa, and if it's as good as this we'll move here for keeps."

The Dragon and the Dry Goods Princess

O nce upon a time, not so very long ago, there was a dragon who lived in a castle in eastern Europe, somewhere near Transylvania, I think. He was happy for the most part, picking off a king's daughter now and again, and spending most of his time sleeping with his head in her lap. Every so often a prince would come by to rescue the king's daughter, and usually he'd just let them go, because after they'd been around too long, they started to complain about the castle and how hard it was to get decent help. So when the prince came, waving his sword and swearing great oaths, the dragon would send the king's daughter out with her suitcase and a purse full of gold. He'd wave good-bye and promise to write, though of course he never did.

But then the communists took over and for a long time it was impossible to find a king's daughter. Just when it looked like things were getting better, democracy arrived, and it's even harder to find a king's daughter in a democracy than in a communist country. Besides, there were a lot of bad feelings with the Bosnians and the Serbs, and one day the dragon's castle was hit by a mortar shell.

"That's it," the dragon said. "I've had it up to here." So he disguised himself as a school teacher, bought an airline ticket, and moved to Canada. He'd always liked remote places, so he found a lake in the Whiteshell area right on the border between Manitoba and Ontario, built himself a castle, and settled down.

For a while everything was perfect. He'd almost forgotten about kings' daughters, it had been so long since he'd seen one, and, besides, the fishing was great. Lots of really big northern pike, and perfect rainbow trout in the river just behind the castle.

Then, one day, there was a knock at the castle door. A beautiful young woman with raven tresses stood there. The dragon's heart nearly stopped. He hadn't seen a princess since 1942.

The young woman was talking almost before the door was fully open. "A bunch of us are camped just down the river," she said, "and I saw this place, and I wondered if you had rooms to rent? One night of tenting is all I need, thanks. I mean, I thought canoeing was supposed to be fun, but there's nothing but bugs and slimy fish, and everybody is supposed to do their share. If I wanted to wash dishes I could have stayed at home and done them in a dishwasher. Look. My nails are all chipped."

The dragon surveyed her. Her voice seemed something quite separate from her beauty. "What's your name?"

"Marcia," she answered. "I mean, I've got this big down-filled sleeping bag and an air mattress and everything, but I can't get a night's sleep. First it was a stone under the mattress. Then last night some joker put a pea under the mattress, and I didn't get a wink of sleep."

"You couldn't sleep because there was a pea under your mattress?" the dragon asked, his voice full of hope.

"That's right," Marcia said. "So, do you have rooms?"

"A hundred rooms at least," the dragon told her with some pride. "This is a castle. I haven't even got around to counting them. Tell me, are you a princess?"

The girl gave him a searching look. "What are you," she asked, "a wise guy?"

"No offence," the dragon told her in his most conciliatory voice, "but you looked to me like the daughter of a king."

"That's us," she said. "King's Wholesale Dry Goods, corner of Logan and Main. Hey, what's that crazy outfit you've got on? You into leather and whips?"

"I'm a dragon," the dragon explained. "It's part of the uniform."

"Hey, neat," the girl said. "I've never actually met a dragon before. Can you breathe fire?"

"Of course. I'm a dragon."

"Show me. Blast that little spruce tree over there."

The dragon drew himself up and took a deep breath. Then he exhaled slowly and said, "I'm sorry. I can't."

"Sure," the girl said. "You're not a real dragon at all. You're just a creepy guy who lives out in the wilderness and dresses funny."

The dragon was upset, but, on the other hand, he couldn't take a chance on offending a princess. "The forest fire index is a hundred and three point five," he explained. "You're not allowed to have open fires."

"Excuses," the girl said, reaching into her purse and taking out a package of cigarettes. It was the dragon's perfect opportunity.

"Here, let me light your cigarette," he said, and he blew a thin line of flame that ignited the girl's cigarette but also startled her so that she jumped back. "There," he said. "That's proof."

"Hey, terrific." The girl fumbled in her purse and pulled out her package of cigarettes again. "You want a cigarette too?"

"No, I don't smoke."

"What do you mean you don't smoke? If you breathe fire then a little smoke isn't going to bother you."

"Smoking causes cancer," the dragon said with a moralistic tone that he regretted but couldn't help. "Breathing fire does not."

"It just causes forest fires?"

"Only if you aren't careful. Do you want to stay?"

"Maybe," the girl said. "What's the deal?"

"You have to let me sleep with my head in your lap every afternoon between three and five," the dragon explained. "You have to bring me cooling drinks before supper on Tuesdays and Thursdays, and I get breakfast in bed on Saturday. You get Sunday off. And in return, you get the run of the castle, an untold fortune in jewellery and gold, and your own telephone and fax."

The girl looked him over critically. "That's the whole deal?"

"Well," the dragon confessed, "there's the usual other stuff."

"What other stuff?"

"Well, you know," the dragon said, shuffling his feet and blushing a little. "The ordinary Dragon-Princess, Beauty-and-the-Beast falling in love stuff. But we can pretty much play it by ear."

"I don't know," Marcia said. "You're kind of cute, but I don't think I'm ready for a relationship."

"Whatever you like. It's just that it's the usual scenario."

And so, Marcia moved in with the dragon, and things worked out pretty well at first. The dragon had been having trouble sleeping without a princess's lap for the past fifty-two years, and so he felt a lot better. Marcia had a lot of fun exploring the castle. There were so many rooms that it was a month before she'd seen them all. She tried on all the jewellery, and counted gold coins until she got sick of counting. The dragon really was handsome, and now that he was getting enough sleep and exercise and eating properly, he cut quite a fine figure. Marcia even fell in love with him, and the Beauty-and-the-Beast thing was more fun than she'd expected.

But by the time summer had gone and fall had passed and they were moving into winter, she started to get restless. The food seemed to be prepared by invisible hands, and the beds made themselves, but she never saw another living soul.

"Look," she told the dragon one day, "it's been thirty below for days. Why don't we slip down to Miami for a couple of weeks? My folks have got a condominium there, it would only cost the airfare."

"I'm sorry," the dragon said, "but I can't leave the castle."

He was practising putting on the castle floor, and it was starting to annoy Marcia.

"Hire a security firm to take care of it," she told him. "There won't be a problem."

"That's not the point," he said, sinking a forty-foot putt. "Dragons have to stay in their castles. They can't just go gallivanting wherever they want."

"Well, I've invited some people out for the weekend," Marcia said. "My folks and my cousin Naomi. I'm going stir crazy here. We haven't even got cable TV." She hadn't actually invited them, but if the dragon didn't object, then she intended to go ahead.

"You'll have to phone them and tell them not to come," the dragon said. He had expected this for some time. About three months was as long as you could keep a princess happy. Then they got bored and were impossible to live with.

"What do you mean?" Marcia said, now angry. "I told them to come, they're coming. End of argument."

"If they come, I'll have to incinerate them."

"Breathe fire on them?"

"Yes. It's what I do."

"What about the forest fires?"

"It's winter," the dragon said. "The risk is low. Anyway, those are the rules. You're my princess. As long as I've got you, I've got to incinerate anyone who comes near."

Marcia rolled her eyes. "That's ridiculous."

"Sorry. I don't make the rules."

"How am I going to spend all that gold? That was part of the deal. What good is all the gold in the world if I can't spend it?"

"Mail order," the dragon said. "Get the Eddie Bauer catalogue, or Ikea, or something. Anyway, the Dragon-Princess relationship is a two-way street. We've all got to make accommodations."

"So I'm trapped. There's no way out?"

"Not unless a prince comes by and rescues you. The rest is non-negotiable."

"A prince," Marcia said.

"Yes," the dragon replied. "A prince."

Marcia brooded in her room for a couple of days. She didn't know many princes. She sent a lot of faxes, but the few men who replied said they weren't into rescuing maidens. One of them even sent her a subscription to a feminist magazine. Finally there was only Arnold. Arnold was an accountant who wore thick glasses but he'd been in love with Marcia since grade one. Marcia sent him a fax.

"Who's that guy standing in the driveway holding a sword?" the dragon asked her one morning a few days later.

Marcia glanced out the window. "Must be a prince," she said, "come to rescue me."

"He doesn't look like a prince," the dragon said. "He looks like an accountant. I guess I'll have to go out and incinerate him."

"I thought you didn't incinerate princes?" Marcia said. She'd played down the dragon's ferocity in her fax to Arnold, and she knew she'd feel really bad if he were charred.

"Well, not as a rule," the dragon said, "not a real prince. But if I let a guy like this get away with my princess, I'll be a laughingstock. Next thing it'll be bakers and taxi drivers. I'd never live it down." He walked out the front door onto the porch.

"Hey, you, at the end of the driveway," he shouted.

"Yes?" Arnold answered. He'd taken off his glasses and was cleaning them with the tail of his white shirt.

"Off the property in ten seconds or you're a cinder," the dragon said. He breathed a little burst of fire, not enough to set anything aflame, but enough to convince Arnold that he was serious.

"Just a minute," Arnold told him. "Turn around and look at that castle."

"Yeah. So what?"

"It's falling apart."

"It's supposed to fall apart," the dragon informed him, "it's turning into a ruined castle."

Arnold saw his chance and moved in quickly. In a second he was at the dragon's side. "But it doesn't have to," he said. "That's the beauty of it. Now if you were to put your liquid assets into mutual funds you could repair that in no time and still have enough interest left over for a little holiday. Let me show you." And he pulled a brochure from his pocket and began to annotate figures with his ball-point pen. The dragon didn't have a chance.

And so the princess was rescued. Arnold took her back

with him along with bagfuls of gold and jewellery, and the dragon invested in high-risk South-East Asian mutuals and became even richer. Marcia and Arnold took over the dry goods wholesale business, bought a condominium in Palm Springs, and lived happily ever after.

And as for the dragon, well, Marcia's cousin Naomi came out to visit him, and it turned out that she was a princess too, and so were several other cousins. In the end, there were enough princesses in Winnipeg for a dozen dragons, so the dragon brought over a bunch of friends from Transylvania and they all lived happily ever after, though some of them are still a little nervous when the forest fire index gets too high.

The Cowboy: A Tale of the Old West

O ut on the prairie, alone on his horse, the cowboy yearns. In all that dust, the hot midday suns of summer, he yearns. He yearns through the rain that drips from his Stetson, yearns through the bitter cold and snowy days of December, yearns through the awful western springs when horseshit starts to peek out from the snow like some obscene early flower.

He yearns for the rancher's daughter, that goes without saying. Susan, the rancher's blonde and blue-eyed daughter, who can rope a calf, geld a steer, ride in the rodeo with the toughest of men. Susan in her soft tan cowboy boots. He imagines her wearing only her boots, naked, swinging in her hand the lariat, the lasso. He imagines the burn of the rope on his skin.

He yearns for the lady teacher, Miz Hawkins, her soft black curls and her big brown eyes. She stands for goodness and wisdom, and he loves her voice. He imagines her naked, wearing only her eastern high-heeled shoes, carrying a book. She tells him over and over, no, that is wrong, you must do it again and again until you get it right.

He yearns in the arroyos, yearns on the burning prairie, yearns on the mountainsides. When he walks along the barbed-wire fence, putting in a new staple here, steadying a post there, he yearns for the bright-lit taverns of the town, yearns for the smooth rye whisky and Seven Up, the polished oak of the bar. He dreams then of Miz Sally and her girls, those high-stepping dancers, flashing flesh under their lacy crinolines.

Around the fire with the other cowboys he makes rude jokes about the rancher's daughter, about the schoolmarm from the East, about Miz Sally and her girls. He eats his bacon and beans, wiping up the juices with fresh bread the cook has just made today, and he leans back on his bedroll and yearns.

When he sleeps, he dreams of houses, ranch houses made from logs, with pine floors and curtains on the windows. He dreams of white stucco houses with brightly coloured furniture, solid brick houses with horsehair chesterfields, glass houses on golden beaches where the waves pound in every day. Sometimes he puts his women in these houses, Susan, the blue-eyed rancher's daughter, Miz Hawkins, the eastern schoolmarm in her high-heeled shoes, Miz Sally and her girls, dancing. When he does, the dreams come apart. Cattle get in them, lowing herds of steers, and cards: diamonds and clubs, the ace of spades. The next morning, his yearning is unfocussed, the weather is bad.

The cowboy's heart is filled with love. It overflows. He has no place to keep so much love, and so he scatters it around him recklessly. He bandages the injured foot of a calf with enough tenderness for an entire orphanage. He finds butterflies made sodden by the rain and carries them to rocks in the sun where they can dry their wings. He comes on a coyote with four kits, and he doesn't kill them, though he has been instructed to do so. It is part of his job. He has so much love that he doesn't even pick up the little ones to cuddle them. He just watches them playing in the light, and he rides on.

He rides on. This is how his days pass. He rubs the flank of his horse, touches the worn leather of his saddle, the worn wooden stock of his gun. He keeps his eyes focussed in the distance because of the unbearable beauty of the prairie. He must get the herd to market. He cannot stop for fringed gentian beside a rock, spotted touch-me-not on the edge of a swamp, Indian paintbrush and wild columbine on the higher slopes. Sometimes he imagines the bouquets he might take to Susan, the rancher's blue-eyed daughter, masses of orange wood lily and purple iris. Miz Hawkins, the eastern school-teacher, will get a single wake-robin, picked before the snow has gone. Blackeyed Susans for Miz Sally, and asters for her girls, depending on the season: white asters in June, yellow in August and blue in September.

And when the rustlers have come by and stolen some of the herd, he yearns for the good old days when he might have followed their trail into the mountains, confronted them, dark-haired slouching men in black hats, and brought them to justice. Then he might have won the heart of the rancher's daughter, he might have shown his sense of justice to the teacher, he might have won the admirations of Miz Sally and her girls.

Now there are only the tracks of the refrigerated trucks that the rustlers drive, a few hooves and horns on the blood-stained grass. The rustlers have even taken the skins to tan. There are not enough entrails left to feed the coyotes for a single night. And when the sheriff comes, the cowboy must fill out forms in triplicate, and have them stamped.

Tumbleweeds drift across the plains. Dust devils whirl and throw dust up into the cowboy's eyes. There is always a thaw in February, a false spring when icicles drip from the eaves of the bunkhouse and the sparrows gather in flocks and twitter their praise. Then the cowboy is filled with desire. Desire gets into his joints, and it makes it hard for him to walk. Desire fills his stomach, so that he cannot eat, and he loses weight. Desire rages in his brain like a fever, like a furnace. He tosses in his bunk and his eyes refuse to see, they keep out the light. Finally, the doctor comes and cures his desire with antibiotics. The cowboy wakes up to see that the rancher's daughter is wiping his brow with a damp cloth, but his desire is gone now, and what he feels for her is gratitude.

The cowboy thinks there must be something wrong with him. He is a creature of excess. He is too tall. His feet are too large. He laughs too loudly. He knows too much about the art of being a cowboy, knows when the herd is restless, where the lost calf has gone, where the wolves are stalking, where there might be bears. He can guess the weight of a steer to a pound. He can break the toughest horse, he can carry a heavier load than any of the other cowboys and be the least exhausted at the end of the day. The problem, he thinks, is that there is too much inside him. There is no room for anything more. And there is no place where he can put the excess he carries with him. He thinks that he needs a wife. And he needs children. That will do the trick, he says to himself. That will do the trick.

The cowboy yearns for his unborn children, the strong-boned boys, the lithe daughters who will spring from his loins. He basks in their future respect, their filial admiration. He imagines the family photo, the four boys and three girls arranged around a cowboy and his wife. Perhaps they will use it on their Christmas card.

Alone on the prairie under a starry sky, the cowboy fears his death, not as an abstraction, but as a real event. His fear is on the edge of panic. He becomes hot and flushed. He feels death on his joints, death as an icy hand gripping his heart, death as a ball of cancer growing in his heavy body. He cannot catch his breath. The horizon is on fire.

Sometimes the cowboy hears wolves in the distance. Sometimes he hears laughter. On summer nights when he is camped near the town he can hear the music from the Saturday-night dance. Then he thinks of the bare arms of women, their calico dresses and their perfume. He yearns to dance, to form a square, to do-si-do, to allemande left, to over-and-under. He wants to give his body to the violins and the accordions.

The cowboy wants to submit to something. He wants to be taken by something larger than he is. He wants to give up all responsibility for himself and hand his life over to someone else so that he needs only to follow orders. But this is impossible. He is a cowboy. One moment of inattention and the herd will be lost.

The cowboy is building up his grubstake. Every payday he sends some money to his mother, he has a night on the town, and he puts a few dollars into a leather wallet he keeps in his bedroll. When he has enough money, he will start his own spread. Then he will no longer be a cowboy, but a rancher himself.

The cowboy rides into sunsets and into sunrises. He rides into the blackness of night and into the brilliance of noon, but something is wrong. When the ride is over, he is still there. Nothing has changed, and no one is watching. The great herd lows softly. Smoke lingers in the air.

When the yearning is too great, the cowboy takes his rifle to the dump. He fires at empty bottles, watching them explode. He fires at the furtive rats, watching them explode beside the broken glass. He shoots out the insulators of the telegraph wires, and the next day there are no messages in the town. The dry grass crackles under his feet.

When he finally acts, it is almost too late. When he asks if he may speak to Susan, the rancher's blue-eyed daughter, he is told that she has gone to law school in the East. The rancher shows him a photograph. The cowboy knows that the woman in the photograph is never coming back. He remembers her cool hands on his forehead the time he was cured of desire. Her soft tan boots are still in the closet.

When he goes to town, the wedding has already begun. Miz Hawkins in a white dress and red high-heeled shoes is marrying the banker. The whole of Main Street has been closed off, and there are free barbecued steaks for everyone, free rye and Seven Up at every corner. The cowboy joins hands with everyone else and sings "Auld Lang Syne," before the banker and his wife leave for a honeymoon in the East.

In the tavern he meets Miz Sally and buys her a drink. She is returning to Boston to open a millinery shop. She has made her grubstake in the West, and now she is returning home. Her girls have no place to go. The cowboy looks the girls over and chooses Dorothy, who is neither plain nor pretty, and he marries her that day in front of the Justice of the Peace.

He buys a ranch and raises sons and daughters. He is saving money to send his daughters to law school in the East. His boys will all be bankers, and they will marry schoolteachers. His house is glass and stucco, and it looks over the river. From where he stands, he cannot see the prairie beyond.

The horizon is on fire. The smell of smoke is everywhere. The grass crackles underfoot. Coyotes howl in the distant hills. Gophers and foxes and deer plunge into the river. The air is filled with whirling birds. The cattle are maddened by the flames and the smoke, and they bellow in rage and fear, but there is no cowboy to save them. The rancher, in his glass and stucco house, is facing east.

The Waitress

The waitress wakes in the grey, hurt dawn. She smells smoke on her clothes, grease on her skin. She has punched her pillow into a tight ball. K.T. Oslin is singing on the clock radio, a song about damaged love. The waitress wouldn't mind damaged love. She would welcome a heartache, because that would mean that for at least a little while someone would have loved her.

She has been reading the advertisements in *Vanity Fair* magazine. She doesn't read the articles. They have nothing to do with her. She doesn't really care about the clothes and perfumes that are being advertised. She cares only about the gestures, the way the models hold their bodies, extend their arms or legs, raise their chins, whirl their hair. She realizes that it is not the clothes that make them beautiful. If that were the case she could never enter that world. But often the clothes are ugly, and the models are nevertheless beautiful. That is the trick she wants to learn.

In the shower, she thinks about love. Her mother does not love her, nor does her stepfather. The men who touch her body as they offer her a tip do not love her. She knows some young, decent men who would fall in love with her if she would let them. But they are all married, and they are all poor. Some of them are good. They are fine and decent and would treat her well. But she does not want to be treated well. She does not want to mother children and be given small gifts on Mother's Day. She does not want to wash the dishes with the other women after the men have barbecued the steaks and are drinking beer out by the garage.

She wants someone who will love her for her gestures, someone who will not even see her behind the gestures. She doesn't mind getting hurt, or doesn't think she will mind, though you can never know for sure. She remembers a Joni Mitchell song with a line about a mean old daddy. That's what she wants. A mean old daddy who will love her and take her to Paris and buy her diamonds, and if he abandons her in Rome or in Athens, she will be ready for it.

She looks in the mirror. She has the body of a model, too thin and too tall. She was afraid for a while that her breasts were too large, but a shift in fashion favours her. Her jaw is angular, her cheekbones high. She knows she is awkward, but she thinks she can use this. Awkward gestures are more powerful than fluid ones. It all depends on the timing.

She looks at herself in the mirror. She prefers her mirror self, a clean surface extended over a smooth plane. She likes the way that mirrors can distort the body, stretching it thin. The polished bodies of cars release a shorter, fatter self. She would like to see herself in a prism, multiplied. She remembers when, as a child, she was a figure skater. This is the only memory she has that satisfies her. She worked very hard at the figures, and though other girls were better at free-style skating, she could inscribe perfect figure eights in the ice, and that was enough to make her happy.

The Waitress

Her skin is the problem. She wants to be free of imperfections, but that is difficult for a waitress. The work is hard, she is often hungry, and the food is greasy. She has tried to live on vegetables, but they will not sustain her through a fourteen-hour shift. Every time she nears perfection, her body betrays her.

She has nearly given up sex. She sometimes goes to movies or dances with Billy, who is left-handed and stutters, who also thinks about getting the gestures right. She does not have sex with Larry, who has never requested it anyway. Sometimes she picks up a man at a singles bar and goes to bed with him, but it is never satisfactory. He believes in profit, or he believes in God. He believes in something, and the waitress finds it hard to listen. The next day she feels violated, as if someone has broken into her home and stolen something she values.

And of course it happens. As soon as she gets the gestures right, the waitress is beautiful, in any way that matters. But there is no point in being loved by truck drivers and construction workers, people who want barbecues and children. And there is no more point in being loved by lawyers who want only more expensive barbecues, or doctors, who want only more demanding children.

The waitress needs an artist or a politician. She needs somebody unencumbered by the real world. A professor would do. Somebody who believes in ideas. Somebody who doesn't care if it works. It would be nice, she thinks, to look over a northern lake, frozen, or an African plain, tattered with the remains of imaginary animals.

She wonders whether, if she were draped over the shoulder of a naked man for an advertisement in *Vanity Fair,* she could achieve the deadness of flesh they would need. She knows she could whirl her hair so that it would obscure her face. She needs only that small confusion that lasts for a second.

She could handle that. She could make love to men who were mean and selfish and only wanted to use her. That would be fair. She would not have to give them anything. Their bodies would be smooth and silken, and they would be gone without apology. That's not so bad.

And, of course, one day the inevitable happens. The waitress is dancing in a dark bar with someone, and later, when she returns to her drink, a man in a suit gives her a business card. Call him or not, he says. It's only business. He doesn't buy her a drink, and a few minutes later he is gone. The next day she calls him, and before long she is a model, nothing big, but she appears on the back page of the second section of the newspaper in a business suit wearing a pair of glasses. She cuts out the ad and frames it and hangs it on her wall. She quits her job as a waitress, and in a few days she no longer smells of cigarette smoke and grease.

Suddenly there is money. She travels on airlines. Around her are men who give curt orders. She works very hard, as hard as when she was a waitress. But now she is a model, and she is taught how to walk, and somebody fixes her teeth. Nobody takes advantage of her. Nobody asks her to sleep with him. She still studies the ads in magazines until one day she imitates a gesture of a model in an ad for hair spray and realizes she is imitating herself. Then later she can no longer pick herself out in ads.

She senses that she is invisible. Clerks take no notice of her in stores until she insists they do. Then they are embarrassed. At parties, nobody comes to talk to her. She feels as if she is stretched tightly across the surface of her life, so thin that she reflects light. She reads articles about finding your true self. What might that be, she wonders, your true self?

And she grows older. There is nothing she can do about that. She doesn't fear the future. The other models are planning to retire soon, in a year or two, and become actresses when their bodies fail. But the waitress who is now a model doesn't worry about that. It is not her body that the world wants, only her gestures, and if she grows older, then she will learn new gestures, the gestures of the old.

What she misses is desire. She sees herself as without depth. There is no absence in her, no gap to be filled. She plays Gorecki's *Symphony of Sorrows* as she goes to sleep. The next morning she plays K.T. Oslin. She prefers K.T. Oslin. She goes to Australia to model dresses in the outback. When she returns, she is interviewed by a newspaper. The reporter asks her what she liked best about Australia. She thinks for a while. The cornflakes, she tells him. They have really good cornflakes.

At some point her stepfather is arrested for molesting young girls. Everyone assumes she has been abused as a child, but that is wrong. Her stepfather, though he does not love her, is a perfect gentleman. She cannot imagine him molesting anyone, and when he is freed, even though it is only on a technicality, she is glad. She buys a dog.

The dog is a mistake, even though he is an Afghan hound, just the right dog for a model. He introduces disorder into her life. He shits on the floor, and after she has cleaned it up, the smell of disinfectant lingers for weeks. He loves her madly. He licks her, nuzzles her, snuffles his nose against her without shame. When she is angry with him he whines and abases himself. He rolls sad eyes at her. When she forgives him he is delirious with joy and breaks the ornaments. She thinks about the dog at work, wonders whether he is happy, and she is angry with herself. He is only a dog. Then he is run over before her eyes, and she weeps for weeks. She does not buy another dog.

And her mother dies. It's impossible, she thinks, she is

much too young to die, a mother who is only fifty-one. Cancer, they tell her, some problem in the reproductive system, something with a Latin name. They should have called her, but her mother wouldn't let them. Leave the girl be, her mother said. She's got problems of her own.

Maybe I am being tested, the model thinks. She tries to remember the story of Job, but she doesn't know the Bible, and she can't find the passage she wants. Besides, she doesn't believe in God. She imagines the universe as one of those glass balls that make it snow when you turn them upside down.

She dresses in black, and every Sunday she places a rose on her mother's grave. Sometimes she thinks that there is something she should have said to her mother when her mother was alive, but she can't imagine what it might be. Her mother is easier to talk to dead, and her daughter comes to love her.

Then a photographer takes a picture of her dressed in black, in an October dawn at her mother's grave. There is even fog. He shoots with a telephoto lens at a fair distance, and the picture is everywhere. It is a perfect picture, all the gestures of grief, but after it is published the model can no longer visit the grave of her mother. There is nobody there she can talk to.

The model has trouble understanding money. She knows exactly what you can do with a waitress's salary, but anything larger bewilders her. She checks her bank account like she checks the oil in her car. If there is money in the account, she spends it. If not, she waits until the account fills itself up again, and then she spends it. She has investments, but somebody else takes care of them. She sends a charitable donation to the university she would have gone to if she'd had enough money.

After that they send her letters every week, so she doesn't give them any more in the hope that they will stop writing

The Waitress

to her. Nothing happens. The model reads about herself in magazine articles, but nothing they tell her is true.

She goes to exotic places: Calcutta, Odessa, Reykjavik. Nothing happens. She parachutes from airplanes. She dives in shark-infested waters. She always comes back to the same place.

Finally she takes to waiting. She waits in airports, she waits in bus depots and train stations. She waits in malls and in theatres. She goes to restaurants and watches the women who serve. They are ordinary people doing a job. She waits by her window when the rain falls steadily in May, and she waits while the first snow falls in November. She is waiting still.

In the Garden of the Medicis

J oe slowed the Toyota and pulled over to the edge of the road. They seemed to have been climbing for a very long time, the Toyota unable to handle the steep grade in anything higher than third gear. Now steam billowed from the engine. Carla turned her attention to the children in the back seat.

"It's okay," she told them. "Daddy will get it fixed in a minute. Just stay still and don't undo your seat belts."

"Daddy's not going to get us out of this one so easy," Joe muttered under his breath, but he only said, "Oh, nothing" when Carla asked what he'd said.

Joe opened the hood of the car and looked at the motor. Steam was still coming from around the radiator cap, but it seemed to have slowed down a bit. A Jeep came from the opposite direction, but it passed without even slowing down, and Joe realized that they hadn't seen any other cars for a quite a while.

Water, he thought. I'll have to get some water to fill up the radiator, then maybe we can limp to a garage.

But there was no water anywhere near, no ditch, no

mountain stream, not even a puddle. There were only the high banks of the rock cut on both sides and a few small rocks that had tumbled onto the road.

"Nothing I can do," Joe told Carla. "We've boiled over. I have to add antifreeze, or at least water, before we can drive anywhere."

"Didn't we pass a garage a while back?" Carla asked. "Or a motel or something? Someplace that might at least have a phone?"

"I don't know," Joe said. "We passed something, but it might have been twenty miles away."

"You can just glide down the hill," Jason said from the back seat. He was eleven and had just recently felt old enough to offer advice to adults. "Just turn around and we'll keep on gliding until we find something."

"Oh, sure," Kerry, his older sister, needled him. "And the brakes will fail and we'll go off the side of a cliff. Besides, we've got power steering and power brakes. Neither of those things works unless the motor is running."

After a half-hour, in which only one vehicle passed, a bus whose passengers apparently thought his appeal for help was simple friendliness and waved at him from the window, Joe was prepared to follow Jason's advice.

"Sure," Kerry said. "Now we'll all die."

"Enough," her mother told her, and that quieted her. Kerry was fifteen and given to unexplained moments of weeping, as if she had suffered some great tragedy but was forbidden to speak of it.

Joe cranked the wheel of the Toyota, and it was much easier to push than he had thought it would be. It also started downhill much faster than he'd expected, and if Carla hadn't pulled on the emergency brake, he would have been left behind watching his family rocket to their fates.

In the Garden of the Medicis

"I'm going to go quite slowly," Joe told the family. "Look for signs. Sometimes there are places that you don't notice until the last second."

And it happened in that way. They had drifted slowly downward for about five minutes when Carla saw a small sign that would have been unreadable to anyone going faster than five miles an hour. It read "Garden of the Medicis" and it marked an almost invisible road that led steeply down. Joe turned without hesitation, and the Toyota bounced over the uneven gravel path. There were hairpin bends he could hardly negotiate and, before long, the brakes were beginning to smell.

There better be something at the bottom, Joe thought to himself, or we'll never get out of here. All that stood between his family and starvation was a couple of Cokes and a large bag of tortilla chips.

There was something at the bottom. A stunning mountain lake that appeared to be half blue and half green with a blur of pink in the centre. They caught glimpses of it through the trees, and, just as they made the final turn, it opened before them in all its glory.

"Wow," Kerry said. "No boats, no cottages, no anything. Just water and sand." The Toyota eased to a final stop just at the very edge of a large sandy beach.

"At least there's water," Joe said. "I can probably get the car started, though I don't know if we'll ever climb out of here without boiling over again."

They all got out to look at the lake, and Jason discovered another sign that said: "Garden of the Medicis," with an arrow that pointed down a narrow path along the shore.

"We may as well find out what it is," Carla said, and they walked single file through the ferns and shrubs that surrounded the pathway. After just a minute of walking, they rounded a little headland and came on another bay and sandy beach. Here, a garish pink building with a false front and a high fence proclaimed itself the "Garden of the Medicis" in ornate lettering. A string of coloured lights hung just above the fence, and a gate that was framed with pillars so that it looked ancient and Roman and was locked with a padlock. The windows of the main building were boarded over, and though a sign on the door said "Open," the building was locked.

Joe rapped on the door, but there was no answer. He rapped again, and a voice from behind them said, "No use knocking. It's closed."

The voice came from a young man of indeterminate age. He might have been in his early twenties, but he might also have been much younger. He wore shorts and a white T-shirt with a baseball cap turned backwards. He was barefoot.

"What is this place?" Jason asked. He seemed to have decided in favour of the man's youth, and there was nothing of awe or respect in his voice.

The young man didn't answer for a while. His eyes were a startling green. "It's a resort," he said finally. "Or at least it used to be. It's been closed for years. I'm the caretaker." Then, as if he had decided that they posed no threat, he confided, "It's just a summer job. I watch that nobody vandalizes the place or sets it on fire or anything. Apparently it was really popular around the time of the First World War, but it's been closed for about ninety years."

Joe turned back to the building. He noticed that what he had first thought was a decorative motif on the pillars of the gate was actually real grape leaves.

The young man's name was Tomaso, and he was working his way through university. He didn't really know much about the place. He'd answered an ad in the newspaper, and the next thing he knew, he was here. Once a week, a truck came by and left him supplies, but the rest of the time, he just read the novels he had brought with him. He helped Joe fill up the radiator with water and waved goodbye as they started up the hill.

About a hundred yards further, the steam from the engine made it impossible to see at all. This time Joe noticed the hole in the hose from which the steam issued. Tomaso could think of no solution. He had no phone, and the truck did not come until Thursday, another four days. He had plenty of food, though, and if they wanted to camp, he'd be glad to help out. The kids loved the idea, and even Carla seemed content.

"You wanted something unspoiled," she said. "You're not going to get much better than this."

They set up their tent back on the first little bay near the car. The kids wanted to set up by the Garden of the Medicis where Tomaso had his tent, but Joe had noticed a bit too much eagerness on Kerry's part, and he wasn't prepared to be caught in the middle of the fantasy of a summer's romance. She was certain to fall in love with Tomaso, and then she'd weep all the way to Vancouver when they left.

Tomaso brought over a bunch of wieners and stale buns, and they ate hot dogs. Joe took out a couple of lawn chairs, and he and Carla read in the shade of an old ponderosa pine. Tomaso and the kids went swimming, Kerry in a bikini, which Joe would certainly have banned if he had seen it before that moment. Then the sun slipped behind a mountain, and though it was only four o'clock, the air was suddenly cold.

Tomaso brought cans of ravioli, and they cooked it in a frying pan over an open fire. Everybody agreed it was one of the finest meals they had ever eaten. Finally, Tomaso said good night and disappeared into the path along the edge of the lake.

He'd be back with breakfast, he said.

Sometime in the night, Joe awoke to the faint sound of music. When he got out of the tent, he could no longer hear it. The night was starry and clear, and the lake was entirely silver. Joe walked to the edge of the lake and dipped his toe. To his surprise, the lake was warm. On an impulse, he slipped off his pyjamas and waded in. The water was as soft and pure as silk. It got deep quickly, but it seemed to have more buoyancy than water should have. Joe had never thought of himself as a good swimmer, but now he moved with ease, slicing his way through the water.

He aimed for the point of land that separated the Garden of the Medicis from the campsite. It was a long swim for him, but he wasn't far from shore, and he could always return along the beach. He rolled over and eased into a gentle backstroke. He felt he could go on for hours. When he thought he must be past the point, he rolled over to see the shore brilliantly lit by hanging lanterns. A shape loomed out of the lake in front of him, and as it passed, he realized it was a gondola, a dark figure in a striped shirt poling it, and lovers clasped in each other's arms at the far end. The music was unmistakable now. Figures flitted along the beach, and he could hear the ripple of laughter above the music. He could make out other craft now, and a barge, brightly lit and decorated with flowers, was anchored in the centre of the bay.

Joe swam in to the shore. As soon as he left the water, he was intensely conscious that he was naked, so he kept very close to the line of trees. A couple came down the beach, and he hid behind a tree as they passed. The man was wearing an elegant three-piece suit with a striped tie and a white shirt, but he was barefoot. The tie-pin and cufflinks gleamed against the darkness of the lake. The woman wore a long white gown and a tiara. She, too, was barefoot. They stopped directly in front of Joe, and the man took the woman in his arms.

"It'll be over in three months," the man told the woman. "That's what everybody says. If I don't go, how will I ever live with myself later?"

"Just don't get yourself killed," the woman said. "They say the Ramsay boy got killed in France a couple of weeks ago."

"I won't get killed," the man said. "Three months. That's a promise." And he folded her in his arms and kissed her. Joe thought the woman was the most beautiful person he had ever seen, and he felt embarrassed at witnessing the intimacy before him. He found the path just back of the beach and continued down it to the Garden of the Medicis. The building was ablaze with light, and dozens of teams of horses still hitched to elegant coaches and wagons stamped their hoofs and whinnied on the night air.

Joe edged his way to the beginning of the fence, then plunged into the undergrowth and followed the line of the fence to a spot where he could climb the low branches of a tree and see over.

Inside was what seemed the balcony of a ballroom. Through a set of open doors, Joe could see dancers whirling to the music of an orchestra. Women with fans cooled themselves behind the pillars of the balcony. Joe listened intently to hear what they were saying, but all he could make out was "The Count. The Count."

Then a man dressed in an elaborate costume that looked like something from a Shakespearean play appeared, accompanied by a tall elegant woman in a jewelled gown. The woman looked amazingly like Carla. Her hair was swept up in an elaborate coiffure that showed off the lines of her neck. A small page in a black uniform with ruffled sleeves brought them glasses of wine on a silver tray. The page looked remarkably like Jason. Joe wished he could get closer, but any further movement would reveal him naked to the dancers.

"Anything you wish, my dear," the Count said. "But it must look like an accident. We shall report him as drowned." These words came sharply and clearly, but it was impossible to hear what the woman answered. The count and the woman followed the page back into the ballroom.

For a while there was no one, only the whirl of distant dancers and the music. Then a young couple emerged from a doorway below the balcony. Joe had not noticed it before. They were laughing, and the young man tried to kiss the woman, who twisted away and ran towards the fence where Joe was hiding. In the light from a lantern, their faces were clear. The young woman was Kerry and the man was Tomaso. He was dressed entirely in black and she in a wispy white dress. He caught her just below the branches of Joe's tree and this time she did not resist his kiss.

"Kerry," Joe shouted. "What are you doing?"

The lovers looked up at the tree and discovered Joe there in all his nakedness. The woman he had thought was Kerry screamed, and in a moment the lawn in front of the balcony was filled with running figures. Joe slipped out of the tree and made his way back through the undergrowth, not daring to walk either on the path or on the beach. Branches whipped into his eyes, and he stepped on sharp roots and stones. There were cobwebs everywhere.

Finally, he made it back to the campsite. He picked up his pyjama bottoms where he had let them fall by the lake, and he put them on. He checked the kids' tent. Kerry and Jason were both sound asleep in their sleeping bags. Carla snored gently in the larger tent. Joe rummaged through his suitcase and found the half bottle of rye he kept there, and he took a long draw directly from the bottle.

The next morning, Tomaso arrived with breakfast, Aunt Jemima pancake mix and some emergency powdered eggs.

Joe asked him if he had heard anything odd last night. Tomaso had. Something, probably a bear, had been crashing around in the underbrush. He'd gone out to check and saw what looked like a naked man, though of course that was impossible. Some trick of the moonlight.

After breakfast, Joe asked Tomaso if they could look inside the Garden of the Medicis.

"I'm not supposed to," Tomaso said. "That's the one rule. I mustn't let anyone in or else I get fired. Besides, there's nothing there to see. Only a few old models in costumes and some ratty furniture. There's a window around the back you can see through if you want, but even I am not allowed to go in there."

By early afternoon, Carla had decided to take a nap, Jason was building a fort, and Tomaso was watching Kerry in her bikini, and not likely to move until she gave up swimming. Joe took a pail from the car and announced he was going to pick huckleberries. Nobody paid any attention to him.

The window around the back was just where Tomaso had said it was. Through the window, Joe could make out tattered furniture and obscure figures in the shadows. The window was locked with a small clasp. Joe took out his Swiss army knife and twisted the clasp. The wood was rotten, and the clasp came out easily. Joe put it in his pocket and crawled through the window into the shadowy room.

The room was apparently a storeroom. Old flowered sofas were piled on top of each other, but they were covered with sheets and appeared to be in better shape than the dust and cobwebs would lead you to expect. Chairs were piled haphazardly, and all along one side of the room costumes hung from hooks on the wall. Like the sofas, the costumes were protected by sheets, and were in much better condition than Joe had expected. He took down a brown three-piece suit that looked like the one the barefoot man on the beach had worn, and tried the jacket on. It fit him perfectly. A batch of parasols stood upside down in an elephant's-foot basket. Ornate gilt mirrors and lamps were propped between the other items.

The figures that Tomaso had mentioned were gathered near a staircase that led upwards. They appeared to be made from papier-mâché, and much of the paint had chipped from them. There were six figures in all, and they represented the serving classes: a cook, a waiter, two maids, a pageboy and a butler. It seemed that the Garden of the Medicis had once been a museum. The top of the stairway was much brighter than the room below, as if it were lit by electric lights.

It was sunlight that lit the room, Joe discovered when he entered it. The stairway led to the ballroom he had seen from his tree the night before. The ballroom was much larger than seemed possible when you looked at the building from outside. Here, figures were gathered in groups. The musicians, complete with instruments, were frozen in mid-song at the far end of the room. Couples swooped and dipped in an elaborate minuet. These figures were far better made than the ones below. They were exquisitely shaped from some material that Joe could not identify. At first glance it looked like wax, but the surface, when you touched it, had all the softness of skin. There was not a speck of dust or a cobweb anywhere.

The Count and the woman Joe had seen with him the night before stood in the opening of the balcony. Seen more closely, the female figure's resemblance to Carla was superficial. It was about the same size with the same colour hair, but the eyes were different. The small page who presented them with wine did look like Jason, but only in the way that an army of small boys in uniform would resemble each other. The expression on the Count's face seemed to be rage. His eyes followed Joe in an eerie way as Joe moved about the room.

From the balcony, Joe could see the tree in which he had hidden the night before. His hiding-place in daylight was obvious, impossible to miss. On the lawn, the figure he had taken to be Tomaso chased Kerry's double in a parody of young love. In a dimmer light, it might be possible to mistake them for the real thing.

Joe was about to leave when he noticed a door behind the musicians, leading to an alcove. He slipped behind the curtains that separated the musicians from the room, and entered. There the beautiful woman he had seen on the beach leaned in a gesture of mourning and grief over a figure who lay on a hospital bed. The figure was dressed in full military uniform, but his chest was covered with blood, and an open hole showed that he had been shot through the heart.

Joe leaned over to see whether the figure was the one he had seen on the beach, the man who had promised to return in three months. It was like looking into a mirror. The face that stared up at him was clearly his own.

On his way back to the camp, Joe decided to confront Tomaso. Tomaso obviously knew more than he had let on. Someone tended those figures daily. Someone vacuumed the dust and the cobwebs, and polished the instruments of the musicians. On an impulse, he turned back and examined the earth in front of the Garden of the Medicis. The prints of horses were everywhere, and the tracks of wagons led up a path into the forest.

Tomaso was not there when Joe arrived. He had told the children that part of his duties included checking on a cabin on the other side of the lake, and he had taken a canoe and paddled off. He had offered to take Kerry for a ride, but Carla had vetoed that plan, and now Kerry was weeping gently in the tent.

"There are no ripe huckleberries yet," Joe told Carla, but he didn't tell her about his visit to the Garden of the Medicis.

"At nine o'clock tomorrow morning the truck comes with the supplies," Carla told him. "Then we can get away from here. It's beautiful and everything, but there's something very strange about this place. I don't think I like it."

Tomaso did not come back with supper, as he had promised, and everyone was a little hungry and a little cranky by dark. Kerry was certain that Tomaso had drowned, and wanted to set out to rescue him. Joe explained that there was no way to rescue him since they had no boat, and Kerry went back to the tent and wept some more.

When the music started that night, Joe vowed to resist it. By nine the next morning, they would be gone, and whatever ghosts inhabited the Garden of the Medicis could go on without him. But the image of the woman looking down at his own dead body haunted him, and he couldn't sleep. He rolled over to put his arm around Carla, seeking comfort, but she was gone. Her sleeping bag was empty. He would probably find her, unable to sleep, sitting on a rock near the beach. He would tell her about the Garden of the Medicis.

But she was not on a rock near the beach. She was nowhere to be found. He looked into the kids' tent on the off chance that one of them was sick and she had gone to comfort them and fallen asleep. The kids' tent, too, was empty. He called their names into the darkness, but no one answered. The distant sound of violins drifted around the point.

Joe put on his bathing suit and walked down to the edge of the water. There was no moonlight, but the stars alone made the lake bright. The water was warm and as smooth as silk. Joe swam steadily until he rounded the point. The scene was nearly identical to what he had seen the other night. Boats flitted back and forth across the water, and people partied on a barge anchored in the bay. Joe swam to land right at the point and made his way along the beach to the brilliantly lit building at the centre of the bay. He heard the whinny of a horse and knew that the carriages were waiting in front. He crept along the fence until he reached the window he had pried open earlier. It swung open now with only the slightest creak.

The light pouring down the staircase from above made the room brighter than it had been during the day. Joe found the three-piece suit he had tried on earlier, and he put it on now. It fit perfectly, and once he had put on the white shirt, the tie, the tie-pin and the cufflinks, he thought he must be indistinguishable from the man he had seen on the beach. He couldn't find any shoes, but he consoled himself that the other man had also been barefoot.

Joe took a deep breath and walked up the stairs into the ballroom. The dancers swirled around so that he had to move back to the wall to avoid being hit. They were dressed in a strange assortment of costumes. Many of the women wore elaborate gowns, but some wore simple pleated white skirts and light sweaters. Flappers, Joe thought. That's what the costume was. Some of the men were dressed as courtiers, but most were in suits very much like Joe's own. Several wore army uniforms.

Joe made his way around the ballroom until he came to the balcony. The Count was standing with his back to the railing, talking to a tall blonde woman.

"It's settled," the Count told her. "Tonight's the night. And it will be perceived as a drowning."

"But won't there be an investigation?" she asked.

"They may investigate all they want," the Count replied. "There will be nothing here for them to investigate."

Just then a small page brought them each a glass of wine.

He handed them the wine on a silver platter, then turned and walked right past Joe into the ballroom. The page was Jason. There was no doubt about it. He looked directly into his father's eyes but gave no hint of recognition.

The Count and the woman turned to go back into the ballroom, and the woman was certainly Carla. In the afternoon, when her features had been frozen, it had been difficult to tell, but now there was no doubt. As soon as they had left the balcony, Joe walked to the railing and looked over. A young couple were in a tight embrace under the tree in which he had sat naked the other night. They pulled apart reluctantly, and in the light that poured from a window he identified them positively. Kerry and Tomaso.

Joe thought he should do something, but there didn't seem to be anything he could do. The music surged and the dancers whirled. From one window, he could see the boats on the lake and the lights from the barge. He moved past the musicians to the alcove where he had seen the woman and the representation of himself, but it was empty. From the window, he could see the teams of horses in front, and a little higher up the bank, Tomaso's tent.

Suddenly, a woman was in his arms. The woman from the beach who had mourned him that very day.

"You're alive," she said. "I saw you dead only a few hours ago, but you're alive."

"No," Joe said. "It's all a mistake." But the woman silenced him with her lips, and he kissed her back, a long, slow, delirious kiss. Then she moved back a little so that she was staring into his face.

"Let me look at you," she said.

Joe looked back at her, but over her shoulder he could see Tomaso's tent and the horses and drivers. People were beginning to leave the Garden of the Medicis and climb into the carriages. One by one, they drove off into the darkness. Then the sun came over the mountain and Tomaso came out of his tent. He stretched languidly and walked out of sight as if to meet someone. In a moment he was back, and a truck towed Joe's Toyota into the clearing. Tomaso and the other man did something under the hood, then Tomaso started the car. Carla appeared then, and from a distance, it looked as if she had been weeping. Jason climbed into the back seat of the car, and Kerry walked over to Tomaso and kissed him a gentle goodbye kiss. Joe could hear their voices, but the only word he could make out was "drowned."

Then a man in a bathing suit rushed into the clearing and Carla flung herself into his arms. Joe couldn't be sure, but it looked like the man he had seen barefoot on the beach. He wished he could move closer to the window, but the woman in his arms was motionless and he didn't dare disturb her. The man in the bathing suit got into the car, and it followed the truck up the pathway the horses had used the night before.

The road up the mountain was even steeper than the road down. The Toyota choked, and the man driving was afraid it might start to boil over again, but after a minute it seemed like the repair was going to work. The children were silent in the back seat.

"You know something?" the man in the driver's seat said, and then he hesitated.

"What?"

"Never mind," he said. He was sure there was something he had to tell his wife. He felt that something terribly important had happened at the Garden of the Medicis, something that would change everything, but he couldn't quite remember what it was. They rounded a bend and popped out onto the highway. He turned on the radio and the car filled with the sound of violins.

Southern Cross

The dogs howled all night. Their din was a comfort to Michael. They reminded him that he was alive. Sarah slept beside him, a heavy lump in the bed. The neighbour's motion-sensor light came on every few minutes, a skunk or a rabbit, or maybe only the leaves on a willow rustling in the breeze that had blown from the south for days now.

A south wind meant low water. Not that it mattered. He hadn't been out on the lake for a dozen years, but he couldn't help searching the sky for signs. He was irrationally happy when the fishing was good.

Now he lurched out of bed and down the hall to the bathroom. His ankles and his knees betrayed him, full of pain. He thought he might fall, but he didn't. His tongue was thick, the taste in his mouth metallic, a sure sign that he had drunk too much. He urinated loudly into the centre of the bowl, shook carefully so as not to dribble onto the floor. The old man's trick, dribbling incontinently, and he wasn't ready for that yet.

The red light on the television in the bedroom had said

259

five o'clock, too early to get up, but not much chance for more sleep. He opened the medicine cabinet and extracted an aspirin from the bottle. Sometimes that worked, and if it didn't help the hangover, at least it was an investment in avoiding a heart attack. As an afterthought, he also chewed a Tums, not because he actually needed one, but as a hedge against indigestion when he got back to bed.

He had turned out the light and was almost into bed before it hit him. Billy had cancer. Forty-four years old, and he was going to die in a stupid, humiliating way. Billy had told him just a few hours ago. As if it were something he had to apologize for, something that had happened as a result of an oversight or carelessness. It was already in his lungs and his liver. The doctor had recommended against even bothering with chemotherapy.

"I haven't got anybody," Billy said the next day over beer. "I'm going to leave it all to you." Then, as he realized there wasn't actually very much, he added, "Such as it is."

"Shit, Billy, don't talk like that," Michael said. "This has all got to be some sort of mistake. You're only forty-four."

"As soon as you're born, you're old enough to die," Billy said. "They're giving me six months, but the doctor admitted that I'd be lucky to make three. And the damnedest thing is, I still feel fine."

"Billy, you're not going to die," Michael said. "The world is a shitty place, but it's not that shitty."

"Australia," Billy said. "I always wanted to go to Australia."

"Well, go," Michael said. "Don't leave anybody any money. Take it and go to Australia."

"It don't work that way," Billy said. "There isn't any money till I die. It's all insurance. I got to be dead for anybody to get at that money, so you got to go for me."

There was thirty thousand dollars in insurance and Billy's

Dodge van, which was actually worth nearly as much, and was also insured so that when he died it was all paid up. Billy died fast, but he died in horrible pain. At the end, he could only speak in whispers, and when Michael answered in a whisper, Billy told him to smarten up.

At the end, Billy would talk about nothing but Australia. He seemed to have an enormous amount of information about the country. "You go to Fiji on the way, and then you spend a couple of weeks in New Zealand," he said. "Then you fly to Tasmania, and you work your way north, up to Cairns and the Daintree Forest. You got to go see the Cathedral Fig Tree."

Billy didn't seem to realize that he was actually going to die, or else he didn't quite know what it meant. He seemed to think that after he was dead and Michael had gone to Australia, they would get together and talk about it. "The Ulysses butterflies," he'd say. "Great big buggers, so blue you can't even imagine it. I can hardly wait." And in the end, he went to die with some cousin in Brandon, and Michael wasn't there to see him through.

Sarah didn't want to go. "We can use the money for a house," she said. "I got my job at the hospital. If I quit, I'll never get another job like that."

"This isn't a choice," Michael told her. "We didn't get the money to buy a house. We got the money to go to Australia. If we don't go, I'll just flush it down the toilet."

But it wasn't as easy as that. Sarah dug in her heels and refused to go. She didn't even like the idea of Australia. If Michael wanted to go, he could have a divorce, but she wasn't budging.

And whoever was bluffing lost. Michael found himself with his separation papers in his pocket along with the ticket to Australia. He hadn't travelled much, once to Toronto on a chance of getting a job in Windsor that didn't work out, and another time to Calgary when his team won the provincial mixed curling. Now he stood in the airport in Nadi talking to a drunken engineer who thought they should get a place together in Suva.

"Sorry," Michael told him. "I've already booked a place down along the Coral Coast." And he went off to meet the mini-bus that would take him to the Fijian beaches, where the pictures showed surf riding in on silver sand.

Along the way, children in uniforms waited for buses, young women in brown or blue dresses with yellow or red scarves. Young boys in suits with caps. There were palm trees everywhere, curving trees with fronds, and giant ferns at the side of the road. The houses were mostly shacks, and old men and women shuffled in their yards, although it was still only seven in the morning.

The hotel was like something out of a fairy tale, but a Japanese fairy tale. There were silver beaches and stunning waves and palm trees and slow-moving Polynesians saying *bulu* all the time, but everyone there was Japanese except for two Australian couples, and Michael was too shy to speak to them. He spent a week in silence except for replying *bulu* to the help and describing the meal he would eat.

New Zealand was better, but Michael still couldn't enter things. The people were friendly and the country was beautiful, but he was going to Australia and he didn't want to take any chances with New Zealand. It was like being married and having a beautiful woman invite you up to her place for coffee. You wanted to go, but something told you it would be a mistake. He remembered the separation papers in his pocket, but they didn't help. It was Australia or nothing.

He rented a car and drove around the Coromandel Peninsula, then up to Rotorua and down to Wellington. He got to Wellington six days early, and he rented a motel as close to the airport as he could. Then he found a spot on the beach where a sign warned that penguins were crossing. He sat there all day for six days, but he never saw a single penguin. Maybe it was the wrong season.

It was raining when his plane pulled into Hobart. Nobody in the airport seemed to know who they were waiting for. They all held signs that read "Auntie Mabel," or "George Day," or "Bishop Andrews." Michael was tempted to claim an identity and have his hand shaken and be ushered out into a waiting car and driven to a meeting of the synod or a family reunion or an early morning business briefing. But he took a taxi instead and went to the Sheraton Hotel overlooking the harbour. In the little magazine shop, he heard a voice that sounded Canadian asking for Tums, but he walked away before he saw who owned it.

That night, he sat in his room drinking Scotch and looking over the harbour. A liner had drifted in at dusk, and it was all lit up and reflected in the water of the harbour. Michael tried to count the lights and estimate how many people were on it. A small town, he figured, and not such a small one at that.

The next day was a Saturday, and he could see the people from the liner massing inside a fenced-off area and moving through a set of gates. Beyond them were the tops of tents and an array of colours that suggested celebration. A circus, he guessed.

It was not a circus, but the Salamanca market, they informed him at the hotel desk. A bellboy or something, a man who seemed in charge and wore a label saying something in French, directed him to the market. It was only a couple of blocks away.

The market was a thriving collection of people selling the kinds of things you found in flea markets, leather and wood and possibly antique pottery, sandals and stuffed animals in the shape of kangaroos and Tasmanian devils. At the centre was a group of Vietnamese gardeners with wonderful vegetables and strange carved wooden boxes. The liner seemed to be Swedish, but all the passengers were German, and the lyric growl of German was everywhere on the air.

At the far corner, just where the German travellers entered, was a table with a couple of frail elderly women. The sign on their table advertised bushwalks. But only for people over fifty. Michael had turned fifty a couple of weeks ago, and he had not yet sampled the special delights reserved for those lucky travellers in time. The women thought he was from the liner, but he told them no. They said that every week they invited someone from another country to join them for a walk in the country. They only accepted six people, but nobody at all had applied today. Did he want to come tomorrow for a walk up a mountain?

He went. They were so pleasant, and he hadn't realized until that moment that he was lonely and he missed Sarah. Since he had left Canada he had felt unstable, floating on the surface, and he was looking for an anchor.

He found his anchor almost before the group had gathered. She didn't look remotely like she was fifty, she laughed almost incessantly, and she had spent ten years in Nanaimo. She was forty, somebody's niece just in from Sydney for the weekend, and she took Michael's hand when they were crossing a small stream on the side of a mountain. His fingers felt as if they had been set on fire. Canada was a great place to visit, she told him, but she was Australian to the core, and she didn't intend to leave the continent again. She extended her vacation for a week, and when she left for Sydney on a Monday morning, Michael was with her, as hopelessly in love as if he had been fifteen.

She was a nurse. One of the last remaining nurses in

Australia, she said. The government had shut down so many hospital beds that nurses were considered an endangered species, like the Tasmanian tiger and the koala. She took Michael to her tiny flat in an area called the Grange, not far from the university. The area was full of little restaurants where you brought your own wine and they uncorked it for you.

Her name was Melba. As in Melba toast, she told Michael. As in peach Melba. Every morning, she went off to work in a hospital, and Michael took bus tours and walked around King's Cross and Circular Quay and took pictures of the Japanese at the Sydney opera house who were taking videos of him. On the weekend, Melba took him out to Bondi Beach and they watched the surfers come crashing in on the surf.

Finally, she asked him what his plans were. He'd been living with her for over a month and seemed, she said, to have no plans at all. She was right. Michael had stopped planning beyond the next day. Even that was an effort. He preferred to get up and get on a bus and see where it took him.

"I guess I'll go back to Canada," he told her. He had been dreaming of skating on the lake, white as far as you could see in any direction. "Why don't you come with me? We could get married or something."

"No," she said. "I'm staying right here. I've been in Canada long enough to know that I don't want to live there. Now, if you decided to stay in Australia, that might be a completely different thing. A carpenter can get a job anywhere."

Michael agreed to think about it for a week, but he knew by the next morning that he was not going to stay. Everything was fine in Australia, but it was only scenery. It didn't have anything to do with him.

"I'm going back," he told Melba. "But first I've got to go to Cairns and the Great Barrier Reef and the Daintree Forest. Why don't you come with me? We could

have a holiday, and maybe one of us will change our mind."
He remembered his promise to Billy, and he intended to fulfil
it, but it wasn't something he could talk to her about.

"It'll have to be you who changes," she said. But she went
anyway. She got ten days off, and they flew up to Cairns and
rented a car, a little blue Daihatsu. They found a place to stay,
a collection of cabins right on the beach in Yorkey's Knob,
just north of Cairns. The woman from whom they rented the
place called them "bures."

"Must be an Australian word," Michael said, but Melba
had never heard it before either. The cabins had no windows,
only metal screens, and though the days were lovely, it rained
all night, every night. Coconuts and giant black beans fell
from the trees onto their tin roof, and the sound was like can-
non balls. It was like being shelled by artillery. Michael was
worried that a coconut might fall on his head, but Melba told
him that never happened, and he believed her, even though
one morning they found a coconut floating in the swimming
pool. He was starting to dream of snow, large soft flakes and
the way light looked through them.

The days were hot, so hot that sweat poured off Michael
whenever he moved, but he loved the heat. He wore a Tilley
hat and smeared himself with sunblock. Everything that was
different about this place reminded him of home. The swel-
tering rain forest made him think of cool dark spruces. The
bougainvillaea reminded him of wild roses.

They went up to the Daintree River and took a tour boat past
mangrove trees and crocodiles sunning themselves on banks.
Thousands of flying foxes hung upside down in the trees, and
when something startled them they darkened the sky, making
sharp, pathetic cries. Pythons were curled in the lower branches,
and the boat came so close to one that Michael thought he might
have reached out and pulled it out of the tree.

Then they went up the Mossman Gorge where the air was so moist that everything, even the leaves and bark on the trees, was damp. There were warnings everywhere of the danger of swimming in the river, but it was full of swimmers nevertheless. Michael thought they might be German, though he had no reason for thinking so except that they were blond and looked in good physical health. They watched for a long time until four swimmers decided to brave the rapids. One of them, a girl of about seventeen, lost her nerve and clung to a rock. The others disappeared down the river and around a bend, and they didn't come back. A half-hour later she was still clinging to the rock. Michael shouted to her, did she need help? She said no, everything was fine, and so they left her there. On the way out, Michael went down to the rapids to feel the temperature of the water. It looked clear and cold, but it was hot, as hot nearly as the water that comes from a tap.

Michael thought he might be able to live in the tropics, but Melba wouldn't even think about it. She couldn't stand the heat and the moisture. Michael told her that one Winnipeg winter would cure all her fear of heat, but she didn't want that either. They went shopping in an air-conditioned supermarket, but neither of them liked that.

The day before the holiday was to end, they took a boat out to the Great Barrier Reef. They still hadn't worked anything out. Somewhere out at sea there was a cyclone, and the seas were heavy and churned up, so that even from the windows of the semi-submersible boat, they didn't see very much. They stopped at a tiny island called Michaelmas Cay where thousands of birds were nesting, and huge frigate birds circled over the others, waiting for a nest to be abandoned for an instant. They reminded Michael of the pictures of helicopters hovering in Vietnam. On the way back, dozens of Japanese tourists were vomiting into paper bags. Michael stood out on the deck and got wet, wondering what it would be like to fish in these waters.

The next day, Melba would fly back to Sydney. Michael's ticket would take him back to Canada. They would both leave at nine o'clock in the evening. They spent the day walking along the beach out to where a small river prevented you from going any farther. It looked like a place where you would find seashells, but there were none. Melba wanted to see an estuary crocodile, but there were none of those either. A kookaburra flew into a tree near them and laughed at them in its mournful, crazed way. Then it flew off. Michael looked very carefully at Melba and wondered if he was really in love with her. He'd know as soon as the airplane left the ground, but by then it might be too late.

When they got back to the bure, Melba announced that she was going to take a swim in the salt-water pool. Somebody had seen an estuary crocodile in the swamp beyond the pool. She took her stuff and walked over. Michael stayed behind and read the paper. Apparently absolutely nothing had happened in Canada, though there was a considerable amount about the royal family, and in particular Charles's infidelities.

Michael didn't feel like swimming, but he decided that he'd better make use of his last chance. He put on his trunks and draped a towel over his shoulders. On the way, a Ulysses butterfly tried to alight on his hand. He identified it immediately, because he'd bought a postcard with a picture of one to take home as a souvenir. It was enormous, brilliant blue as if it were lit from inside, and Michael thought about Billy. This was what Billy had wanted, but Billy was buried under the frozen Manitoba earth. Under three feet of snow.

Melba was sitting in a deck chair reading a magazine. Michael swam the length of the pool using a slow butterfly stroke. Then he swam back with a sidestroke. He was on his way to the far end of the pool again using a lazy breaststroke when he saw them. Two brilliant green butterflies and an enormous black one with polka dots on it. Their beauty took his breath away. They danced at the edge of the forest beyond the pool. It was like watching a fire that had escaped from a fireplace and was dancing in the air. He thought to himself, I am going to remember this moment for as long as I live.

"Sure are nice, aren't they?" said a familiar voice from the edge of the pool. Billy was sitting there, his feet trailing in the water.

"You're dead," Michael said. "You are dead, aren't you?"

"Well, no," Billy told him. "Not exactly. I mean, I'm officially dead as far as the government is concerned. But I'm here breathing and eating, if you see what I mean."

"No, I don't," Michael said. "I don't see what you mean at all. You are either dead or you are alive." Billy seemed fully human sitting there. Nothing about him seemed at all like a ghost, and Michael didn't believe in ghosts anyway.

"It's a remission," Billy said. "The cancer went into remission, and so I came here. That sure is a beautiful girl you've got with you."

"Melba," Michael told him.

"Yes, I know. I was talking to her earlier. You know, Michael, I never got married because I could never find the right girl. Now this is exactly the girl I wanted to marry. She tells me you're going back to Canada. That true?"

"Yes. My plane leaves at nine o'clock."

"Then I suppose you won't be upset if I marry her?"

"Have you asked her to marry you?"

"No, no. I've hardly met her. But I'm going back to Sydney, and if you have no objections, I'd like to court her."

Michael looked over at the far end of the pool. The butterflies were still dancing, still as beautiful as before. "No," he told Billy. "You go ahead. But you'll never get her to leave Australia and come to Canada."

"No," Billy agreed, "she can't." A Ulysses butterfly drifted over and landed on Billy's shoulder, a brilliant blue patch. He didn't seem to notice. Michael turned to where the other butterflies had been dancing, but they were gone, and when he turned back to Billy, he was gone as well.

All the way to the airport, they hardly spoke until Melba said, "Well, I guess that's it."

"Yes," Michael said. "Do you regret it?"

"No," Melba said. "It wasn't a thing that had a future. It was just something that happened." Her flight was a few minutes later than his, and she had seen him to the gate.

He kissed her goodbye and just as he was going through the gate to security, he called out to her, "Take good care of Billy."

"What?" she called. "What did you say?" But Michael was already too far away to answer. He followed a crowd of people onto the airplane and found his seat. All the way to Hawaii, and all the way from Hawaii to Vancouver, and all the way from Vancouver to Winnipeg the flight was as smooth as a butterfly.

In Paraguay

In Paraguay the buildings insist on history. They are not content to merely refer to a time that has gone. No, they sit there implacably containing their history, self-satisfied and solid. Eliza Lynch walks through the hallways of the Gran Hotel de Paraguay searching for her lost lover, Lopez, the grand dictator. This place was once her palace. It still is.

From the balcony overlooking her private zoo, I can see monkeys and deer. Eliza is not a ghost. She is as real as you or me, though that's not such a large claim. She refuses to talk to me. The parrots speak, but that's no help since I cannot speak Spanish and they know no English. A tortoise dreams by the edge of the pond.

In Pilar, a dog slept in the middle of the sand street. He raised his head when we approached, but didn't think us important enough for him to move, and so he went back to sleep. We drove up onto the sidewalk to avoid him, or at least we drove where there would have been a sidewalk if Pilar had sidewalks. But it doesn't.

In the wetlands, cows stand up to their waists in water.

They look like strange cow-shaped boats. Yes, I know they don't have waists in the ordinary sense, but you know what I mean. A flotilla of Paraguayan cows. I think they must be eating water lilies, white water lilies, to be precise, though precision is not considered a virtue in Paraguay.

I have apparently stolen the key to room 21, a heavy brass key that reeks of history. The management will be angry. They have gone to great trouble to ensure that keys are not stolen. Each key weighs nearly a pound and is deliberately designed not to fit in a pocket. Nevertheless, I have inadvertently made off with it, though inadvertence is not a defence in Paraguay. There are many statues of martyrs to attest to that.

It is August, and the Lapacho trees are in bloom, purple and pink and yellow and white. In Pilar, a monkey climbed in the high branches of a pink tree where he could look across the river to Argentina. I thought of you then, imagined you climbing high in the branches of a pink tree and yearning for Argentina. I know you don't like that image of yourself, but it was my fantasy, and I can do pretty well what I want in my fantasies. I don't think a lot about other people's feelings when I am imagining things, though normally I am considerate.

And consideration is a virtue in Paraguay. Paraguayans consider carefully the various options open to them, though to tell the truth there are not really that many options. Things are inexpensive in our terms, though of course the Paraguayans themselves have so little money that they cannot buy a lot. Funerals are sombre, but the Paraguayans like a party, especially if there is a gaucho around to barbecue some meat, a leg of lamb, say, or a roast of beef, or a mess of pork ribs, and preferably all of the above with a side dish of guava and some *guaraná* to wash it down.

I know that you are suspicious of altruism, and your argument that people are only good because it makes them feel good is a tough philosophical nut to crack, but I think you are wrong. The crosses in front of the Assembly building where the young martyrs were shot down by the dictator's bullets are a sort of argument, not a particularly good argument, I acknowledge, but better than dreaming of Argentina, of which I have not actually accused you.

When it rains in Paraguay, the water fills the streets, and traffic comes to a stop. Don't wait till the last minute to go to the airport when it has just rained. You will not miss your plane, because the planes do not fly on time in Paraguay, but the tension of fearing that you will be left alone in the airport, dreaming of Argentina, is too much to bear.

The waterfalls! You have not seen waterfalls until you have been to Paraguay!

Paraguay is in early Technicolor. All the colours, whether of buildings or trees or birds, fail. They do not quite reach the point where red could properly be called red, or green, green, or even white, white. Everything in Paraguay is on a blurred edge of becoming, just about there but not quite.

In Paraguay, the shadows have substance. They have weight. A shadow may choose to stay in the same spot for days and nothing you say will convince it to leave. Or there may be no shadows at all.

The birds of Paraguay do not have Latin names. They are given local names that imitate the sounds they make, like *tooratoora* or *kikiki*. It is the great hope of the Assembly of Paraguay that the birds will receive Latin names either late this year or early next year.

Many young women of Paraguay spend their days dancing and gliding. It is of no use to tell them that life is not all dancing and gliding, that there is serious work to be done, equations to be solved and books of poetry to be written. They will dance and glide right past you.

I know of the problem with your knee and the unsightly birthmark on your shoulder. There is nothing I can do about either of them.

The Paraguayans would dance the tango if they could but they cannot, and so they envy the Argentinians. The tango is very sad, they say. Very sad. But they like sadness.

That's why I think you might be happy there. You would like all the failed buildings, the failed dictators, the failed lovers. You could forget about Argentina, just across the river, and even the winters are warm in Paraguay. In Paraguay, nothing much happens, but everything is possible.

And that's all we want, really, the thought that everything might be possible. Don't you think?

Over and Over

And he knew it would never be any different, that he would go on and on, endlessly planning escapes he hadn't the courage to make, endlessly lusting and desiring, endlessly hopeful with the taste of ashes in his mouth. But that's the end of the story, the end of all stories. It's a beginning I'm after, and so I'll start in the middle, after Marion had left him. You wouldn't have cared for Marion anyway, though Tom did, and her leaving had hurt him. At least, he told himself and everyone else who would listen that he had been hurt, though to be perfectly honest, he wasn't so much hurt as paralyzed, numbed, humiliated. I suppose it was the way she had left, the cool precision of her leaving, that had done the damage. She had mixed each of them a drink, Scotch for her, rum and Coke for him. She sat him down in the living room, and over the top of her glass, fixed him with a look of contempt, that, cliché though it may be, was mixed with pity. What she said was, "Tom, I'm in love with Bill Simpson. We've been having an affair for the last eighteen months, and we've decided to move in together."

Tom felt exactly as he had a couple of months ago when he had suddenly realized that he had lost his wallet. It was time for complex emotions, for jealousy and rage, and Tom felt cheated later that the best he'd been able to come up with was curiosity and bewilderment. When had this started? Where? Bill had a wife who was home all the time, had they done it in Tom's bed when he was at work? Who was he going to golf with now that Bill was no longer his friend? Where was he going to spend Christmas? Why? Where had he failed? Who was going to iron his clothes now?

She told him she didn't care to discuss details.

And then she was gone. The house was empty. The closets looked bare and he realized he didn't own very many clothes. She'd taken sausages out of the freezer and placed them, along with two eggs, beside the frying pan. For a moment he felt a swell of affection and self-pity, then he fried the sausages and eggs and ate them.

The next day she came and took the freezer. And the dining room table. She took half of the sectional chesterfield, most of the kitchen appliances and all of the pictures. She left the bed, but she took the dresser, leaving Tom's clothes in a pile on the rug. And then she was completely gone, without leaving an address or a phone number.

Tom phoned Bill's wife. She blamed him. "If you'd kept control of the little bitch, this would never have happened," she said. It was unfair, but she was hurt, Tom told himself, and you couldn't expect her to be polite.

So now, where we begin, three months later, Tom is talking on the telephone to Marion. She has just announced to Tom that she is coming back. She and Bill are spending one last weekend together and she will be back on Monday. Tom, of course, is ecstatic, and finally, also, jealous.

"No. Dammit. If you're coming back, you come back right now. No last weekend."

She reasons with him, what difference can it possibly make, Bill's wife understands, she isn't making things difficult. Tom is adamant. So is Marion. On Monday, Bill drops her off at the house. Tom gets a peck on the cheek, and Marion complains about the terrible mess and starts doing the laundry.

On Tuesday a van arrives, and now they have two freezers, two dressers, two stoves, two kettles, and a whole chesterfield. The pictures Tom has bought during Marion's absence are taken down and hung in the basement.

Things came back to normal with appalling speed. They had dinner with Marion's parents. They shopped together on Saturday afternoons at the Safeway store. They played bridge with the Gibsons and went to parties at the neighbours'. They even picked up their desultory sex life pretty well where they had left off. Marion seemed happy, though she treated Tom with a certain condescension. Tom brooded. He had a used wife. He imagined that people at the parties looked at him with contempt. The word "cuckold" hovered at the back of his mind, and so he combed his hair very carefully.

Then one day he fell in love. It happened like this. Tom worked in a government office, shuffling forms from amateur sports organizations, giving money to some of them and denying it to others. He didn't have his own secretary, but there were several girls whose desks were together in a large ante-room. One or the other would type things for him if she didn't have more serious things to do for higher-ranking people. One of the girls was named Andrea. She had taken a commercial secretary's course in high school, where she had also been an athlete. She had taken a job as a secretary for the Sports Branch under the mistaken notion that in this way she could bring the two things she was interested in together.

It all happened very quickly. Andrea had been in the office for six months, but Tom hadn't noticed her. He was too busy worrying about Marion and Bill to need anything typed. After Marion came back, he decided that he had better do some work, because even in a government office you have to do something or eventually they will fire you.

So, when he looked over all the paper on his desk, it turned out that he needed quite a bit of typing done. Andrea did it. One night she agreed to stay for a couple of hours after work and finish all the letters of acceptance and rejection for rural sports organizations, because they were due the following day. After they finished, Tom offered to drive her home. When they got to her apartment block she said, "You want to come in or something?" Tom didn't know how to answer that, so he followed her into the building. She unlocked the door and led him into a small, messy living room. She turned around and looked at him as if she expected him to say something. Tom didn't know what to say, so he kissed her. Then she took off all her clothes and so did Tom, and they made love right there on the living room floor. It turned out that she had never made love with anyone else before, and that fact, combined with her tiny, powerful athlete's body, was enough. Love struck Tom like a sixteen-pound sledgehammer.

Andrea started working half time, afternoons only. Tom announced he was undertaking a series of field trips to see the amateur sports organizations that applied for money. Every morning they met at Andrea's apartment and made love. They gathered together a little library of books about sexual technique, and worked their way through them. They had picnics with wine and exotic cheeses, and they took baths together, sharing a bottle of champagne as they washed each other. They were cleaner than they had ever been in their lives.

Apparently, the chances of being found out in an adulterous affair are only one in thirty-three, but the odds are considerably worse when the finder-out has already been in one herself and knows the signs. Marion noticed how clean Tom had become. She heard him whistling popular love songs. She noticed that when they went to restaurants, he knew the names of the wines. And, of course, he had completely stopped making love to her, which is always a giveaway.

One day she sat him down in the living room, mixed them each a drink, Scotch for her, rum and Coke for him, and said, "I know you're having an affair with someone. Who is it?"

Tom told her all about Andrea, of course. He was a little proud of himself. He hadn't been able to tell anyone before, and though he couldn't expect Marion to be sympathetic, it was better than keeping it all bottled up. Marion responded much better than Tom had done when it was his turn. She screamed and raged and tried to kill him with a half-full bottle of Johnny Walker Red. She vowed that she would emasculate him with a rusty tin can lid as he slept. Then she ordered him to break up his affair with Andrea.

So he did. He told Andrea it would have to end. She wept but was very reasonable about everything, making no claims and leaving him completely alone. She didn't even talk to him at the office. Tom felt as if his heart and liver had been removed, but he became much better at his job, and got a small promotion.

Then, about six months later, Marion threw him out. In the settlement she claimed the house and all the furniture, and Tom was too exhausted to fight. He called up Andrea instead, and went over and made love to her, but it wasn't the same. Since he had left, she had made love to several of the other men at the office and she knew things Tom hadn't taught her. When they got married, the men from the office chipped in and bought them a gas barbecue, and congratulated Tom heartily. It made him sick, and every time he had to use the barbecue he got into a rage and sulked for the rest of the evening. Finally, they had a garage sale and sold it. Tom bought a little Hibachi, and for a while they were happy, because they both loved barbecues.

Then, one day, Tom noticed how clean Andrea was. She was humming a love song and drinking a glass of white wine from a bottle she had bought herself. And it all started again.

Driving Through Montana

We were driving through Montana, counting the white crosses where people had been killed driving off the road. Susan was sleeping, or pretending to be asleep, it was hard to tell. I negotiated a great curve, seven crosses, two of them doubles. I wanted to wake her up so she could see them, but there wasn't enough time. I added them to my score. Thirty-nine, one with flowers. I was listening to a country and western station, the only kind of station in Montana. A girl was singing, "I got a cowboy in the saddle and another one holding my horse." Then there was a kind of yodel. Susan stirred.

"You hear that song?" I asked her.

"Mnhhh."

"Mnhhh, yes or mnhhh, no," I asked her.

"Mnhhh, yes."

"You think they recognize the erotic implications of the words?"

"Sure. She wasn't yodelling for nothing."

I brooded on the song. The world is full of erotic invitations, but you usually can't do anything about them. Montana

281

was yellow. In the distance there were buttes, the kind you see a horse and rider at the top of, in old western movies.

"I'm going to buy you a horse," I told Susan. "A sorrel mare, spirited but gentle."

"I want a stallion," she said. "A big black stallion named Lightning."

"Don't be disgusting," I answered. Women are like that. You try to be romantic and they turn it into a dirty joke. "I'm going to buy you a sorrel mare so that you can ride to the top of a butte and look over the land below. I'll wait in the truck and watch you, a distant rider outlined against the sky."

"I had this boyfriend," Susan said, "an American. He used to come for skiing weekends, and he'd ask me out. I didn't like him very much, but he was good looking and the only reason I went out with him was because they were always playing 'Canadian Sunset' on the radio, and it made all my friends jealous."

"I don't want to hear about it," I told her.

"Once he asked me to spend a weekend at his college for a big dance they were having."

"I knew a girl once," I told her, "who used to wear chains on her ankles so that she could tear holes in the backs of boy's shirts."

"I didn't go," Susan said. "You don't have to get huffy. I was supposed to stay with his parents anyway."

"I lied about the girl, too. She didn't actually wear chains. She just had long toenails."

"You're a pig, you know. I was telling you an interesting story about my innocent past, young love and all that, and you get foul mouthed."

"You started it," I said. "You and your black stallion."

"I was thinking of Elizabeth Taylor in *My Friend Flicka*."

"OK, I'm sorry. Anyway, we haven't got room for a horse in the duplex."

There are hardly any trees in Montana, and the few there are don't have any leaves. To be fair, there were some trees with leaves beside the rivers, but there aren't a lot of rivers. Susan hunched up the pillow and went back to sleep. I stopped at a bar by the side of the road and bought a six-pack of Coors. It was 94 degrees in Montana, so I opened the window and let in the heat as I drove along drinking my Coors. I tried singing all the cowboy songs I knew, but that didn't take me very far. I know only the first couple of lines of most of them. There were buttes in every direction.

The sun was shining on my crotch, giving me an erection. I pointed this out to Susan, and she said we could fix that later when we stopped to camp.

"It may be gone by then," I pointed out.

"It'll come back, I promise," she said. She took my cap off my head and put it on my crotch.

"There, just keep the sun off it and you'll be OK." She changed the radio to another station where they told us it was going to be 94 again tomorrow. We passed a sign that said "WILLISTON 256."

"Let's have a baby," I said, "a bouncing baby boy that we can dress in a sailor suit. He could follow me around holding my thumb and saying 'Right, Dad?' And when he got bigger we could buy him a pony and an English sheepdog."

"No English sheepdog," Susan insisted. "They shed hair everywhere. And if there isn't enough room in the duplex for my stallion, then there's no room for a pony or a sheepdog. There isn't even room for a bouncing baby boy. Besides, he'd crawl into bed with you when you were hung over and poke his fingers in your eye. He'd vomit curdled milk onto your silk dressing gown when you were walking him to sleep."

"Maybe we should just get a cat."

"Or a trip to Europe. That'd be great. We could look at cathedrals."

"We've already been to Europe. You hated the cathedrals. You said they made your feet sore."

"I only hated them at the time. In retrospect, I love them. Remember the one in Strasbourg with the great soaring steeple?"

"They weren't finished building it. Nine hundred years and they still weren't done."

"It's a big job."

"Yes."

"Hey, there's a tree," Susan said. "Let's count trees."

"You just want to count trees because I'm winning at crosses." The tree actually had some leaves on it, though they didn't look healthy. Montana was still yellow, except for the strip of black road and the few green leaves on the tree.

"You are not," she argued. "I got thirteen crosses when you were sleeping earlier. I just haven't marked them down yet." I hadn't really been sleeping and I knew that she hadn't marked some down, but I thought she had missed them. Actually, I had put them on my own score, but there were only seven, not thirteen. Still, I wasn't in any position to take a moral stance on the issue. We declared it a tie.

"It's a pretty morbid game anyway," Susan said.

"No more morbid than trying to count trees in Montana," I told her. "I'll only play if we just count live trees." A few minutes later we drove into a little valley. You could see the Milk River and the line of green trees that surrounded it.

"Ten thousand," Susan said as we crossed the brim of the hill. "I win." There were quite a few trees, but no ten thousand. I conceded anyway, because I wanted to stop and change drivers.

The lady who served us sandwiches at the roadside bar was from Norway. "It nearly rained in June," she said. "There were about a dozen great big drops on the window, but I haven't seen a cloud since." I asked her about the fjords. She said they weren't what they're cracked up to be. "Once you've seen one fjord," she said, "you've seen 'em all." She'd grown up on a fjord and hated the isolation. "Now here," she said, "it's different. People drop in for a beer and a sandwich from all over the world. Just the other day there were a couple of Russian tourists in here."

I told her I didn't know there were any Russian tourists. I thought they couldn't leave the country.

"Oh, no," she said. "We get them all the time."

I had to go the washroom, because I'd drunk the entire six-pack of Coors. You couldn't use the indoor toilet, because they needed all the water for drinking. The outdoor toilet had COWBOYS and COWGIRLS carved into the doors, but they were clean and smelled of disinfectant.

A little later we passed a sign that indicated we were entering an Indian reservation. Susan was driving. She has long slim legs and one of them was extended so that she could reach the gas pedal. She was wearing shorts, and when the sunlight shone on her legs, I could see tiny golden hairs.

"You have tiny golden hairs on your legs," I told her.

"Go to sleep," she said. "We're going to camp for the night at Wolf Point. It's another sixty miles." The road was better in the Indian reservation than it had been before. The shoulder was paved.

"Do you think it's wise," I asked Susan, "to camp in the middle of an Indian reservation? If I remember my history correctly, several massacres have taken place in this immediate area."

"None recently. Anyway, it's marked with a little green

triangle on the map. It's the only little triangle between here and North Dakota. Unless you want to fork out fifty bucks for a cheap motel."

I would, in fact, have preferred that option, but we had decided that this trip was to be done on the cheap, and I felt a sort of existential commitment to tenting. I'd even bought a little battery-powered light you could hang up in a tent so you could read at night, and I hadn't had a chance to use it.

The campground turned out to be seven miles south of Wolf Point, on the Missouri River. A couple of hundred Indians were holding a party, or perhaps a series of parties. They were divided into several groups, each of which had its own radio and campfire. All the radios were tuned to different stations and were being run at full volume. Nasal voices mourned lost love in every direction. We paid our two dollars and were given a slip of paper to put under the windshield wiper. The man who took our money explained that he was a deputy sheriff, and that he would kick all the Indians out of the campground at ten o'clock. I wasn't sure that was a good idea.

"We are on a reservation," I explained to Susan. "The Indians in this area don't have a history of responding kindly to being kicked off their own land."

"It'll be fine," she said, and it was. At ten o'clock all the Indians left and we turned out to be the only people in the campground. The deputy sheriff drove by a couple of times and shone his spotlight in our tent. Susan took out the cooler and mixed us rum and Cokes and I made sandwiches with the pastrami we had bought in Idaho. Idaho is not particularly known for the quality of its pastrami, and it was soon apparent why.

"This pastrami tastes like rubber boots," Susan said, a hint of accusation in her voice.

I agreed. "It's not up to the *foie gras* we had in Les Voges," I told her, "but the Meyer's dark rum has a certain *je ne sais quoi.*"

"Dark tropical joy," she added. "Caribbean moonlight. Jacinth blossoms. Swarthy lovers."

"Watch the dirty talk," I warned her. "Besides, you've never even been to the Caribbean. You don't even know what colour jacinth blossoms are. You don't even know if they grow there."

"Red," she said. "Great tuberous red blossoms."

I was suspicious. "Are you sure?"

"I'm a woman," she told me. "Knowledge of flowers comes with the territory. Along with perfect discrimination of what colour goes with what other colour, and a soul so sensitive that your poor brute male mind couldn't even begin to grasp its subtlety."

"Let's go in the tent and make love," I suggested, "just to take the edge off that sensitivity."

"You're so gross," she answered. "A woman wants to be wooed and won."

Still, she headed for the tent. I'd hung up my special light, but I didn't feel like reading. The memory of the hot sun in my lap was still close. The ground wasn't very smooth, and even through the foamies you could feel tiny stones. I offered to flip a coin to see who got the top, but Susan insisted that the traditions of gallantry demanded that she have her choice. I conceded, and she chose the top.

A little while later I had reached that perfect state of withheld expectation that makes it all worthwhile. Susan stopped and said, "I wonder whether the zucchini will be ready when we get back."

"We are making love," I reminded her. "We are in the

heat of passion. I don't want to turn this into a disquisition on gourds."

"I'm sorry," she told me. "I'll just finish you off, and then we can discuss the garden."

"I don't want to be finished off," I informed her. "I want a mutual passionate explosion of joy."

"You've been reading too much D.H. Lawrence," she warned me. "I'm not in the mood. I just want to think about the garden for a while and then go to sleep."

"If you're not in the mood, then why are we doing this?" I asked. She didn't answer, but in a few seconds the question was redundant anyway.

"There," she said. "Wasn't that nice?"

I agreed that it had been nice, but pointed out that it would have been a lot nicer if both parties had taken the business seriously. I rolled over to sulk, but I must have fallen asleep immediately, because the next thing I knew, the tent was hot and bright, Susan was gone, and I could smell bacon and eggs.

I crawled out of the tent, blinking. A few yards away, some woman was washing her car. "Where did you get the bacon and eggs?" I asked Susan. She was wearing a halter and a pair of white shorts and looked amazingly fresh and beautiful. I decided to forgive her for last night.

"They've got a little store here that sells groceries," she said. "Sorry about last night. It's just Montana isn't a great place for passion. We'll do better in North Dakota."

I apologized too. We don't have any rule about it, but we usually both apologize at the same time. The bacon and eggs were great, though we didn't have any coffee. We picked up some coffee in Styrofoam cups in Wolf Point, and headed east into the rising sun. Montana was still yellow. The buttes were lower and farther away, and the air was full of grasshoppers. The radio announced that it was already 94 degrees.

"I'm pregnant," Susan announced.

"When did this happen?" I asked.

"Last night."

"You can't tell if you're pregnant that fast," I informed her. "You have to go to a doctor and have tests. It has something to do with a dead rabbit."

Susan was adamant. "I'm pregnant all right," she said. "The tests will only confirm it."

I asked her if she wanted ice cream and pickles, but she only wrinkled her nose in disgust. A sign by the side of the road said North Dakota five miles. I asked whether it was a boy or a girl. Susan said it was a boy, and I told her I'd prefer a girl. "Too late," she said. "You should have thought of that last night. Now you'll have to wait until the next one."

Just then we came over a rise and an enormous sign said "North Dakota." The grasshoppers had disappeared. The grain by the side of the road was thick and green, not yet ripe. There were trees everywhere, shimmering green in the bright, clean morning light. Roses and morning glories bloomed along the fence line. A small lake shone brilliant blue in the distance. Everywhere birds skimmed in the air. I turned to Susan. Her long blonde hair was golden in the sunlight, her skin was as white as ivory, her stomach already beginning to swell. She leaned over to whisper to me. "Hurry home," she said, "It's almost time."

The truck was lighter now. The wheels barely touched the road as we swept into North Dakota. Behind us, without a sound, Montana sunk, yellow and dry, into the faded and disappearing west.

Do Astronauts Have Sex Fantasies?

Do astronauts have sex fantasies? They must, of course, but has this been taken into account by the planners of space missions? Is any provision made for masturbation during long flights? What would be the effect of gamma rays on a foetus conceived and delivered in space? Is anybody in charge of this kind of investigation? We know these things are too important to be left to chance, but how are we to find out what's going on?

And what about the greenhouse effect? The melting of the polar ice caps will mean the flooding of New York and London, but isn't that a small price to pay for bananas in Manitoba? Who is going to work on the plantations in the Northwest Territories? How many Eskimos are there, and are they willing to pick things? What are we going to do with all those leftover Massey-Harris combines and four-wheel-drive Case tractors?

Are ballet dancers promiscuous? If not, how did all those rumours about them get started? Why do they walk in that funny way, even when they have quit dancing many years ago and now only teach a few of the neighbourhood girls while their husbands, who are lawyers, mix themselves Scotches and watch reruns on TV? Why do they only marry lawyers? Where do they meet these lawyers? Do the lawyers send dozens of long-stemmed roses backstage after the performances, or are there restaurants frequented only by lawyers and ballet dancers?

Is the French language really in danger? Are English words, like viruses, creeping into French and corrupting whole sentences? Why are crêpes tastier than pancakes? How does one become a member of the French Academy? Is it possible that the president of the French Academy is a mole, an Englishman who started working in a lycée in Provence after the war, then slowly worked his way up to a teaching job at the Sorbonne, wrote a couple of books on structural linguistics, and was appointed to the French Academy? Does he dream in English?

Is it true that, because of the principles of natural selection, in eighty years all cats will be tabby? Should a cat be allowed one litter before she is spayed? Is there any way of keeping a spayed or neutered cat from growing fat? Do people think less of you if, instead of naming your cat something interesting like Oedipus or Charles, you simply call it White Cat?

What do well drillers do in winter when the ground is frozen? Do they hang around in rural cafes, having coffee with the electricians and plumbers? When the electricians and plumbers go off to work, do the well drillers hang around and tease the waitresses? Or do they take on odd jobs, cleaning a garage here, mending the shingles there? Do they sometimes wonder whether it is all worthwhile? Are their children proud of them?

How do Marxists in the United States stand up to all the contempt they face? Are they, like dentists, inclined to depression and suicide? When they lie in bed at night, thinking about death and fantasizing about all the opportunities to have sex they have missed, do they think with words like "proletariat" and "praxis"? Do they become suspicious that all their friends are working for the FBI? Are they sometimes grateful that the FBI sends beautiful female spies to seduce them and learn their secrets, women much more beautiful than they would ever have expected to sleep with? Do they sometimes marry these spies and get jobs teaching political science in small mid-western universities?

Is there any money to be made in lawn furniture? The aluminum lawn furniture with plastic webbing always breaks, and the wooden lawn furniture is always uncomfortable, so you'd think there would be room for someone to create a whole new kind of lawn furniture, wouldn't you? Is any research lab working on this question? Are there secret patents, like the patents for gas-saving carburetors which the oil companies buy up and destroy? Are these patents held by the aluminum, plastic and wood industries, while they go on turning out breakable and uncomfortable lawn furniture?

Why are piano tuners so often blind? Why do strong young men, possibly their sons, take them by the arms and lead them to pianos? Are blindness and an ear for music somehow intertwined? And what of those muscular sons, have they any plans for the future? What will they do when their frail, blind fathers die? Will they find other blind men, or will they weep with joy at their release from their fathers' musical obsessions? Will they, perhaps, holiday in Mexico for a month, then go back to school to retrain themselves as bakers or clerks?

And what of love? Must that first fierce passion decay into tolerance and mild aversion? Can love be kept alive by flowers and meals in fancy French restaurants as the newspapers tell us? Are the wealthy happier in love than we? Does regular sex help, even when neither party much cares? Do outside liaisons, amours and affairs help put the spice back in a fading relationship? Do people in the final stages of debilitating cancer still feel lust? Is anybody looking into this?

Where is Chad? Why are the Chaddians fighting one another? What is the gross national product of Chad, or is it so remote and agricultural that it does not even have a gross national product? What do they drink in Chad when they want to get drunk? Does some importer supply them with Scotch and bourbon, or do they make themselves a lusty native beer from the leaves of some native tree? What is the most popular musical group in Chad? Has any Chaddian ever written a novel of manners that chronicles a young man's rise to power?

Are the underground pipes that bring water to our houses made from asbestos? Are things being added to our water that we do not know about? Is some of our sewage seeping into the river? If things are going wrong, as we all suspect, how much money will it cost to set them right? Can we afford not to be poisoned? Does the city council know all these things but not care? Do the councillors keep bottles of pristine water from deep underground springs in their refrigerators at home?

What has become of Kohoutek's comet? Is somebody still keeping track of it, watching it dwindle into space? Do we sometimes lose discoveries because a scientist is making love to his assistant just at the moment when some life-saving but short-lived compound has precipitated in a beaker or petri jar? Who actually buys books of poetry and reads them? What happens to all the paintings of failed artists when they die? Why do you keep smoking when you know what it is doing to your lungs? Why can't you resist that extra glass of wine with supper, that extra glass of brandy after dessert, when you know what it is doing to your liver? Why are you so filled with lust and yearning and desire? Why does your weakness threaten to overwhelm everything you do? Doesn't anybody care?

The Raffle

In Canada, you get a kind of conviction that you can speak French, even if you can't. You get it from the packages, which have English on one side and French on the other. *Mouchoirs* Kleenex. Kellogg's *flocons de blé. Cigarettes filtres.* Mostly, you read French at breakfast, when it's okay to put the packages on the table instead of putting the food into pottery bowls and jugs. You read *orignal,* then turn over the package to find out that it's a moose.

"Why do you read the packages?" Carol asks me. She takes life seriously, and likes to read about massacres, disasters and wars, though she prefers local murders.

"It's the French," I tell her. "I like to read French." Then she takes the package from me and disguises the English side. She makes me try to translate the French and I always get it wrong, even though I studied it at the university and have a certificate from Princeton saying I am fluent.

"It's the wrong kind of French," I tell her. "Ask me something about poetry. Read a description of the Corsican countryside. Let me define *crépuscule* for you."

"No," she says. "If you can't read the cornflakes box, then you can't speak French." She draws fine distinctions, which is what drew me to her in the first place, but she has a mean streak. One of our friends is an anthropology professor. She asked him a question about Claude Levi-Strauss that he couldn't answer. She sniffed in that way some women can sniff, and he hasn't been able to write an article since. He spends all his time studying Levi-Strauss, hoping she'll ask him another question, but she never does. I've begged her to give him another chance. I even picked out questions for her, but she says he's just a big baby, and if he were a real anthropologist he wouldn't be worried.

Orage. That's a thunderstorm. And *guimauve*, I think might be pineapple, though I'm not sure. I'll have to check next time I shop for groceries. I don't like pineapple, or at least I don't like very much pineapple, which is quite a different thing. We live in a French neighbourhood, but nobody will speak French to us. There was even a *quincaillerie* just a few doors down from us until it went broke when the Co-op opened another hardware store across the street. Now the Co-op has gone broke too, and you have to drive all the way into the city to buy wood screws.

I was wrong. *Guimauves* are marshmallows. Pineapples are *ananas*. I told Carol about the story I'm writing and she explained the correct words, even though she doesn't know any French. I told her I was going to demonstrate her innate mean streak. She said that a concern for getting things right was not the sign of a mean streak. She pointed out some of her good points, her generosity, her concern for other people's feelings as long as they didn't pretend they were something they weren't, her admirable restraint in not pointing out to me that I have fallen down in my commitment to do half the housework. I tried to point out that a mean streak was very different from essential meanness, of which I had not accused her. "A mean streak," I told her, "is a kind of aberrant and occasional occurrence, which by its very difference sets off essential goodness." She called it a distinction without a difference, but I think she was quoting somebody.

It was like our discussion of arrogance the other night. She often calls men arrogant, and says she doesn't like them. She called the host of a TV program arrogant last night, and I asked her what she meant. She defined the word perfectly, as good as any dictionary, but I've noticed that she only thinks that physically attractive men are arrogant. I think she finds them sexy but, since she's committed to the women's movement, she doesn't like to admit this, even to herself. I didn't tell her that, because it might be true and I don't want it to be true, and besides, she hates to be psychoanalyzed.

Anyway, the reason I bring this all up is because I won a raffle. It was a French raffle, and apparently I have won the *deuxième prix.* There were three prix, and I am supposed to go over to the church and pick up my *patente.* The problem is, I don't have the slightest idea what a *patente* actually is. I've consulted my *Larousse de poche,* but it doesn't list the word. I even got into the Volkswagen and drove all the way to the public library, but none of the dictionaries includes the word *patente.* And I'm not going to ask Carol, just in case she knows.

I decided to brazen it out. I went to the church and told the priest I'd come to pick up my *patente.* "Oh yes," he said, "just go down to the basement and pick it up." The basement looked as if it had been set up for a garage sale. Tables were covered with assorted objects: toasters, irons, clothes hampers, electric mixers, you name it, it was there. Everything was new, but everything looked like the cheapest model of its kind. There was nothing labelled *patente,* but it was clear that one or the other of these bits of merchandise was my prize. I went upstairs again and was leaving the church when the priest asked me, "Aren't you going to pick up your *patente?*" "No," I told him. "My car's too full. I'll pick it up later." He looked a little bewildered, but he didn't stop me, and I rushed out before I could make a fool of myself.

It's about here I start sounding paranoid. I've never won a raffle before. In fact, I've never won anything in my life, and I'll be damned if now that I've finally won, I'm going to be cheated out of my prize by the failures of the French language. I've got a stubborn streak, or at least that's what Carol says, though I don't think standing up for your rights is a sign of stubbornness. She won't let me repair things in the house anymore, because she says I get into such a foul temper that it's easier to hire someone else.

I went to France once. I couldn't understand any of the conversations that went on around me. If people were talking at the next table, they might just as well have been speaking Urdu or Hindi, but the funny thing was that when I asked for things, they had no difficulty understanding me, and I could hold long conversations with innkeepers and waiters about all sorts of things. I only seemed to be able to speak the language when they were talking directly to me.

I even learned a French joke once. It was about three kittens floating down a river on a log. The log tipped over and *un deux trois* cat sank. French people don't think that joke is funny. At first they don't understand it, and when you explain, they never laugh. They seem to take their language very seriously, and they don't like people making fun of it.

Carol likes really expensive clothes. She doesn't believe in sales, because, she says, what you really get is either cheaper merchandise that looks like the real thing or clothes with flaws in them. She claims she can pick out people wearing clothes that were bought on sale. Most of the labels in her clothes are written in French. She says it's better to have fewer good clothes than a lot of cheap ugly clothes. I pointed out once that her closet was as full as anyone else's, but she said it just proved her point. Expensive clothes last longer.

She's not going to like my *patente*, whatever it turns out to be, because if it's one of the things the priest has sitting on a table in the basement of the church, then it's going to be the cheapest *patente* you can buy, and Carol feels the same way about appliances as she does about clothes. I don't care. It's my *patente*, and I'm not giving it to Oxfam for a garage sale.

I grew up almost poor. We lived on a farm out in the country, and Mom bought most of the kids' clothes at rummage sales or ordered them out of the Eaton's catalogue. She said buying expensive things was sheer vanity. Dad said that if you were going to get something that was really important, you ought to get the very best, and although most of our farm machinery was tied together with baling wire, Dad had the most expensive Case tractor they make.

I suppose that's why I married Carol. She was the Freshie queen at university when I was in my final year. I passed her in the hallway and she smelled so good I fell in love with her right there. All the other girls I'd ever taken out smelled like lavender soap, and in high school, some of them even smelled like Lifebuoy. If you're going to spend your life with someone, you've got to be careful about things like that. It's a little like buying a tractor.

It's expensive though. Some of that French perfume costs over a hundred dollars an ounce. You're probably wondering why Carol would even consider marrying me given her tastes. Well, it turned out that after she was voted Freshie queen, the market completely dried out. Nobody asked her for a date for six months. When I finally got up enough nerve to ask for a date she would have been grateful for Attila the Hun. Now, she says it was because I had a certain barnyard appeal. All her women friends laugh when she says that. I'm not certain I've figured out exactly what she means.

I phoned my old French professor at the university to find out what *patente* means. He's actually an Italian, and I'm not sure I completely trust him. He told me once that all French cooking was based on the cuisine of northern Italy, but I read an article that said that the cuisine of northern Italy was a corruption of French cooking. He told me there was no such word as *patente*. I told him it was written right on my ticket. Then he said it must be some local patois, but it wasn't real French.

We're always on a diet, me and Carol, twelve months a year. If you pay two hundred dollars for a blouse, you can't afford to grow out of it. Mom always had two complete outfits, one for when she was thin and one for when she was fat. Carol thinks fat people are morally decadent. We eat a lot of vegetables. I never liked vegetables very much, and in particular, I can't stand those white asparaguses that you eat cold. They're always covered with a thin layer of slime. Even if the slime exists only in my imagination, as Carol says, I'm still not going to eat any more of them.

I didn't think Mom was going to like Carol, but she did. Carol was so sweet and helpful when she came out to the farm that Mom couldn't talk about anything else for days. And it turned out that Mom really did like expensive things. Now she comes to the city and the two of them go shopping together. Dad grumbles, but since he sold a quarter section when it became clear that I was not going to come home and take over the farm, he's got plenty of money. He's the one who got a little upset when I got married. He told me I'd got a lot of woman there, and I might have bit off more than I could chew. I think he wanted me to marry Jim Harper's daughter, she of the Lifebuoy soap, but Linda decided when she went into nursing school that she was going to be a lesbian, and that's not the kind of thing you can tell your dad.

Patente means something or other. I should have put that in quotation marks. *Patente* means "something or other." Apparently it's a catch-all term that can mean almost anything you want it to. The fellow at the service station that gives out free glasses explained it to me when I gassed up this morning. It seems I can choose any of the things sitting on the table in the church basement. They're all bingo prizes, and whenever you win a raffle at the church, you get your choice of bingo prizes. This doesn't make things much easier. I don't actually want any of those prizes, and I certainly don't need any of them. And I'm not certain how I'm going to get it into the house without causing a row.

Carol read Nancy Friday's book, *My Mother, My Self.* Now she's afraid that she's going to turn into her mother. I said that was perfectly okay, her mother is a nice lady, but could she do it gradually? Like her mother, she does not like to be teased. She pointed out her own faults with a lot more accuracy than I would have dared, then she blamed them all on her mother. Deep down, apparently, Carol is not like that at all. That was last week. This week she's reading a book called *Don't Say Yes When You Want To Say No.* I've never noticed that she had a problem in that line, but she says people are always getting her to do things she doesn't want to, like going to showers and Tupperware parties. I've noticed, though, that she only goes to ones where you bring your own bottle of wine.

I chose *une bouilloire électrique*, an electric kettle, a very small brown one with a short cord. Carol loves it. She banished the big chrome kettle to a box in the basement where it awaits emergencies. All I did was confess the whole thing, my failures in French, my humiliation at the hands of the priest, my own stubbornness. She gave me a little cuddle and said it was okay, she really liked the kettle. I personally can't stand the machine. It sits there primly on the cupboard while I eat my *flocons de blé* and ponder the French on the cornflakes box. When it boils, it does so with a nasty nasal whistle, and if you listen carefully, you can tell it is trying to sing "Frère Jacques."